Amanda MacAndrew was born in 1 .... gshire on her farm. She has three children and her husband is a photographer.

BY THE SAME AUTHOR

Passing Places

PARTY PIECES

Amanda MacAndrew

ARROW

Published by Arrow Books in 1996

1 3 5 7 9 10 8 6 4 2

© Amanda MacAndrew 1996

First published in the United Kingdom by

Century Books
Random House UK Limited
20 Vauxhall Bridge Road, London SW1V 2SA

Random House Australia (Pty) Limited
20 Alfred Street, Milsons Point, Sydney,
New South Wales 2061, Australia

Random House New Zealand Limited
18 Poland Road, Glenfield
Auckland 10, New Zealand

Random House South Africa (Pty) Limited
PO Box 337, Bergvlei, South Africa

Random House UK Limited Reg. No. 954009

A CIP catalogue record for this book is available from
the British Library

Papers used by Random House UK Limited
are natural, recyclable products made from wood grown in
sustainable forests. The manufacturing processes conform to
the environmental regulations of the country of origin.

ISBN 0 09 963281 0

Printed and bound in Great Britain by
Cox & Wyman Ltd, Reading, Berkshire

Dedication

My grateful thanks go to Sarah Molloy of A. M. Heath and
Mary Loring of Random House

With deepest gratitude to all those who helped me and answered
my questions during the writing of this book
which is dedicated to

John and Jo Nicholson

with all my love and thanks for not being in it.

I

October 1994

'SELECT, THAT IS what we are. A select circle like choice vegetables.'

'You are no vegetable, Mother.'

'No, maybe not, but I am beginning to feel like one, especially when I look at the rest of the select circle. Today we are to be talked at about bats. Bats – what are bats to a select circle of rich old women? Nothing but flea-ridden flying rodents with mackintosh wings and loose bowels.'

'Are you saying you don't want me to drive you to this lecture?'

Charlotte was being a chauffeur while her mother's car was in the garage following yet another collision. Mrs Winifred Forth often collided with spiteful inanimate objects, her garage doors and gateposts were badly bruised. She hadn't yet collided with anything breathing or more precious than a resin version of the Three Graces. The damage, so far, was inconvenient rather than tragic. Her mother's driving was yet another worry for Charlotte.

'Oh darling, I saw a picture of Robin on the television at lunchtime.'

'Did you? What was he on about?'

'I don't know, I had the sound turned down. I do hate all that cross shouting, it is so embarrassing. What exactly does he hold forth on now? Not bats, I hope.'

'No, Mother, you know perfectly well he has been shuffled off the environment and on to Youth.'

'How sweet.'

Charlotte drove Winifred to All Saints where the church hall had been cunningly done up to provide all manner of secular institutions with a venue for their activities from kick-boxing to country dancing for the under-fives. Today the Godleham Culture Society was to hear about bats.

'Muriel will bring me home, dear. Thank you for the lift. Give my love to the children.' Winifred kissed her daughter affectionately. Of her son-in-law she made no mention.

Charlotte was under-occupied and under par. It wasn't the weather, her age or a vile virus that caused the deep feeling of gloom that kept her from wanting to go home. She didn't mind being alone; she seldom missed her twins or her husband when they were off and about their own lives. She just couldn't face the reproachful neglected garden tubs and the pestering fawning of the overbred and dippy spaniel.

She rang Peta. Peta was out, probably to a smart lunch or else otherwise engaged, possibly in bed. Peta, comfortably single again and permanently thirty, had an appetite well catered for by her skilful powers of seduction. Charlotte was not jealous of Peta; in fact jealousy was not an issue with Charlotte. She had been born with and retained much of a most enviable amount of life's best things. Charlotte was rich, and despite some snags and unscheduled demands she had remained so. In middle age she was insulated from the fear of penury, provided her desires were reasonable. The last time she had gone to church, on some occasion demanding a display of the united family in quest of old-fashioned values, the sermon had been on the Parable of the Talents. Charlotte did so hope that God would not rebuke her for lack of zeal. Her funds were invested prudently, unadventurously, and had not multiplied pro-digiously, but at least she had not buried them in the garden. Being reasonable was the pivot of her life. Maybe it was a virtue. However, Charlotte never acknowledged any virtue in herself and was permanently racked by a nagging guilt. It was years since she had slept well or been able to make her own oblivion. She could turn on a light of fun and happiness, she could sparkle and amuse because these were tricks she had learnt. Her face was lined from laughter but she couldn't remember experiencing the sensation of spontaneity. Now that she no longer had hangovers, bright dawns would wake her. Each day had its promise but as her eyes opened she would remember and regret. Like the condemned, she had learnt to expect no joy from the mornings.

At the library she looked up the life of William Godwin. Godwin had crammed lots into his span and seemed to have been at the hub of much at the end of the eighteenth century. It was an intriguing subject and formed part of her correspondence course in journalism. Unlike many of her contemporaries she was not studying more erudite subjects through the Open University. Charlotte did not consider herself sufficiently dedicated to be a serious student. Her concentration was dreadful. There would be no degree ceremony and certainly no burstingly lusty summer school for her, just a remote relationship with a tutor conducted by post. Charlotte was uncertain of the age, appearance and even the sex of Julian Peabody but liked to assume that the person from whom she got such good marks was male. Julian Peabody had declared himself much entertained by her piece on funeral parlours; maybe they shared a macabre sense of humour.

The librarian stamped a biography of Mary Wollstonecraft and handed it back to Charlotte with a most unexpected 'Thank you, madam.'

She had been called madam twice in the same day. The first had been the policeman who had booked her for speeding.

'Were you aware, madam, that you have been driving in excess of the prescribed speed limit?' he had enquired courteously.

Lying, Charlotte had replied, 'No, Officer, really? I am so sorry.'

Sorrow was no good. She was booked and requested to pay a fixed penalty.

'Name please, madam, and can I see your licence?'

'My name is Charlotte Brand,' she replied, handing him her licence all pink and unsullied like a baby before vaccination. She smiled ingratiatingly at the young policeman and reflected that if Piers was less of a rebel he too might look all fresh and wholesome like this serious upholder of the law.

'There should be no problems, as you have no previous convictions.' Charlotte heard these words with some remorse, for she did indeed have no previous convictions of any kind. Original thought had been smothered in favour of a smooth-running life.

'Thank you Lady Brand. Please drive carefully.'

'I will, Officer.'

Charlotte was angry with herself for getting a ticket, the local paper was constantly on the prowl for news of misdemeanours in the model home life of the local Member. Piers and the bikers and the bottles beneath the golf course bridge had been bad enough to get to the front page. Robin expected a high standard of behaviour from all. Coral and Piers chose to spend much time away from home for that very reason.

It was still only two-thirty when she arrived at Hair by Immaculata. No appointment was necessary or advisable as Mahmood, who manned the phone and saw off intruders, said yes to everything.

Spanish Immaculata's finances were rocky. Her current protector kept her solvent provided she followed the path of Islam, so she did the hair of others whilst keeping her own modestly covered. This compliance secured a better understanding with the bank and a new Swiss cheese plant. The tiny salon catered for all and was as uncomfortable as it was cheap. Immaculata had threatened to kill herself if Charlotte went elsewhere. 'The choice is yours,' said Immaculata with an expressive shrug, having listed an amazing catalogue of personal misfortunes. Of course there was no choice.

An hour and a half later Charlotte's grey had been transformed into a golden halo, several shades too yellow, Immaculata having gone to the bank for a protracted interview during the highlighting process. Peta would be horrified yet again by Charlotte's lack of style.

Immaculata sighed as she waved a mirror behind Charlotte so she could admire her striped rear view.

'You are lucky, you have a nice lord to look after you, and

not be throwing rocks through your windows like my ex-husband is doing.'

Mahmood produced two half-bricks for Charlotte's scrutiny and delight.

'He isn't a lord, Immaculata, he is only a knight.'

'No matter, he is not throwing stones.'

No, Robin had not thrown stones.

Charlotte found Maureen already busy in the Memorial Hall putting out the chairs. It was too early for the meeting, and anyway she didn't feel like attending that day. The afternoon glowed and sunshine was precious in a fading year. Afternoon meetings were seldom well attended in Godleham. Perhaps no one would come at all and Maureen's time would have been wasted. Only it wouldn't have been wasted because the very fact that she had to be there and get things straight kept Maureen from the insanity of addiction.

'Are you sure you can cope, Charlotte? Do you not want any support? Things can be harder when your life goes wrong.'

'I know, Maureen, but everything is pretty good just now, and I haven't really got the time.' Charlotte had plenty of time, she just lacked the inclination to spend any of it with the other group members. She did not feel like hearing all those stories yet again.

'You know best, dear. Just remember we are here. Don't forget to take one day at a time.'

'I won't forget, Maureen. Thank you, good luck.'

At Oak Court Hospital the sister had seemed somewhat flustered. 'We weren't expecting you today, Lady Brand,' she said as if such a visit was likely to merit extra polish on the vinyl and welcoming aldermen.

'I just thought I would pop in to see Wally. That is all right, isn't it?'

'Oh yes, that is quite, quite all right.'

Wally was propped up in his chair as usual, his face a blank and a tube coming out from underneath connected to a bag hooked on to the chair frame. Charlotte wheeled him to the sunshine which was streaming through the windows warmly despite the chilliness of the autumn afternoon.

'You like the sun, don't you, Wally?' She squeezed his hand. 'I meant to bring you *The Diary of a Provincial Lady* because it makes me laugh, but I am afraid you will have to make do with Mary Wollstonecraft instead.'

Charlotte read aloud for about half an hour. As usual no flicker of interest or recognition crossed Wally's pasty damaged features, but she enjoyed reading and felt that he might like it too. Mary Wollstonecraft was dead at thirty-eight, having done a hundred times more than Charlotte had managed by the age of forty-seven. For Wally life had been over when he was forty-one, only unlike Mary he had failed to die. He breathed unaided. That was all he could do for himself eight years later.

Cedar Lodge had entrances back and front. The iron front gates remained shut most of the time as the garage was approached from behind via a small lane used by walkers of all sorts including Phyllis Potter and her brace of medal-winning Labradors. They earned prizes for obedience.

With dread Charlotte noticed Phyllis standing squarely mid-lane: she must wish to speak to her, or, to put it more accurately, to speak at her and tell her what was to be done. Charlotte always thought of Phyllis as Mrs Morning because her sons were the brightest and the best.

Phyllis wished to know whether Cedar Lodge would still be available for the Conservative bazaar.

'I am sure that will be fine,' Charlotte replied. 'I will just have to check it with Robin.'

'Really? I would have thought he could have safely left that sort of thing to you,' Phyllis replied. Mr Morning was never consulted on anything: he was instructed to attend the many brilliant occasions devised to honour and recognise the Potter sons and their countless outstanding achievements.

Zoe, the dimmest of dogs, greeted Charlotte with much silly wagging and not a vestige of shame. A tapestry cushion was now too distressed even to appeal to the most aesthetic of decorators and several stinking sausages and unexpected puddles were dotted about on the better carpets. For a medium-sized bitch equipped with standard bowel and bladder Zoe certainly had a prodigious output. Zoe was a chronic guest but really belonged to Robin's sister, Laura whose clever lover had announced that either he or Zoe would have to go. Unfortunately Laura had settled for love and sent Zoe to Charlotte as an unwelcome replacement for her late, much loved mongrel Pandemonium.

Piers and Coral were having a year off. She before continuing her degree in languages at Oxford and he before – well no one knew what Piers was taking a year off from. Piers was idle and uninspired and delightful, Coral was earnest, clever, dedicated and nothing like as pretty as her brother, though apparently far sexier. Coral was doing a year of her Oxford degree in Paris and though Piers would have liked to travel, lack of funds and indolence kept him frequently in bed, mostly alone, attached only to his music and exuding an endless stream of cigarette smoke. He had been driven to take a job at a garden centre.

'Hello darling, you are home early,' said Charlotte as she cleared the last mess and squirted the stained area with the camouflaging stench of disinfectant.

'I have been let go,' said Piers.

'Oh.'

The bell rang: the front door bell, so it wouldn't be a friend or the post. Charlotte went to answer it warily. She hated being doorstepped by anyone and was in no mood to be polite to evangelists or pollsters.

A young man with a black case and a file stood before her, a couple more people were on the gravel behind.

'Lady Brand, I am Cliff Heath of Radio Thames and I am recording an interview with you now.'

Charlotte wondered whether this was the sort of chap that chanced past to ask whether one was satisfied with one's wash.

'Could you tell the listeners, Lady Brand, what your views are on your husband's resignation and whether you intend to stand by him?'

2

Summer 1968

CHARLOTTE HAD BEEN twenty-one, newly out of love and work. She had made the mistake of becoming involved with her boss, a young, enterprising rat who revelled in trawling women, extracting his own enjoyment then tossing them back to flounder like surplus fish, which was harsh. It had not been much of a quasi-secretarial job and was certainly an insignificant affair from her employer's point of view but Charlotte's virginity, heart and self-respect had all been annihilated in 1968. She hid her unhappiness behind dark glasses and most of her face was obliterated by a silk scarf knotted, as was then the rage, beneath her pale pink lips like a guardsman's bearskin chinstrap, as she trailed listlessly down the King's Road and bought lots of short frocks. There would be other jobs and other men. Both were easy to come by then. However, she had plenty of money and only wanted the man who had so carelessly replaced her with a fresh bed-mate.

She had a flat that smelt throughout of stale fridge contents in the musty basement of an excellent address. Felicity and Henrietta with whom she shared were older, wiser and well sorted. They had captured baby merchant bankers of their own and were rarely at home except to change their little linen shifts, hang pearly chandeliers from their ears, pin on hairpieces, iron their Hermès scarves and launch themselves into their lovers' MGBs and TR4s for a night of dining at Parkes or the Mirabelle, invariably ending up at Annabel's where, unlike Charlotte, they were on friendly terms with all and intimate with the loo attendant. They both had vague jobs connected with art, about which they knew but a modicum. They had been engaged for their charm, giraffe legs and self-confident establishment hauteur rather than their qualifications, which had been expensively and acceptably procured at the Victoria and Albert and the British Institute in Florence.

Charlotte had wondered whether Greyhounding around the States and seeing Haight Ashbury for herself would be fun, or if joining the draft-dodgers at some university for foreigners in Italy or France would be worth while. She had pondered on learning to cook, to mend china, to restore pictures or even going to work in a kibbutz. All these options were possible but none of them appealed. Daily she became more listless, permanently suffering from a malaise and fatigue that could not be blamed entirely on the depression of having been ditched. Then one day in July when the heat was great and the cloying stench from Price's candle factory (or was it Young's brewery?) had wafted across the river on the southwesterly breeze, she had become really ill. Her glands were swollen in her neck, armpits and groin and the heat of the stuffy day was enhanced by her own fever.

Charlotte was yet another victim of fashionable glandular fever and was so unwell that she was removed from London by her parents and taken home to Dorset to recover.

She was an only child of parents who had hoped for further heirs to share their considerable wealth, which had been cleverly amassed by timely investment in the gramophone record industry and Canadian railway tracks. It was not to be, and Charlotte remained their solitary offspring. Though several further pregnancies had raised their hopes, all had ended in the devastating disappointment of miscarriage. She grew up realising that all her parents' hopes and, more importantly, their fears were vested in her alone. They made a conscious effort to give Charlotte her freedom, to let her go and grow up independent of their immense anxiety, but the shadow of their concern was always there. When she returned home ill and dispirited she experienced the awful sight of her father in tears. It would be the end of him if something happened to his precious daughter. Her mother had a more pragmatic attitude born of the fortitude she had displayed throughout her earlier life as a nurse. She had seen the most harrowing sights and worked in the worst conditions with the most distressed and distressing casualties whilst with the Red Cross. She had seen the Holocaust aftermath for herself. She never spoke of this, opting instead, because of her medical knowledge and obstetric experiences, to become with age a notable hypochondriac and flippant cynic.

Charlotte's father had been named Fraser by his foolish parents, who felt ashamed of their roots and wished to pass their son off as a Scot and not the heir to a grandfather who had laid such a firm foundation for their wealth with his remarkable business acumen in Whitechapel. Fraser's war was uneventfully blameless, after which he set up as a rather idle solicitor in deepest Dorset and spent more time playing the Stock Exchange than handling conveyances, divorces and grievances for locals of litigious intent, preferring to leave these tediums to his cautious partner, Cyril Brand. By the cultivation of a most aristocratic drawl and much leisureliness, Fraser rose within local society until he was well accepted everywhere (like Simon Smith's amazing dancing bear). Cyril Brand remained the junior partner and lesser mortal despite his greater age, legal knowledge, professional zeal and guile.

Summer advanced and while London emptied for the holidays and the beginning of the aspiring class's northern migration Charlotte recovered slowly through the restful inertia of untroubled rural life. All exertion was forbidden and all emotional upheaval banned. With excitement proscribed, Charlotte began to enjoy passive tranquillity once the fever had subsided and her glands dwindled to their proper size. For the first time in her life she appreciated the smell of grass, the sound of birds and the placid security of home. She had received a glimpse of an ideal of domestic bliss. It was an attractive prospect and seemed to be a delightful alternative to searching for a career or holding down a tedious job. She was her father's daughter and, like Fraser Forth, enjoyed being idle.

However by September inertia was starting to pall, she was no longer ill and it was time to get out and on with life once more. She realised that she wanted to test her recovered health against something more demanding than drinks with the grounded natives whose eyes were already twinkling in anticipation of the partridge and pheasant shooting to come.

The Brands' eldest and brilliant son was home too. He was six years older than Charlotte, a first-class Oxford graduate and embryo barrister who had been engaged by an urbane cabinet minister as a political researcher whilst nursing covert opposing parliamentary ambitions of his own. Immediately after his boss had discovered these treacherous aspirations, young Brand had not only been sacked but had become quite ill. He too was painfully afflicted by many very swollen glands.

Winifred Forth, Charlotte's mother, thought it might be nice for the two young people to meet. Naturally they had known each other when young, but six years is a century of an age difference between children and Charlotte had been dispatched to a socially elevated boarding-school while all the Brands had got their education via the state and won scholarships to assisted places at academically elevated day schools. The Brand children (two girls and a boy) were poor and brilliant; Charlotte Forth was rich and not clever, at least not so you would notice. Laura and Fenella Brand, who flanked Charlotte in age by a year, were both at Sussex University. 'Whatever you do, please don't talk about glands.' Winifred implored. She knew a thing or two about such things and wished the subject kept private.

'I promise,' Charlotte replied. 'I am utterly cheesed off with glands,'

Charlotte had never warmed to Mrs Brand, who made a virtue of being poor but provident and held the opinion that the Forths were abominably vulgar. For all her professed Christianity and puritan frugality (no collar remained unturned, no sock undarned) Elizabeth Brand was profoundly xenophobic, loathing all who had not been English since before the Armada had threatened and been defeated by doughty mariners reared in Devon and Dorset. She despised the Forth lineage and would have done so even if they had really hailed from Scotland. No good ever did come from up there.

'Were not the children of Israel told to go forth and multiply?' she asked guilelessly. 'I was only asking. Don't worry. I was just thinking aloud.' She smiled at her husband's senior partner's wife with a patronising smirk while making an accurate estimate of the cost of all Winifred's clothes: no replaced knicker elastic there, she'd be bound.

When next Winifred gave a dinner party (the Forths were constant entertainers; the Brands made a virtue of being unable to afford such indulgences) Robin Brand was asked to come and balance the numbers and represent the younger generation with Charlotte. Long after Charlotte had forgotten the identity of the other guests, what was eaten and what she wore, she could recall exactly the way in which her future husband made his entrance.

'Good evening Mrs Forth,' he announced openly and frankly, extending a warm hand for a firm and honest shaking. 'What a truly beautiful room,' he said beaming and inhaling the atmosphere with which he was evidently much in sympathy.

Winifred Forth was floored by this handsome young man's self-confident charm.

'Thank you, sir,' Robin said with natural good manners as Fraser handed him a glass of sherry. He tasted it and the approval he registered was not just politeness but the appreciation of one well up in wines, having often lingered over equally fine samples in England's most venerable institutions.

'Ah Charlotte, how lovely to see you again.' Robin smiled with truthful warmth and kissed her cheek. All the Forths were captivated. Had they been constituents, their votes would have been assured. As it was, Robin knew that from then onwards financial backing for his political ambitions was within reach and Charlotte would make an excellent wife for a Tory MP.

Rather incongruously he reflected that not only did Charlotte have one of the healthiest bank accounts but she also possessed ideal ankles for appearing in supporting roles on political platforms and would look good in the sensible flat shoes needed for pounding about constituencies demonstrating loyalty and devotion to a spouse so utterly worthy of receiving the votes of all. Robin boasted an ability to read ankles. When times were tough, in years to come, Charlotte would recall how her heart had jumped as Robin bent to give her that first courteous kiss. She would reason with herself that such a man could not possibly be all bad, and if he was, did it matter so long as he could, just now and again, bestow such devastating pleasure? Charlotte often despised herself . . . in years to come.

★

Apart from Robin's mother, most people seemed thrilled and even Elizabeth Brand was heard to say that in view of the circumstances, it was probably one of her son's soundest schemes. On the nature of the circumstances she was silent, but Cyril Brand expressed no qualms and was already casting about among his relatives for a successor to the practice once his own soliciting days and those of Fraser Forth were done. Family ties must count, and welding oneself to the daughter of the senior partner must be wise especially as the Forths had no male heirs of their own, and the Brands had several diligent nephews.

Charlotte was relieved to have no further decisions to make about her future career and spent the winter learning elegant cookery and agonising over which colour of hessian would suit which wall of the delightful house in Chelsea which her parents had bought for her and where she and Robin would set up home after their marriage. Till the wedding day in April they pretended that they were living apart. Robin would leave for his own shared and rented flat as the milk float hummed down Markham Street and was regularly sighted by the Household Cavalry as they exercised their horses around early morning London.

After Robin had crept away Charlotte would lie in bed listening to the pigeons copulating on the window-ledges and waiting for Peta, who was a temporary tenant, to return from whatever profitable conquest she had embarked upon the night before. Peta had been in Oxford rather than at it when Robin was completing his final year; she had known him and had reason to dislike him. Birds of a fortune-hunting feather do not flock well together.

Henrietta who had shared with Charlotte in Cadogan Lane was now married to Roddy MacPhail. She had made a beautiful Christmas bride in a romantic cloak of virginal blue velvet trimmed with ermine salvaged from a deceased aunt's presentation ensemble. The wedding had been in Scotland where both she and Roddy had families descended through aeons of bloodthirstiness to acquire, by dint of sword and guile, stark castles apiece. Charlotte alone had been invited to the wedding, a gaffe on Henrietta's part, but not one that gave her much grief. As she was officially engaged by then Charlotte had refused: it wasn't worth igniting the injured wrath of her future mother-in-law by setting off to the heathen north alone.

In February the MacPhails came to dinner in Markham Street. They were still healthily tanned from their Kenyan honeymoon which contrasted with Charlotte's winter weary pallor.

Peta's skirt only just skimmed her buttocks and her glow came from deft use of blusher. Henrietta looked on Charlotte's friend with matronly disapproval, and on her fiancé with faint misgivings. Robin Brand was no Roddy MacPhail, there was something almost imperceptible of the bounder about him, but Charlotte looked happy and he was most devoted and attentive; suspiciously so.

Henrietta had much to impart about present lists. Thomas Goode for china, Heals for beds, General Trading Company for pretty furnishings. 'No one can have too many Ali Baba baskets or too few chicken bricks,' she advised.

During dinner she warmed to Robin and rebuked herself for being a snob. He was indeed a charmer. First impressions can be deceptive.

The dinner was bridal white, vichyssoise, followed by fricassée of chicken and *crème brûlée*. During the Brie the telephone rang. It was for Peta. A man of great wealth, shiftily procured, wanted to take her out.

'But you have already eaten, Peta,' Charlotte protested. 'How are you going to manage Boulestin's on top?'

'Don't fret. When it comes to millionaires I can manage everything.'

Peta left for her date in a minuscule black frock, and a pre-paid minicab.

'Charlotte, where *did* you find that?' Henrietta asked.

'Peta was a couple of years ahead of me at school, and has recently become a good friend. I like her a lot.'

'She's frightful.'

'No, she is honest. She doesn't pretend. She admits that she craves money.'

'She is mercenary,' Henrietta persisted.

'I can't help admiring her,' Charlotte replied.

'Oh I admire her,' said Roddy.

'Of course you do, darling. She is a walking man-trap. I don't think Charlotte meant her admiration to be taken that way.'

'I admire her for being straightforward. She can be mercenary but she is no hypocrite.'

'Luckily she will be moving out, when we are married,' said Robin.

'I'm fond of her' Charlotte said firmly. 'I can be friends with whoever I please.'

'We'll see about that, my sweet,' said Robin kissing the back of Charlotte's neck as she poured the coffee.

When April came and Charlotte returned home for the wedding which had been such fun for her mother to organise, the Brands' first home was completely decorated and right ready for use by the newly-weds. The soul of William Morris had invaded the basement, coral-coloured parrots climbed the glazed chintz of the drawing room which had been cunningly crafted out of two small rooms in the primrose-painted house which had once been an artisan's cottage. Peta moved out, leaving both tiny spare rooms free for the unmentioned future baby Brands while the master bedroom and bathroom had been built on the flat roof. Many Chelsea houses had been extended upwards. Residents could gaze in a medieval way across the road into each other's bedrooms, most of which were similarly and fashionably decorated, all matching walls and curtains swamped by little meadow flowers.

Charlotte was happy but wondered whether she should be happier. She did love Robin, and he said he loved her. Whenever she expressed doubts he would look at her with hurt doggy eyes and say that if that was how she felt she must do what was best but that he would always be waiting for her, and she knew where to find him. Robin never got further than the door before Charlotte would implore him to come back. It became a game; the reassuring reconciliations served to convince Charlotte that she was doing the right thing and that she was also rather silly. Robin's eyes were hazel brown, his glasses gave him gravitas.

However, right up to the day of the wedding she continued to be knobbled by doubts and pestered by anxiety. She told herself that every bride felt like that, didn't they? In theory there was still a possibility of cancelling everything, but in reality she told herself there was no going back now. She just wished that the whole rigmarole was over and the burden of choice eliminated.

The proportion of Brand to Forth at the wedding was four to one. The lesser faction owned most of the wealth but few of the brains. Clever Brands had gathered from all over in shabby posses while sparkling Forths, newly got up in quite the latest rage, shone out at the reception like the sparse Christmas lights of a thrifty local authority. Old Brands were staggered at the brevity of the girls' skirts and wondered whether Charlotte and her friends were really as silly as they looked. When it was done, and the doing of it had been lots of fun, Charlotte was mightily relieved. She had committed herself. A photograph of Brands and Forths happily posed with assorted Kate Greenaway attendants in front of the portrait of the invented ancestor proved that Robin had taken Charlotte for his lawful wedded wife. They had made, as they say, a lovely couple. Charlotte's doubts were slain, Robin was indeed a wonderful man. What more could she possibly want? What more could she reasonably deserve?

'Well Mrs Brand, what does it feel like?'
  'Wonderful, Mr Brand.'
  'I'll make you a lady one day.'
  'I'm fine as an honest woman.'
  'Wait and see.'

3

Summer 1969

THE HONEYMOON WAS a present from her parents, the choice of New York was Robin's. They stayed at the Plaza and after a week they would return to England aboard the QE2.

Fraser was pleased that his daughter had married a man with such decisive ideas but even he, who could easily afford to pay for several such trips, did think that this offer to finance the entire affair had been grasped with too much alacrity. Still, he had only one child's wedding to fund, and that he had done without stinting in any way. He and Winifred were relieved as well as happy for Charlotte: they were apprehensive about the impending seventies and feared for their daughter, who had not coped too well with the sixties on her own. Charlotte was like a climbing plant, inclined to topple without a stable support. Now that she had an upright husband she would surely flower.

Charlotte loved New York. The Plaza she knew from *The Adventures of Eloïse*, it gave her great joy to find that one did indeed have to 'step on it' in the Rest Room. The potted palms, the lobby, the ladies who shopped, they were all there. She told Robin about it and how Eloïse did love Room Service, but he didn't appear to understand and said that he thought the idea of a little girl living in the Plaza in the care of an Irish nanny sounded rather sad.

They trotted round Central Park in a carriage and Robin charged it, they dined at the Four Seasons and Robin entered the bill on his expenses sheet, but air was free, the spring well advanced and the trees were all performing nicely. They walked down to Greenwich Village, took the ferry to Staten Island and marvelled at the marble splendours of Grand Central

Station. Robin had a great-uncle, an elderly man more at home in the New York of Edith Wharton or Henry James than that of Mayor Lindsay. He was an alumnus of Harvard and had combined the career of attorney with much serious wealth-gathering on Wall Street. He lived in widowed and murky brownstone splendour on East 72nd but spent most of his days at his club. Robin and Charlotte were invited to lunch. For dignity and gloom this club was the champion, beating even the most repressed and exclusive male retreats in London. The Hedera Club did however tolerate women provided they were decorative, discreet, ladylike and silent.

Ludlow Brand believed that America should be for the Americans. Ludlow's Americans were white Anglo-Saxons. He couldn't be doing with blacks, Hispanics, Orientals or Jews.

'The idea of this country as a melting-pot is just so much liberal garbage. I want this great land cleared of all these god-damn immigrants and left to the proper natives.'

'Do you mean the Indians?' Charlotte asked.

'Don't try and be smart with me, young lady,' Ludlow replied, glowering at Charlotte. 'Now tell me, Robin, what do you intend to do with your life? I understand you are at the bar, a fine calling for a young man. Are you aiming to become a judge or make your fortune as an attorney?'

'I am going to become a politician. I'm on the lookout for a constituency right now. I'm a Conservative, Uncle Ludlow.'

'So I should damn well hope,' Ludlow replied. 'In the mean time will you continue with the law?'

'Well yes, but probably just on a consultancy basis.'

This was the first that Charlotte had heard of Robin's plans. He had never suggested giving up speaking up for the unspeak-able and defending the defenceless before. He had grumbled about days wasted in provincial towns doing his best for tire-some flashers and drunk inadequates but that was his calling, his skill, he was good at it. It was how he got his livelihood.

'Your ideas sound expensive, my nephew.'

'Yes, well we will get by, won't we, darling?' Robin patted Charlotte's hand.

'I see,' said Uncle Ludlow. 'Tell me, my dear, what do your

folks do? Your father is a lawyer too, I take it? What is his name? Maybe I should have heard of him.'

'I doubt it. His name is Fraser Forth; my mother is called Winifred.'

'Yes, yes, I'm sure she is a fine woman, but Fraser – I figure that is a Scottish name. A great race the Scotch, some of our best citizens originated in Scotland. Mind you, many of those who want to be our best citizens kid us that they are Scotch just to hide the fact that they are goddamn Greeks or Jews.'

'My great-grandfather was called Mordecai. He was a pawnbroker.'

In the yellow cab, on the way back to the hotel, Robin and Charlotte had their first row.

'Where are you going?'

'Nowhere, just out.'

'Wait Charlotte, darling I'm sorry.'

Charlotte turned to look at Robin, who did indeed appear contrite. He caught her hand and put on his guilty dog look. 'Of course you are quite right. It was silly of Uncle Ludlow to make such an issue of it.'

'I didn't know it was an issue,' Charlotte replied.

'Oh you are so sweet.' Robin held her and gave her a kiss. 'Come on let's go to the MOMA, it's only round the corner, then we can meet Martin for supper.'

'Martin?'

'Yes, Martin Fable. Remember, I told you, I met him at law school, he's working here in the Pan Am building. He is also a freelance journalist and just about the only satirist who admits to being of the Right. His father is the member for Godleham. We'll have a drink with him in the bar here, then he wants to take us to some place in Chinatown.'

They sat in the sculpture garden in silence. Robin had bought himself a *Times* and Charlotte amused herself with watching mother birds twitter about in the neat greenery quite impervious to having set up home amongst such erudition. Most of this sculpture left Charlotte unmoved. She preferred such things to be safely sweet or gloriously heroic: Peter Pan and Boadicea suited her. Robin had told her about *Guernica*; he had said that it was the most seminal work in the gallery, encapsulating the horrors of all wars, civil or otherwise, and that it represented a watershed in twentieth-century art, mores and philosophy. Charlotte was sure that he had got this all mugged up from a book. She was haunted by Rousseau's *Sleeping Gipsy*. Was the lion that stood over the girl friendly or savage, protector or predator? It puzzled and worried her. She had bought herself a postcard of the picture.

Charlotte looked good in plain colours; her shoulder-length hair had auburn lights, was reasonably thick and hung obligingly straight. Being tallish, slender and the owner of good legs meant she was quite striking but her large mouth and long nose prevented her from being thought pretty, despite her beautiful eyes. Her complexion, clear as it was, could look sickly pallid in fluorescent lighting and throughout her childhood all the invigorating tonics her mother could muster and the brisk walks in all weathers had failed to give her rosy cheeks.

When she came down to join Robin in the bar she looked marvellous, in a ginger-coloured short-sleeved gabardine dress. Martin Fable had arrived some few minutes before and he and Robin were drinking Martinis for which Robin had signed.

Martin was the antithesis of Robin in appearance, possessing neither height nor urbane good looks. Without his glasses, Robin was the American idea of the definitive English gent, similar to Steed of *The Avengers* and likely to grow older looking like the smoothie who advertised shirts, but without the eyepatch. Martin could have been a mad scientist crossed with a Russian writer. He was quite short, slight and had a cloud of undisciplined, upright frizzy hair. He wore small round metal-rimmed glasses, not because he wanted to affect the granny look of the Beatles but because he had been kitted out with them ever since his parents had realised that their five-year-old was extremely short-sighted. Once he could see properly Martin became happy, hardworking and alarmingly bright. He was four years younger than Robin but at only twenty-four was well able to keep pace intellectually with those many years his senior. Like Charlotte he had been an only child. His mother had died and his father was forever on the prowl for a replacement, which entertained Martin enormously.

When Robin was collecting coats after dinner Martin asked Charlotte what it felt like to be married to the next prime minister but three.

'Fine,' she answered, 'Fine, great.'

'You will have to manage to be more beamish about it than that when you are waving to us plebs from the steps of Number Ten.'

'Uncle Ludlow has arranged for me to meet some prominent Republican politicians in Washington.'

'When?'

'This weekend.'

'But the boat – we'll miss the boat!'

'Can't be helped; we will just have to fly home.'

'But Daddy will be so offended.'

'You go alone, then.'

'But darling, this is our honeymoon.'

'Yes my sweet, the beginning of a long lifetime together, not a dirty weekend.'

'I'm not going home on the QE2 alone. I hate being on the sea, and anyway it was your idea to travel that way.'

'Yes, but that was before I got this great chance to further my career. It means a lot to me.'

'More than me?'

'I'm not going to answer that, you silly ass. Look, you go and buy some air tickets, we can be home at exactly the same time and no one will be one bit the wiser. I'll ring Mum and make sure that she smooths things over with your parents. She's very tactful when necessary.'

'They will be very hurt.'

'Look darling, let me make one thing quite clear. I am not going to let your family's feelings come between me and my future, do you understand?'

'Yes.'

'Good. Now I must go and arrange for you to keep the room on for the extra nights.'

'Why?'

'Because, you fool, I can't leave you behind here to sleep on the Bowery.'

'Aren't I invited to Washington too?'

'No. Uncle Ludlow felt you wouldn't fit in, you would be bored.'

'What am I to do then by myself?'

'Oh for God's sake! Read a book, go shopping.'

'What with?'

'Money, of course. You have got plenty of that even if you are a bit short on imagination. Oh for Christ's sake, Charlotte don't start crying!'

'Is this how it is always going to be?'

'Probably. Now, come on, cheer up. It is only a long weekend after all, and you would hate it. Look how drowsy you got last night at dinner when I was talking to Martin.'

'I was tired.'

'Well then, you can have a lovely rest while I'm gone and be bright and cheerful for the flight home. Look I've an idea. I will ring Martin and see if he can take you about a bit, show you the sights and that. He's just the person to help you sort out the flight.'

'You want me to buy the air tickets?'

'Of course. It will give you something to do. Now I must get on and get organised, I'll take you wherever you like for dinner tonight and then I'll creep away first thing in the morning. The weekend will pass in a flash, you'll see.'

Martin's office was pretty near the top of the Pan Am building which towered above the teeming railroad station below and carried a heliport on its roof. The building shuddered with technology and swayed in the wind. The office in which Martin worked was oak panelled and well furnished with brass and leather upholstery.

'Isn't it great?' he said as he welcomed Charlotte. 'All this genius of modernity dressed up to look like a bit of kitsch Dickensiana. I am glad you can come and meet the Van Schumachers, they are thrilled to have you and me for the weekend.'

'It is terribly kind of you to organise it. I was dreading being in the Plaza by myself.'

'Of course you were. You'll enjoy this, though.'

They drove past the United Nations and 59th Street Bridge. 'You know the song?' Martin asked.

'I do.'

'Good, then you can sing to me. I'm sure you can sing beautifully, you've got such a fine strong neck.'

'You make me sound like a chicken.'

'No I don't. You are a swan.'

'Swans only sing before they die.'

'Oh dear. No singing then.'

The Van Schumachers did 'cook-outs' most of the time: it was an easy way of coping with all their guests who dropped by to stay anything from an hour to a month at will. It also kept their animals happy to scavenge in packs and brawl over the scraps. A small piglet had recently joined the throng of odd dogs, four cats and a mean-tempered goose who patrolled the garden and possessed no social graces of any kind. The pool wasn't ready for summer, which was a relief to Charlotte who didn't really fancy sharing it with the piglet. In its brief life it had become a remarkably exuberant swimmer.

'My, have you seen surgical procedures! Floydie, just take a look at Martin's scars. They are awesome!' Mariana-Louise van Schumacher had no problem about making personal remarks. Martin was helping Floyd, her husband, to chop some wood that had blown down during the winter. They worked shirtless, as summer was definitely coming even if the pool wasn't prepared for it.

'You are like Wallace,' Charlotte said. She was carrying an enormous ice bucket down to the barbecue terrace. The Van Schumachers lived in woodland seclusion far from tidy suburbia in what was called a French château style home.

'Wallis Simpson? I thought all her scars were hidden in her hairline,' said Mariana-Louise who was always called Mallow, or Mellow Mallow after Floyd had fixed her third daiquiri.

'No Wallace the lion whose nose was all covered with scars. He ate Our Albert.'

'Tell us about it, Charlotte. Do you know this beast that ate Alfred, Martin?'

'Albert, Mallow. Yes of course I know all about Young Albert Ramsbottom. He had a stick with a horse's-head handle.'

'And shoved it in Wallace's ear,' Charlotte announced in triumph.

'Can you remember it all, Charlotte?' Martin asked.

'Yes, I hope so.'

After the doleful tale was done with – Charlotte narrating and Martin doing all the voices and the magistrate chap who had hoped the Ramsbottoms would add further sons to their name – Mallow burst into wild applause. 'Isn't that just darling, Floydie? Don't you just love that?'

For the rest of the weekend Martin and Charlotte were stars. Between them they knew most of Stanley Holloway's monologues and got quite exhausted with reciting the doings of Sam and his musket and Anne Boleyn's ghost.

Charlotte was a hit with Pike and Clemency, the little Van Schumachers. Pike was mostly interested in baseball but Clemency, aged only eight, was already terribly pretty, bright and totally self-assured. 'You'll make a lovely mommie, Charlotte,' said Mallow.

'One day, maybe.'

'What are you going to do till then?'

'I don't know, I'm not sure.'

'You can't just be a lady of leisure, play house and arrange the flowers, you know. You'll get bored.'

'I know.'

'I'd just die if I didn't have a job,' said Mallow.

'You work? I thought the children would take up all your time.'

'No, I work. When they are in school I work, Juanita and Pedro look after the house and the animals and we all stay in the apartment during the week. Floydie and I both have jobs, that's why we get on so well.'

'What do you do?' Charlotte asked. Mallow just didn't seem the sort of woman to have a career.

'I'm a social worker in Bellevue Hospital. You should come and see it, I'll be there Tuesday, quite a contrast to the Plaza. I work mostly with alcoholics. We get a lot of bums in from the Lower East Side and the Bowery. Floydie is in advertising. We met at graduate school. What did you read at college?'

Charlotte explained that she hadn't been to university.

'What you mean is you haven't been *yet*,' Mallow replied. 'This world isn't a fit place for *hausfraus* any more.'

Martin wasn't due at his office till late on Monday so they were able to spend Sunday night with the Van Schumachers too.

'We have garbage-can hash on Sundays,' said Mallow. 'Floydie gets to cook. It can be bizarre.'

It was, in fact, delicious. Charlotte found the crème de menthe frappé utterly flooring, but a great confidence enhancer. She and Martin were still the stars of the weekend. She had never laughed so much.

Clemency and Pike seemed to have no fixed bedtimes. 'Say, Charlotte, what are you going to be?'

'Happy, Clemency, I hope, as happy as I am now. What are you going to be? Tell me.'

'I'm going to be President of the United States,' Clemency replied.

Darkness had enveloped the barbecue terrace, large winged insects danced in the beams from the surrounding lights and a busy chorus of nocturnal nature had struck up during the garbage-can supper.

'At last!' said Floydie. 'At last we will get to have a president who is not a garter-snapper.'

'I'll snap garters if I want to. So!' Clemency replied.

'Sure, honey,' Mallow interjected. 'You just get out there and snap whatever you want.'

'She will, Mallow, she will,' said Martin. 'In ten years' time your Clemency will slay all in her path. She will be a dangerous woman. Dangerous but fascinating.'

Charlotte's enthusiastic thanks were not just the gushings of the gently reared but came from her heart. The generous happiness of the chaotic household had delighted her. She found the conversation not only brilliant but stimulating and was astounded to find that she too had something to contribute; she was included and given credit for being herself and not patronised in any way. She implored Mallow and Floyd to come and visit her in England. She longed to see them again but couldn't help being apprehensive about the reception Robin might give them. She feared he might not be one to mix well with swimming pigs, perpetual barbecues and barefoot children.

'You are very quiet, Charlotte. What is worrying you?' Martin was driving them back down the freeway.

'Nothing. Well, almost nothing. That's it: I feel so beastly inadequate.'

'In what way?'

'I'm nothing.'

'You are Robin's wife.'

'Is that enough?'

'Yes, for Robin.'

'I don't think it is enough for me. All I can do are things to fall back on.'

'Well then Sam, perhaps you should pick up thy musket,' said Martin.

Charlotte knew what he meant. 'And let battle commence?' she enquired. Despite having far more than many other women (even Mallow) in looks, wealth and possibly social status, she often felt herself to be profoundly inferior in company. Charlotte feared that she was no more significant than a decorative feature, a handy coffer and a sweet thing who smiled and saw to putting fresh soap in spare bathrooms; the sort of wife whose price was above rubies only because she had inherited all the rubies in the first place.

She looked to her left at Martin who was sitting up close to the steering wheel and staring intently at the multi-lanes ahead through his essential glasses, wild hair dishevelled and flying in the down-draught from the sunshine roof. He did look scruffily leonine, but not the kind of beast that went about ripping flesh or savaging. Maybe that was the essence of his guile or charm. Like Le Douanier's sniffer lion his intentions were a mystery.

'Do you mind if I call you Wallace?'

'I'd be flattered, Sam.'

'Where have you been? More shopping?'

Robin was waiting in the bedroom when Charlotte got back to the hotel.

She kissed him. 'I've missed you, darling, but I have had the most wonderful time. Martin took me to stay with some friends of his for the weekend. It was marvellous. I had such fun. You can't imagine how much I loved it there. So unstuffy, so interesting. I feel inspired, I have such plans.'

'Oh?'

'Yes, I am going to get myself a degree, a career. It isn't too late, I know it isn't. Some people don't even start their education till they are older than me.'

'Don't be ridiculous.'

'Oh Robin. You mustn't be so damning. You haven't given me a chance.'

'You are dotty, Charlotte. Come on, let me give you lunch.'

'I don't feel like lunch yet. Won't you come with me to the Guggenheim and then I would like to get bagels and lox from a deli.'

'No.'

'Oh why not?'

'No.'

Charlotte never did hear how Robin had got on in Washington. He chose not to tell her and dismissed all her enquiries by saying it would bore her. He did, however, get over his obstinate bad temper and made sure that what time was left to them in New York was congenial.

Robin had one more political engagement from which Charlotte was excluded. She didn't mind; instead she went to Bellevue to visit Mallow that afternoon. The experience shocked and fascinated her: she realised then that she had never encountered anyone really poor before. The total lack of money that makes a subway token one third of a passport to a brief, happy alcoholic stupor; the mother of ten children by different fathers who has to leave hospital a couple of hours after giving birth; the gun-toting cops on the wards, and the American citizens without any English pleading as best they could for free colostomy bags and a chance to cry.

Robin even managed to get tickets to the Opera. Charlotte wept unrestrained, mascara coursing down her cheeks.

'You must learn a bit more self-control. You are far too emotional,' Robin scolded. He was not sympathetic.

'La ci darem la Mano' had done for her. The simple tune and the simple deception masking the complexities of betrayal and enchanting harmony had unexpectedly touched her in a spot she had not known she owned.

Robin cleaned her dirty face with his handkerchief as one would a grubby child.

'For God's sake buy yourself some waterproof mascara; you are letting me down.'

Back in England the telephone was ringing even as they got out of the taxi. Fumbling with keys Charlotte opened the door, skipped over the accumulated post and snatched up the receiver.

'Darling!'

'Mummy!'

Winifred's voice was shaky, not cross exactly, more relieved and angry like a parent who has been driven wild with anxiety by a naughty child discovered mischievously hiding after all manner of disasters and abductions had been imagined.

'Where have you been? Why were you not on the boat?'

Charlotte explained as best she could why they had chosen to ignore her father's present and return by air. It sounded most unlikely. She had assumed that Robin had told his mother to inform her own parents as to their movements. This had not happened.

'I am so sorry, Mum. I really am.'

'Never mind, my lamb, it wasn't your fault.'

'Mum, I am longing to see you.'

'Us too. Make it soon.'

Later Charlotte heard that Robin had sent the bill for the additional nights at the Plaza to Fraser along with a meticulously minute list of incidental expenses – dinners, opera tickets, the lot. He was only doing what he had been told. Robin hadn't wished to deprive Fraser of any chance to display his generosity. Charlotte had bought the air tickets home with the money in her current account. Her wordly goods were there for the sharing.

Fraser and Winifred had gone to Southampton to welcome their daughter and son-in-law off the boat. Winifred had taken flowers: the bouquet had become a mockery, so she dumped it in a litter bin.

Man had visited the moon before Charlotte could persuade Robin to find time for them to go to Dorset.

October 1994

'Lady Brand? Lady Brand, could you please tell the listeners whether you intend to stand by your husband following this afternoon's revelations, or do you have other plans?'

Charlotte looked beyond the reporter at the leafy gravel. She never knew if it was better to keep getting the leaves swept up or to wait until they had all dropped off. She knew that she did not want a vacuum cleaner for the leaves like the one Mrs Morning recommended. Garden machinery was forever breaking down or failing to start; besides, one might suck up all manner of undesirables – dead birds, dog turds, small mammals, it didn't bear thinking about. A silver thread waved in the breeze from the railings that led up the front steps, a relic of the silver wedding party. Charlotte noticed that the microphone was being impatiently waggled. According to Cliff Heath, the listeners to Radio Thames were all agog for her views.

'There is no question of it,' Charlotte said.

'No question of what, Lady Brand?'

'I have no more to say, thank you so much.'

The door was shut firmly on Cliff and his crew.

'Lady Brand!' he shouted through the letterbox. 'Your dog has bitten me.'

'Then bite her back! It is the only way.'

4

Autumn 1969

'YOU WILL LOVE him, Charlotte, he really worships me. He is utterly sweet and terribly fit for his age, not stooping or drooping or grotty like other men over fifty.'

'But he could be your father.'

'He isn't, though. Anyway I haven't had one of those for years.'

'Won't you get bored?'

'I'm not bored yet, and I don't intend to get bored or let him bore me. We understand each other, perfectly.'

Peta had caught a new man, a widower with money, position and all the bits that make age, hair loss and retreating gums irrelevant. She was secretly engaged and wore a mighty diamond on a chain round her neck. She looked happy in her fun fur, a garment which would only have brought amusement to someone well dug into affluence.

'The only problem is that he would like us to live in the country near his beastly suburban constituency. You know the sort of place – all houses called after the trees that grow in their well-fenced gardens where the Tories get voted in, even if they fart in public and promote genocide.'

'You didn't say he was an MP. Robin will be fascinated: he's trying desperately to get adopted by the Tories anywhere.'

'Well when he does just make sure you keep a flat in London, like us. I would die if you ran off to somewhere awful like Lincolnshire and got swamped in a fen.'

'He has hopes of a seat in Scotland.'

'Christ! How terrible. I just refuse to fester anywhere further than Fulham. Hurlingham is dangerously exposed.'

'Come on, Peta. Do tell me his name.'

'I can't. I promised. Not yet. Not till he has told his son.'

'Oh Peta, you will make a really wicked stepmother. Poor little thing.'

'Little be damned, he's about the same age as me!'

'Your man must be well over fifty.'

'I never said he wasn't.'

Charlotte's plans for self-improvement had withered. She was not to become further educated: Robin fixed that. 'I need you, my darling, you are perfect as you are. Please don't spoil it. Everything is so right, just as it is.'

Robin liked things kept right. A wife with a stirring brain might get diverted from his life's route, which he had planned to run straight to the top without irritating diversions. His wife must be prepared to devote everything to his maintenance and adapt to all his ways. Charlotte was perfect: malleable, kind and not in a position to question much.

Once home in London the call to self-fulfilment was not so blatant. Old friends, content with the way things were going on, did not stimulate her to be restless or search for greater horizons. Instead of working for a degree Charlotte got a job of sorts helping a friend make and distribute entertaining draught excluders. Draft Dodgers did well, especially at Christmas: there was scarcely a family in SW3 who did not buy a dachshund, worm or fish with a dopey smile to stop the wind whistling under the ill-fitting doors of their country retreats. The Clever Dick was the most daring of their range and not suitable for the prudish but outrageously popular amongst the young. Robin was uncertain whether it was funny or not: he needed guidance on this point, and at twenty-eight he was no longer young in years. He had never been young in demeanour.

Apart from Charlotte's job making felt sausages, Robin had asked her to do some work for him. She had been flattered and delighted and really enjoyed what he asked her to do. He needed research done into the wives of prime ministers from Robert Walpole to Harold Wilson. That, he thought, should keep her well occupied. He was working on the Great Reform Bill himself; at least that is what he told anyone enquiring to how he filled his days now that he had virtually given up work. By the Monday of Christmas week Caroline Loam and Charlotte had completed their last orders. Any draught that sprang after 22 December would not be excluded till the New Year. Draft Dodgers would have made more money had they sold more of their stock but as both girls had decided to give all their relatives their handiwork for Christmas the profits were minimal after the overheads had been calculated.

It was strange staying in her old room with Robin. Winifred had kindly pushed twin beds together and linked them with double sheets and blankets. The castors were well oiled and the beds skidded apart if anything strenuous happened in the middle. The floors creaked and the windows rattled disapprovingly, convincing both Robin and Charlotte that even the household germs were watching. Every eye was trained on them from her old school photograph where straight tiers of gym-tuniced girls smirked in front of a strangely convex Gothic building. The lacrosse team thought the whole performance unlikely and unhealthy. China horses, wounded teddies and dreadfully old and tawdry treasures of her childhood remained on their shelves as comforts to Winifred, who liked to remember how much she had loved her only spell of being a mother. As the mother of a grown child she still worried.

'My lamb, are you happy?'

'Yes, Mum, I'm very happy. Why do you ask?'

'What a joy to have so many of our dear, dear family with us.' Elizabeth Brand had worked herself into a pulp of benevolence to secure a place for herself in the good providers hall of fame. She was to do Christmas lunch that year. Thrift had not been abandoned: season of goodwill or not, there was no need for extravagance. A plentiful spread could be got by stuffing most edible cavities with well-breaded forcemeat and enhancing the pudding with grated carrot and crumbs to make an ample feast for all. Her peppermints were only slightly grubby and much cheerfulness could be created with chicken netting, tinfoil and fir cones dangling from wire coat hangers. Evergreenery was everywhere.

The Forth household, to which all had been invited for champagne, smoked salmon and mince pies on Christmas Eve, had been warm and sparkling but, according to Elizabeth, lacking in soul.

The Brand table was laid for thirteen. The number worried Winifred, so Fraser, who had fortified himself at home with several stiff drinks, asked Elizabeth Brand if another place could be set.

'Of course, you want a place for the stranger. How nice.'

'No, Elizabeth we are just superstitious about thirteen at table. The Last Supper, you know.'

'Yes, yes. The Passover, I remember.'

Various Brand relatives had appeared for Christmas including a cross aunt with a pug. In the interests of Christian charity and worldwide brotherhood Elizabeth was pleased to have got hold of a Finn.

'That woman talks just like someone who has managed to get a pork chop on the black market,' Fraser grumbled.

The Finn was frozen. He offered to chop wood for the empty dining-room grate and would gladly have swept the flue, but all to no avail. The Brands had thick blood as well as skin.

'Nonsense Lars, you are our guest. Enjoy yourself,' Elizabeth commanded.

Fenella's fiancé was a Marxist called Jake Cleaver. He felt very insecure about Christmas.

Charlotte naturally had intended the Clever Dick for Laura, who was young and still entertained by humorous genitalia. The robin upon the yule log was for her mother-in-law. Getting those presents muddled was most unfortunate. As a *faux pas* it was substantial and no good as a joke.

'How facile,' was all Elizabeth would say on the subject.

Winifred chattered, saying little but preventing awkward silence; Jake made no effort whatsoever. Charlotte and Robin had become fixtures. Fenella's forthcoming marriage to Jake was the new focal point of Brand family interest, and especially popular in that ten minutes' worth of Registry Office made such economic sense.

'These lavish weddings are so often such vulgar hypocrisy,'

33

Elizabeth told Fraser who was still floating on his home-poured alcohol and agreed with her on all subjects while trying to remember what it was about the cross aunt that reminded him of Halifax.

'So what did you see in New York?' Jake had put a mirthless paper hat on his dirty hair. The hat did not detract from the piercing dedication of his eyes.

Charlotte told him what she had seen.

'A typical conditioned response,' he sneered. 'What did you really see?'

Trying hard to please, she mentioned her visit to Bellevue.

'Spare me the slumming. Don't fob me off with that over-privileged garbage about the possession of material wealth imposing obligations.'

Charlotte shrugged. There was nothing she could say. Jake took her silence for superior insolence.

He thumped the table. Berries plopped off the holly decoration into the brandy-free butter. 'How dare you insult me, you running sore of the bourgeoisie!' He tore off his paper hat and slamming the door left the room in a shower of dislodged glitter, floating like the tinfoil scattered to puzzle enemy radar.

'Poor Jake,' said Fenella, 'he is very sensitive.' She went off to reassure him. She returned in an hour, ruffled but with her man much appeased.

'You will have to learn more tact, Charlotte dear, if you are to become a politician's wife,' Elizabeth said. 'I can't be doing with an atmosphere. Do have another mince pie, Laura my sweet, they contain parsnips.'

'Can I be of assistance?'

'Sit down, Lars. Relax. Have fun.'

Clever games followed lunch. Apart from the pug, Charlotte's score was the lowest. A forfeit must be paid: she must recite, or sing. Charlotte did 'Albert and the Lion'. No comedian getting the bird could have met with such a wretched response.

'Please, is the eating of children by lions considered entertaining in England?'

'No, not in the slightest, Lars,' said Elizabeth.

'I think it is hilarious,' said Fraser. 'Well done, Charlotte.'

'You would say that, Fraser.'

'It is time we left,' said Winifred.

'Laura darling, find Mrs Forth's coat for her, there's a dear.'

'Don't trouble her, Elizabeth, I never took my jacket off. You must all call me Winifred. Goodbye everyone, it has been a memorable Christmas,' Winifred beamed at all, much cheered by the prospect of home comforts. 'You have gone to so much trouble, Elizabeth, you must be shattered. Next year . . .' Here she faltered: she knew that she was expected to reciprocate the hospitality but she could see Fraser's martyred expression. 'Next year . . .' she faltered again. 'Next year . . .'

'In Jerusalem?' Elizabeth suggested.

Winifred attempted a laugh. 'No, next year . . .'

'Next year,' Fraser announced, 'we are going on a cruise.'

Robin had been quiet during lunch. He had made no attempt to be jolly and certainly none to make Charlotte feel at ease. Once back home with her he asked whether she had enjoyed Christmas.

'No, I thought it was hell. Every one of your family except that pug was out to make me look a fool.'

'You will have to get used to that.'

'Why? Because I am a fool?'

'No, not entirely.'

'Well then what?'

'Envy, jealousy.'

'What of?'

'For having married me.'

'You are bloody conceited.'

'Joke, darling.'

'I never know when you are being serious, Robin.'

'I'm always serious, deadly serious.'

'Laura told Jake, in my hearing, that you married me for my money.'

'So?'

'Did you, Robin?'

'It helped.'

'Really?'

'No, not really. Here, let me give you a kiss.'

'I can't tell when you are speaking the truth either.'
'That is why I will make a brilliant politician.'

Two weddings followed each other closely that spring. First Fenella and Jake had a subdued ceremony at Chelsea Register Office which was not then in the splendour of the Town Hall but in a joyless room up some stone stairs in the building opposite. Fenella seemed happy in her tent-shaped minidress; Jake looked resigned. Charlotte felt very silly in her fur hat. Possibly fatherhood would make Jake more amenable. His parents were much respected in Maidstone. Somehow no one had really expected Jake to have parents, least of all a pair of churchwardens.

The second wedding took place round the corner in St Luke's, Sydney Street and caused quite a to-do amongst the groom's constituents. Godfrey Fable, DSO, MP, widower of the parish of Godleham and aged fifty-five was remarrying. His bride was twenty-four. Charlotte's ex-flatmate Peta was to become stepmother to Martin. Her stepson was the same age as her and found the whole affair thoroughly uplifting.

Martin was his father's best man and Charlotte was matron of honour. Peta appeared to have no sane relatives apart from a hippie brother who was usually stoned, and some unreliable uncles, so Robin was recruited to give her away which he did with devastating condescension, though bride and her substitute father both had reason to dislike each other profoundly. Robin, as always, was prepared to plumb all depths in search of a constituency, and the groom, after all, had clung to his seat since 1951. A knight of the shires without a knighthood, keen rider to hounds and chaser of women, Godfrey had managed to stride through life endearingly. His wife, Martin's mother, had been a dear sweet soul who grew lovely flowers and died as quietly as she had lived at the age of forty-seven, a patiently resigned cancer victim. Martin had adored her. He loved his father too and was happy for him to have found Peta. Her motives for marrying his father he considered to be none of his business. He hoped they would make each other happy one way or the other. Martin was lucky not to be plagued by jealousy or greed: his own needs were well met by his own salary, he did not hanker after his inheritance. Peta was dressed by Valerie Goad as Supervirgin.

'Listen Sam.'

'What to, Wallace?'

'The sound of hands wringing, teeth gnashing and garments being rent.'

Charlotte and Martin were observing the guests from behind the mountainous wedding cake at the reception in the House of Commons. Ponderous paintings of dignitaries hung from the dark panelled walls and spring sunshine insinuated itself through the stained-glass mullioned windows. Lots of champagne and canapés circulated amongst the knots of guests, most of whom seemed to be well over forty and inclined to talk out of the sides of their mouths while glaring at the bride.

'They do all look cross,' Charlotte said.

'They are,' Martin replied. 'The fury of a scorned Tory lady is quite beyond Hell's scope. Ever since Mum died Dad has been pursued by herds of true blue widows and spinsters. I can't think what he will do for constituency workers now. There was nothing those women wouldn't do for him when it came to canvassing, stuffing envelopes, raising money and forcing people into polling booths. You watch out when you become a candidate's wife. Those women will destroy you, given a chance, like worker bees with too many queens.'

'It's a wonder no one caught your father before now.'

'He is too canny for that.'

'But not canny enough to dodge Peta.'

'Dad will be fine. He knows what he is taking on. He has always been a terrible philanderer. I reckon they will do each other very well. Tell me about yourselves.'

'We're all right. Robin is very busy trying to get a seat.'

'So I see. He was ardently making himself known to just about every important or influential guest at this wedding before we had even left the church. He'll be great and make you proud.'

Charlotte watched her husband at work: it was an awe-inspiring display of social dexterity.

'And what about you, Sam. Have you got yourself an education yet?'

Charlotte confessed she had not. She felt stupid explaining to Martin why she had shelved her ambitions and turned her energies to making draught excluders. 'I do some research for Robin. I thought I might try and do something on prime ministers' wives.'

'Ending with you?'

'Maybe.'

Roddy MacPhail, deftly urbane even when spearing a sausage, waved at Charlotte; his parents had known Godfrey for years. Henrietta, who looked radiant in all-over Elegance Maternelle, remained most sceptical about the bride.

'Well Sam, when is Robin going to make you a mummy?'

'Oh Wallace, not for a while I hope. I'm not happy being in charge of a Hoover yet, let alone a baby. I'd leave it somewhere or let it get at the gin.'

'Robin will be anxious to be a father soon. Family men are favourite when it comes to selection committees. They are thought to be well behaved and reliable.'

One of Peta's vague relatives was the solitary bridesmaid. A snotty child with a fractious temperament that certainly did not detract from the beauty of the bride. The child's name was Ocean and she was four.

'I'm bored,' whined Ocean.

'Well go and find your Mummy.'

'Mummy told me to come and see you. Will you play with me?'

'No,' said Charlotte.

Ocean glared and stamped her patent-leathered foot on Charlotte's satin slipper.

'Ow!'

'Now will you play with me?'

Charlotte crouched down till her eyes were level with Ocean's sulky face. 'Do you see those cage things?' Charlotte pointed at a portcullis embossed on a chair-back.

'Yes,' said Ocean.

'Well my little chicken, those are the doors to the prisons where they put extremely naughty people.' The child stared at

Charlotte. 'The sort of people that stamp on other people's feet. Do you understand?'

'Yes.'

'Can you count, Ocean?'

'Yes.'

'Well I want you to go away and count them. There are lots and lots of them and don't come back till you have counted them all.'

'You will make a rare mother, Sam,' said Martin.

Robin was having a wonderfully useful time making himself charming and playing the part of the future redeemer of Conservatism. Dark and handsome, he could slay any Tory lady with ease; the men he could charm without appearing to fawn. His academic and social records were faultless.

'Darling, come and meet Sir Edward Peerless. Sir Edward, may I introduce my wife Charlotte.'

Charlotte shook hands with a bluff, bloated man, whose face was familiar from the newspapers. No amount of press exposure had prepared her for his breath, which was a nasty blend of putrefaction and port. Sir Edward was also high in Central Office.

Later when they were waving the happy couple off outside Westminster Hall Robin kissed Charlotte. 'Well done, darling. You made a very good impression.'

A camera flashed. The picture of Robin with his young bride made a good impression too. Now all he needed was a child to make him into a dream candidate.

October 1994

Charlotte felt besieged. Luckily Piers consented to collect Zoe from the front garden. The little bitch's jaws were not obviously bloodstained even though the ladies and gentlemen of the press remained firmly planted on the lawn.

'Piers, do you know about what has happened to Daddy today?'

'No, not really,' Piers replied.

'Nothing?'

'Well only that a bloke at work said my dad would have to be looking for a new job too, like me.'

'Ah, I see. Did this bloke say why?'

'Why don't you turn on the telly. It's bound to be on the news.'

Before Charlotte could follow her son's suggestion the telephone rang.

'Charlotte darling, it's me, Peta.'

'Peta, what has happened?'

'You haven't heard?'

'No. Quick, tell me.'

'You know about those reports that Robin was taking sweeteners, and I don't mean saccharine.'

'Yes, but I thought all that talk of bribes was a rumour trumped up by a load of bored and hungry hacks.'

'Maybe. Well anyway it looks as if the Parliamentary Privileges Committee have reason to be curious.'

'I see,' said Charlotte. 'So Robin has resigned?'

'Yes, but that isn't all. Oh Charlotte I feel dreadful telling this to you of all people, over the phone.'

'Go on, Peta. I've got to know. I'm not an idiot and I don't want to look like one. Everyone else seems to know.'

'That bitch told her story, that's what.'

'What bitch?'

'Clemency van Schumacher, of course. She has revealed all to coincide with the publication of my vile little cousin's frightful book.'

'Your cousin? Which cousin?'

'I've only got one, Ocean Bray. She has written what purports to be a work of fiction based on her time spent employed in the House of Commons. Names have been changed but the title isn't too kind to Robin.'

'Why, what is it called?'

'Branded in Blue.'

'I see.'

There was a pause.

'Charlotte, are you still there?'

'Yes Peta. You haven't said anything about Clemency.'

'She has had a son. He's called Merlin.'

'Well I suppose she has got to the age when babies are looked upon as right-on accessories amongst the sisterhood. She went back to the States ages ago, just after the accident.'

'Charlotte, Clemency's son is not a baby, he is eight years old.'

5

Spring 1970

WHY THE CONSERVATIVES bothered to fight Kirkbeggie at all was a triumph for pig-headedness. Apart from a handful of the faithful the only crosses the Tory ever got were scrawled by illiterates and drunks, of which there were a lot, but not quite enough, in Kirkbeggie. The virtue of the constituency from the Conservative angle was that it served as a sieve. Any candidate who fought in the blue corner and survived was keen indeed and could then apply to be considered for somewhere a bit safer.

No one felt safe in Kirkbeggie unless they were part of a gang. The cats and dogs strolled in packs, children formed lifetime allegiance to their peer groups and football teams while still in Bogview lying-in hospital, their mothers being prepared to fight a woman from a rival close for anything from a seat on the bus to respect in the queue down the Co-op. The lucky men of Kirkbeggie were spasmodically employed by Isis Metals, Grieg's Rope, and Curtis Curley Chemicals which gave forth a sulphurous smell and lit the neon sky with yellow and blue flame plumes. Occasionally a loud blast would be heard coming from Curtis Curley but most of the noise in Kirkbeggie was caused by the relentless passage of lorries on the greasy cobbles, the thump of the dye-stamp at Isis, and Grieg's twelve o'clock hooter.

The unions were the strongest thing in Kirkbeggie, the men being for the most part scrawny, bent, paunchy, tobacco-stained specimens in flat hats while their wives were either large and stuffed with scones or meanly thin with Woodbines stuck to ratty lips. Most women, fat or thin, kept their hair in curlers and tied their heads up in scarves to be released for bingo and the occasional Friday night at the working men's club. Only the Fair fortnight relieved the depression that hung over Kirkbeggie even when the sun shone.

Robin sat before the selection panel in the Conservative and Unionist Party office which was a Nissen hut with gridded windows at the end of a row of prefabs of long standing. A signed photograph of Sir Alec Douglas-Home gloated like confident Death above the chairman's seat; no one had got round to getting a picture of Ted Heath.

'You are a married man I see, Mr Brand.'

'Yes, I have a most supportive wife.'

'Any children?'

'No.'

There was a silence while the chairman referred to his colleagues, Mr Waxman the oculist and Mrs Curley who though not a resident of the constituency had been recruited to join the committee on the strength of her husband's family firm providing the area with much of its employment and most of its odours. The Curleys lived up the Campsies.

Robin answered the questions put to him with skill acquired from his legal training. He said yes to law and order, peaceful co-existence and full employment; no to crime, joblessness and strife. He wore his glasses for earnestness and to delight Mr Waxman, taking them off to woo Mrs Curley. The chairman demanded to know where he stood on capital punishment, to which Robin replied he was only moderately keen.

'I take it you are prepared to swing either way?'

'Yes, sir.' Robin answered, appearing to give this much consideration.

'That was my little joke,' the chairman pointed out gravely, while scribbling on his pad.

Robin laughed but it was too late.

'And you say you have no children?' enquired Mrs Curley again just to confirm his failure.

'Thank you for coming, Mr Brand. Perhaps you would ask the next gentleman to come in.'

The next gentleman was Roderick MacPhail, merchant banker husband to Henrietta, mother of one and pregnant.

Robin drove down James Brown Avenue and away from Kirkbeggie for ever to the sound of Roddy's laughter as he displayed snaps of young Leonora MacPhail to the delighted committee.

Seatless Robin helped to get Godfrey Fable re-elected for Godleham. Charlotte and Peta didn't do much except be there to celebrate Godfrey's inevitable triumph. The overall Conservative victory, however, came as a big surprise.

Hungover and jaded the following afternoon, Charlotte sat watching the John Lewis removal van on the television drawing up outside Number Eleven to ship Roy Jenkins out of Downing Street, when Robin's new and most portentous desk arrived from Peter Jones. It was pompous reproduction much embossed with tooled leather and polished to a tawny sheen. Robin had bought it as a consolation prize for himself and charged it to Charlotte's account, home furnishing being the wife's affair. 'If only Roy had stuck to his job with us instead of larking about being Chancellor of the bleeding Exchequer,' the delivery man remarked sorrowfully, 'he could have been head of department by now.'

Winifred was up in town. She needed lots of things, the sales were on so she needed even more than she had first thought. Laden with parcels she called on Charlotte.

'Mother, you look like something out of a Hollywood movie.'

'Nonsense darling, they always have bellhops and lovers to carry their parcels.'

'OK, let me help.' Charlotte kissed her mother: 'You look wonderful, and smell gorgeous.'

'You don't, darling. Look wonderful, I mean. You smell all right though.'

'That is something, I suppose. I just haven't been sleeping too well and we had a heavy night celebrating the election yet again.'

'Is Robin being horrid to you?'

'Shh . . . He's upstairs.'

'Doing what?'

'Working, he is writing a book.'

Winifred didn't believe a word of it but kept quiet. Fraser had implored her not to interfere but sometimes there is nothing else to do, especially when a beloved daughter looks all fraught.

'I am going to start a new job,' said Charlotte. 'Well it isn't really a job, more an occupation. Caroline Loam and I have stopped the Draft Dodgers and now we are going to do flowers.'

'But darling, you know practically nothing about flowers.'

'I can learn more, and Caroline went to Winkfield. I can be a bucket carrier anyway. We are called Loambrand Bouquets. It has a good earthy ring to it, don't you think?'

'You know best, darling. Anyway my lamb, tell me how you really are. Are you happy?'

'Of course.'

'You always say that.'

'Well I am. We are going to have a baby.'

'Oh my love, how wonderful! Oh what heaven, I long to be a granny. When is it due?'

'Well at least nine months from now. We only decided I should stop taking the pill yesterday.'

The years passed and Loambrand fell apart with Caroline's marriage to an Orcadian in 1972.

Fenella and Jake remained together and bred between rows. Jake was father of three in late 1973 and also looking for a seat in Parliament but on the opposite side of the House to his brother-in-law. Jake had made himself a thorough nuisance in local government since his marriage. He was the bane of the East Blenchworth Conservatives and a champion of that borough's downtrodden. The country was all of a heap, Ted Heath was in a fix and soon the cunning wheeze of the three-day week would do his cause no good at all. An election was a growing inevitability.

Still Charlotte did not conceive. Nightly, often daily, Robin went about his marital business. The anxiety was destroying them both, and certainly annihilating the rapture. Copulation was a duty, best performed at a favourable time. Robin insisted on taking Charlotte's temperature to ascertain the most auspicious moment to pounce. They both ate a lot of fish. Fish might be the answer, only it wasn't.

Peta had no babies either. She couldn't anyway, even if her husband had been younger.

Martin Fable was on a brief visit from Hong Kong when he told Charlotte this.

'But she never told me, and I am her best friend.'

'Aha, but Sam, I'm her stepson.'

Peta had a past which had done for her future as a mother. She and Godfrey lived an idyllic life, they doted on each other and asked no questions.

Robin insisted that Charlotte visit a specialist. The doctor charged a lot to say that all was well; relaxation was the key, he opined and presented a three-figure bill, which Charlotte settled, the womb being the wife's department.

'There is nothing wrong with me,' Robin said when Charlotte suggested that it might be as well for him to visit a man of the testicle.

'How do you know?'

'I do.'

'But how?'

Robin would not be drawn. Suffice it, he told her, that he had paid out considerably for the evidence of his fecundity to be removed. 'I was still at Oxford, just.'

'Oh Robin, how dreadful.'

'It happens all the time, you goose.'

'I know, but . . . did you love her? Why didn't you marry her?'

'She wasn't suitable. I didn't love her, and anyway I wouldn't have then been able to marry you. Come on, why don't we go upstairs now, and I'll show you.'

Sometimes Charlotte felt it would have been better if she hadn't been suitable either, suitability being so much embroiled with being well off. Sometimes while gazing at the ceiling Charlotte wondered whether she would be better off without Robin altogether. She was getting pretty bored with him being on top of her all the time.

'Relax!' he commanded between the thumping lurches. 'Relax! There now, what did I say, nothing wrong with me!'

'Yes darling, Peta told me you were the Cock of the Walk at Oxford.'

That seemed to please Robin. Actually Peta had said that Robin was a randy little jerk.

Robin's hard work for the Conservatives paid off just before their fourth wedding anniversary. Their hard work at procreation had not. Heals were to be congratulated on the resilience of the bedsprings, but still no small Brand got itself conceived. However, Pittenfirth and Netherloch Conservative Association decided that Robin was just the thing. He was young, bright, a barrister with an advance on a scholarly book as well as having a splendid wife. Robin had told the committee that his wife was a Scot; that went down well. To a question on the rights of minorities he pointed out that she was also Jewish, and a keen churchgoer, a tireless worker and great enthusiast for all things Tory, a historian with a particular interest in political wives, a botanist and, remembering Draft Dodgers, a notable craftswoman, and mad keen on golf. Everything in fact but not, alas, a mother. But all was not lost, said Robin, as negotiations were, even as he spoke, under way for the adoption of one or two Vietnamese orphans.

'What?' shrieked Charlotte, when Robin had returned to London triumphant with his seat almost assured. 'I know nothing about that!'

'Well you do now. I just thought of it, and why not?' Robin replied. 'It is a splendid idea; noble too.'

Before consenting to give Robin the candidature, Pittenfirth and Netherloch wanted to vet Charlotte for themselves.

'I have never felt more humiliated in my life, Robin,' she told him in the train going home. 'Do you know, they actually asked me to turn round so they could see my back view, and whatever made them think we were about to move up there to live?'

'I did,' said Robin, looking at his wife's ankles. They were ideal.

Whatever happened, Charlotte insisted that a move to Scotland would not mean a pebbledash semi beneath a flightpath overlooking a forbidding reservoir such as Henrietta and Roddy MacPhail had rented when fighting the lost cause of Kirkbeggie.

Little Caspar's nanny had left the moment Henrietta had been diagnosed as suffering from impetigo, got while electioneering in the boning-out department of the abattoir.

An elegant flat in Edinburgh or some authentic crofty sort of thing but well set up with plumbing, heating, communications and a matchless view would do. In the end they got a seaside cottage, pebbledashed certainly but quite well appointed, at the end of a golf links.

'I hate golf, it bores me. I know nothing about it.'

'Nonsense, darling, you adore the game, you know you do.' Robin had bought Charlotte an enormous Afghan sheepskin coat to cheer her up. As a fashion it was out; the poorly cured hide was off, but its price was down.

They had withstood the horrors of Links Cottage for about a week before Robin's mother visited to help them settle in and to admire her son's magnetic performance on the platform. Nightly Robin spoke to the same handful of faithful followers and daily he traipsed about shaking hands and being terribly impressed with local industry and the beautiful children of the locality while tutting his tongue sorrowfully over shortcomings in the cleansing department, the sorry state of the pavements and the rise of petty crime amongst the insubordinate youth of Pittenfirth and Netherloch. Elizabeth and Charlotte followed behind, beaming and being healthily concerned with all. After her spell in Scotland Elizabeth was to go to furthest Essex to do the same for Fenella and Jake, only there she would have to be a good granny as well as listening to more electioneering rhetoric, this time for the Labour Party. Jake's chances of success at Mireness were as tenuous as those of his wife's brother at Pittenfirth and Netherloch.

With Laura nursing a crush on Dick Taverne and gunning for the Democratic Labour Party, Elizabeth Brand tended to look upon herself as the womb of modern politics. Cyril Brand stayed at home, minded the practice and voted Liberal.

Winifred and Fraser Forth also came north, spent one night in the howling cottage and clocked in at Gleneagles.

Robin needed to increase his general popularity.

'Darling, do you think your father could possibly manage to be a bit more Scottish?'

'I don't think so,' Charlotte replied. She and Robin were trying to keep the North Sea gales at bay with insulating tape round the windows. Never was there such a rattler of a building as Links Cottage. 'He just isn't the sort for the kilt.'

'Well perhaps he could be a touch more Jewish. Rabbi Pearlman tells me his synagogue is crammed with Tories in need of encouragement.'

'I can't see Dad in a skull cap either and he has only got one hair, but at least he does play golf, that ought to do something for your credibility.'

'You aren't taking this seriously.'

'No, Robin, to be honest with you I can't. How much longer have we got to stay here?'

'Till after the election, of course.'

'And if you get in?'

'We'll see.'

'Well I tell you one thing: I am not going to stay in this cottage, it is terrifying.'

The party agent was a dear, sweet man, meeker than a dormouse and constantly plagued by the most crippling anxieties. Once he confided in Charlotte that he too had wanted to get into Parliament but public speaking was not his line. In fact if he spoke to more than two or three friends or one mild foe he was apt to panic and had been known to cry. Phil Fleet was zealous and worried about everything, especially protocol.

'Oh please,' he would implore. 'Please do not follow too closely in your cars. More than one Vote Brand car at a time could be misconstrued as a motorcade.'

For some reason Phil Fleet felt motorcades should not be allowed to form at random moments. He also worried a lot about the size of rosettes. Only Robin was allowed a real breastplate of a blue monstrosity. There was an ongoing bouquet of flowers that got itself repeatedly thrust at Charlotte. Phil would confiscate it almost at the moment of presentation lest it should wilt in the heat. The budget ran to just one such bunch per week. Everybody wilted not from heat but from tedium and the monotony of keeping constantly cheerful and up to the top with loyal optimism.

Charlotte was sick and Robin's hopes were raised: pregnancy

might catch the floating voting housewife. Charlotte was not pregnant. Both she and Phil Fleet had been mildly poisoned by some malign meat paste.

Pie 'n' pâté party, cheese 'n' wine party, soup 'n' sandwich party, tea 'n' biscuits party – Charlotte found herself at one or another every day. 'I'm sick 'n' tired of all these bloody apostrophe n's.'

'Wait till you go to a conference,' Robin warned. 'You will have to learn to do ten parties, chat, be intelligent and remain sober all in half an hour.'

'We all think you're damn plucky, Charlotte,' said Lady Begg.

Sir Tam Begg had been member on and off for Pittenfirth and Netherloch since before little Phil Fleet had timidly got himself born, and was only relinquishing his seat in 1974 on doctor's orders. Sir Tam had been flirting with senility for quite some time but his wife was indestructible and much looking forward to the time when her husband would succeed his father in the House of Lords. The Beggs were long lived and often mad, descended as they were from Begg the Deranged of Auchenkirk.

'I suppose you get used to it,' Charlotte said.

'I'm damned if I would,' replied Lady Begg.

Charlotte was puzzled. 'But you were an MP's wife for years and years. I heard you were magnificent. I know I will never come up to the mark.'

'I wasn't talking about that, my dear. I meant Links Cottage. You wouldn't catch me living there.'

'Why?'

'Didn't anyone tell you?'

'Tell me what?'

'Never mind. Oh look, here comes dear wee Phil with something troublesome.'

That night the wind rattled through every crack even though there was just a slight breeze disturbing the whin grass outside. At two o'clock the front door flew open and the insulating tape fell from the window-frame like a dead snake. Charlotte clung to Robin. At moments like this she knew why she stayed married. 'I am not going to live here for another night. Get me out of here.'

'Calm down, darling.'

'I can't stand this place. It seems to be haunted.'

'Yes, but very cheap.'

'You knew?'

'There had to be some reason for the low rent. I'm not made of money, you know.'

'But I am?'

The next day Robin and Charlotte moved to a comfortable and hideous bungalow costing three times as much as Links Cottage. Charlotte paid the bill: the inflated rent was worth every penny.

On 28 February 1974 the Acting Deputy Returning Officer for Pittenfirth and Netherloch announced that Robin Birtwhistle Brand was duly elected to represent the said constituency. There had been a recount. Robin had failed to attract the loyalty that had marked Sir Tam's years of dithering silent presence in Parliament, but no matter. Robin was so elated that he neglected to jump on Charlotte even though it was the optimum time of the month.

The Conservatives, however, were no longer in power. The election had been hastily and unwisely called and their proportion of seats had been reduced to below that held by Labour. Ted Heath's Tories went a-wooing but there were no brides to be got amongst the Liberals or Independents. On 6 March hands were kissed and the socialists were back. The Wilsons flitted into Number Ten Downing Street; the miners were appeased.

Jake Cleaver, a new boy on the winning side, had been returned for Mireness. Robin started his parliamentary career in opposition.

6

March 1974

'LET ME INTRODUCE you to Tim Renton. He is another new member for our side – a rare beast.'

Robin smiled graciously at Godfrey Fable, hoping to make it perfectly clear that while he appreciated the older man's efforts to get him settled and organised he would prefer to make his own friends, in his own time. He wanted to be noticed by the prefects, not be seen chumming up with New Boys.

His first encounter with the ex-Prime Minister in the corridors of power had been a bit anticlimactic. Gone were the grin and the shaking shoulders beloved of impersonators; instead of studied joviality a natural grim surliness permeated the familiar fleshy features of his party leader.

'Never mind, darling,' said Charlotte on hearing of this disappointing incident. 'Moving house can be utterly ghastly, it knocks the stuffing right out of one.'

'Try not to be too silly, Charlotte,' Robin replied.

Godfrey Fable had offered to give Jake Cleaver and his entourage lunch in the House of Commons too. He was a generous man and believed in civility.

'Now can you understand why I adore Godfrey?' Peta asked Charlotte.

Charlotte said she did. She too liked Godfrey, though not of course with such passionate intensity. Peta and Godfrey Fable had been married for four years, she was an old man's darling and her heart belonged to her father figure. Mostly her body did too. Charlotte did not like to admit that it was Godfrey's resemblance to Martin, his son, that made him attractive to her.

'Oh no thank you, Godfrey,' said Robin hastily on hearing of the proposed invitation. 'Jake may be my brother-in-law but there is no need for fraternisation.'

'Still, I shouldn't be too dismissive, Robin. He might make a useful pair. Believe me, it is very handy to have an opposite number.'

Robin wasn't listening. He was observing the ex-Secretary of State for Education: there was something worth following about her.

Earlier that day, Robin had found his first experience of life at the Palace of Westminster quite horrendous. Family Members, Brothers in Arms, Rule of In-Law, the press had swooped upon the family interest aspect of Jake and Robin both entering Parliament on the same day on opposite sides of the House.

Elizabeth Brand, besotted by their success, aimed to get herself photographed linking arms with her son and her son-in-law lots of times all over the Palace of Westminster. Snapping within the building is forbidden, so she had to settle for a shot of her with Robin and Jake below the statue of Mrs Pankhurst giving rise to the theory that she, not her men, had been elected. MOTHER OF PARLIAMENT the caption proclaimed when that picture appeared in the *Evening News*.

A family group was posed with the Burghers of Calais as backdrop. Charlotte stood by Robin, neat in navy coat-dress while Fenella and her messy children clung to bearded Jake. All three and their mother were got up in loose cotton garments assembled at home from a kit, and looked like a condensed Family Von Trapp. Cyril Brand had remained in Dorset: the practice needed an eye kept upon it, he did not like leaving its custody to Fraser Forth, the senior partner, alone. One reads so much of coups occurring when those in power go on excursions, entrusting the palace to lax viziers.

Mr and Mrs Cleaver senior had come from Maidstone for the day and felt snubbed. Jake's mother had forced his father to get a new suit and drive all the way to Tunbridge Wells for the buying of her outfit with hat to match plus gloves, shoes and bag to tone.

'How nice you look in your demob suit,' Elizabeth remarked, kindly condescending to beam at Mr Cleaver. She had absolutely nothing against her daughter's parents-in-law, nothing at all, she wanted that to be understood.

Robin too would have liked to have given a display of offspring, and even wondered whether Caspar and Leonora MacPhail could be borrowed complete with traditional shorts and smocked frock to add tone to his image. Roddy MacPhail would have to continue merchant banking yet a while. Kirkbeggie, much to Henrietta's relief, had rejected him again.

Elizabeth, her daughter and grandchildren eventually disappeared to feed the wintry ducks in St James's Park and eat a disappointing lunch in a Wimpy bar.

The Cleaver parents returned to Kent disgruntled. Jake's father was minded to get the money back on his suit, especially as his son had turned up for the big day in old trousers, corduroy jacket and flowered tie.

Meanwhile Jake Cleaver took the oath. 'Them what's keen gets fell in previous,' Robin had remarked sarcastically on observing his brother-in-law's unseemly eagerness. He, himself, planned to saunter down later and get sworn in in his own time, with the sophisticated detachment of one accustomed to these things.

Despite his efforts to appear self-assured there were a multitude of things that Robin needed to know and even he had to admit he was grateful to have a veteran like Godfrey to show him around. Peta and Charlotte enjoyed the lunch enormously and chatted with the kind of girlish animation that made Godfrey glow with delight and pride at being seen entertaining two pretty women, young enough to be, but decidedly not, his daughters.

Robin resisted the temptation to take notes. There was much to remember and lots to absorb but by the time two bottles of claret were dead even the fact that Jake would be sitting on Mr Speaker's right and he would have to skulk on the left seemed to jar less. He had, after all, achieved his ambition: he had been elected to Parliament before reaching the watershed of thirty-five.

Charlotte sat alone outside the post office in the Central

Lobby. Of the four marble statues of great statesmen only Gladstone was familiar to her. She looked up at the ornate dome and the mosaics in its surrounding arches. St Andrew, quite properly, faced north, and stared down from above the corridor that led to the dining room. St David and St George faced each other from above the passages to the Commons and Lords respectively. Beneath St Patrick was St Stephen's Hall, one-time chamber of the House of Commons where pioneering and politically inflamed Margot Hume had chained herself to the statue of the second Viscount Falkland in 1909. Charlotte doubted if any political issue could ever ignite a similar passion in her. She was just an observer, a bit-part player and member of the chorus who adapted emotions to match and reflect those of the show's stars.

Robin was taking ages to get sworn in. There was much purposeful scurrying going on; everybody appeared to be on errands of utmost national importance. Everyone, that is, except for her and Jake Cleaver.

'How is it going, Jake?'

'Fine. Just fine. How about you?'

'I'm waiting for Robin. He has gone to get sworn in.'

'Oh.'

Jake looked untidy and dishevelled but not nearly so angry any more. There was something quite sensitive about him. Perhaps such precipitous fatherhood had made him gentler.

'I'm sorry, Jake, I never congratulated you this morning. I think it is a tremendous achievement. I really admire you.'

'What for?'

'For having convictions worth fighting for.'

'Oh yes? You surprise me.'

'Jake, please don't be snide. I'm not trying to be patronising or sarcastic. Incidentally, I thought Robin was horribly rude to you, it wasn't necessary.'

'No, it wasn't. Anyway, maybe he didn't realise that the order in which you take the oath fixes your parliamentary seniority for ever.'

Charlotte laughed. 'No, I'm sure he didn't. Poor Robin.'

Jake looked at Charlotte and said, 'I'm sorry I was so rude to you at that Christmas do.'

'That was years ago, Jake. The whole affair was sheer hell anyway. Forget it.'

'You haven't, I'm sure. I had no business calling you what I did.'

'It wasn't awfully nice being classed as a suppurating sore and festering wound or whatever on the body of humanity.'

'I said that? Well I apologise. I can get carried away, it was an exaggeration.'

'That is a comfort. Am I now no worse than a tiresome rash?'

The new Prime Minister and some disciples were passing through the lobby. Prompted by an aide, he came up and shook Jake's hand. The bags beneath his eyes were vast indeed and he came complete with trademarks of both pipe and mac. Having finished with Jake he turned to Charlotte with outstretched hand. 'You must be very proud of him Mrs Cleaver.'

'Oh, I am, we all are. It has been a great day,' she replied, shaking the premier's hand with perfect frankness.

'A great day for the country too,' said the Prime Minister. He passed on down to the Commons, chivvied by a blonde sheepdog, with teeth.

Robin wasn't pleased when Charlotte told him what had happened.

'I don't believe you,' he said. 'No one could take you for a socialist's wife.'

'Why not, darling?'

'You are far too stupid.'

Charlotte was told that they must move. She objected. Markham Street was her house, the first place she had made into her own, she was loath to leave. Boldly Robin told her she must choose between him or the house. Charlotte conceded, it was a silly choice to ask her to make. She told him so. He said it was a joke. She supposed it was.

A tiny flat in division bell range was essential as well as a home in the constituency. Both could be bought with the proceeds from Markham Street.

'You don't want to live in London,' Robin told her.

But Charlotte did. She loved London and would miss

her friends. Besides, she had begun to work in earnest on research into prime ministerial wives and found that she got more than just information out of study. She enjoyed herself in the London Library and the reading room of the British Museum. Though she would have been delighted to have been taken for someone more profound than a rich flower arranger her interest and enthusiasm were genuine. The work she did was not a pose.

'We are turning ourself into quite the little bluestocking, aren't we,' Robin remarked to Charlotte in Peta's hearing. To repay Godfrey for his kindness Charlotte and Robin gave the Fables dinner at the Casse Croute in an atmosphere thick with garlic and cigarette smoke. It was no place to be pregnant, which was fine as nobody was.

'Robin, you could patronise for England,' Peta said. 'Poor Charlotte, she has got her own mind, you know.'

'Charlotte is not poor,' Robin replied.

'You said it, Robin.'

'Now then children, no squabbling!' Godfrey pleaded, giving Peta a wink. She nudged his knee and they both laughed, delighting in each other like young lovers. While their fidelity might be the stuff of speculation, their happiness was never hindered by the difference in their ages, provided nobody asked questions. Peta was discreet and kind-hearted, Godfrey prided himself on being deaf to gossip and confined his reading to *Horse and Hound* or *The Times*. What he didn't learn during his days at Westminster he got from watching *Nationwide* and *Panorama*. He was also a most popular MP of the old-fashioned paternal backbencher school.

When Robin went to be affable with a senior Tory dining with his wife at another table (her worthy air labelled her clearly as his wife) Godfrey said that Martin sent his love and had been utterly delighted that Robin had managed to get elected but had been particularly keen to know how Charlotte was getting on. 'He is very fond of you, of you both.'

'Martin and Charlotte are a great double act,' said Peta.

'How is he? What is he doing?' Charlotte asked. 'I, we haven't heard a thing from him since Christmas. He sent a card showing some Hindu goings-on, it made a change from holly.'

Martin was enjoying his posting as Eastern correspondent to an American international English language broadsheet; he would be home for a while at the end of the summer.

Charlotte was tearful when her precious house was handed over to a couple who had begun sneering at the hessian even before their offer had been accepted.

The next time Charlotte went to Westminster was to hear Robin's maiden speech. He was called at about four and the House was not packed; the subject being debated was fairly anodyne and Robin followed the tradition of starting his political career with a non-controversial speech. Elizabeth Brand thought she had mothered the next Edmund Burke.

From the gallery the chamber appeared disappointingly drab, swampy green and surprisingly small. Not many stars were there that day but the few Charlotte could recognise looked quite benignly disposed towards her husband, who spoke from below where she and Elizabeth had been seated and was not easy to see. His voice was good, he spoke well; no need for him to take elocution lessons. The speech was like a sermon, against wrong, about virtue and ten minutes. An honourable member opposite rose and congratulated Robin before continuing his own speech in a similar vein. Charlotte longed for tea.

Jake was clearly visible to Charlotte and his mother-in-law who beamed upon him encouragingly, but his eyes remained firmly downcast studying his order paper with unusual intensity. No member of the family had witnessed his maiden speech which, while being firmly on the side of improving mankind's lot, had been fiery and decidedly provocative, earning his début reports in the national press. Robin's loss of virginity languished unremarked upon, safely tucked away in the pages of Hansard.

Meanwhile Fenella was delighted to be left alone. Three children under five was dreadfully wearing and a lusty husband whose mind was on speeches while his body was on top of his wife just made things worse. The Cleavers lived in a heap not far from the only proposed site for the third London airport that did not elicit anguish from the heritage lobby. Only seabirds and the Cleavers looked on that marsh as home.

7

IN SCOTLAND FLORENCE Begg was finding the planning of her father-in-law's funeral tedious. Lord Begg, though well over ninety, was in remarkably fine fettle. His daughter-in-law wished him no ill but did so long to wear her peeress's robes just once. She wished no ill to the monarch either and hoped that a sumptuous celebration of her jubilee would provide the opportunity she craved. The next coronation would probably be long after her own death. Tam Begg was happy hacking at the rhododendrons with a machete and seemed to miss little of his parliamentary life, but Florence Begg was bored.

Auchenkirk with crenellations and battlements was not a cosy house. Only a quarter of it was maintained: Lord Begg and his manservant Prime lived in the east wing and watched the sun rise over the Firth of Tay leaving the west end and the view of the sun setting into the loch to Tam and Florence. On the death of this, the twelfth Begg of Auchenkirk, the main doors would be opened and the great hall would reverberate to its Victorian hammerbeams with the chatter of the flower of Scotland. Bats lived amongst the antlers and mice had nibbled at the displays of stuffed game; Florence would need to get that sorted.

Nothing much had happened to the house since it had been thoroughly rebuilt and done over in the 1870s. Florence Begg had persuaded her husband to make Auchenkirk's façade less forbidding by painting the window-frames a merry crimson. The house now looked red-eyed and hungover.

Florence felt she need be in no rush with the mousetraps and feather dusters provided Prime appeared from his Lordship with his weekly Donald McGill postcard on a tarnished salver. Fat ladies and weedy men on one side and 'I.N.D.Y. Begg' written in green ink on the back. Green ink, because the blue and black were exhausted and Lord Begg believed in thrift, one's nineties being no age to dash out and invest in fripperies. I.N.D.Y. stood for I'm Not Dead Yet. Prime's sister provided the cards; she lived in Portobello.

The deranged Beggs had descended crabwise for several centuries. Tam would be the first son to inherit the title from his father, if the reaper got going. If not, Florence feared she would never even be a dowager and the title would continue on its crooked way to a lumberjack in the Yukon. The two Begg daughters were married and far away in Australia and County Kerry.

To help Charlotte find a house was a joy and delight to Florence.

'Don't look downcast. You will find we are very central, everything to hand you might say. All that golf, savage history, the Byre Theatre putting on such jolly plays about girls in soup, and Dundee so handy for marmalade and jute.'

Robin had also told Charlotte of the wonderful life to be lived up north and flattered her by saying that she must be the one to choose the house, her taste being so astute. He did not embarrass her by dwelling on who would sign the cheque. Being keen to be seen and spotted as a rising star by the elder statesman of his party occupied him so much that he barely managed to have any time off to be with Charlotte except when he came north on sporadic constituency business.

Charlotte was grateful to Florence for her concern. Without her help she might easily have got herself a house beneath the RAF's most aggressive planes or within sniffing distance of the sugarbeet processing plant.

'What exactly did go on at Links Cottage?' Charlotte asked.

'Dark doings, dear. It is built on the site of the torching of Torquil of Netherdrew and lots more besides. One's forebears were most irascible. Bloody Begg ordered his wife's maid to be cooked for insolence and his son Begg the Mad ate his hounds as a mark of respect. It is a damn awful spot.' Florence would be drawn no further.

Florence went away to visit her daughter for Easter and it was nearing the end of the recess when the estate agent came up with Charlotte's ideal house. Robin was already packed once more for England when she burst into the lodgings' front room and announced her great find.

Robin kissed Charlotte goodbye as he got into his new car for the journey south. 'You are a clever girl, it is a lovely house. Well done. I am sure I can leave you to tie things up with the agents.'

'It isn't ours yet, darling.'

'No, but it will be. Determination will get you there, do not let anything stand in your way.'

'What about the tenant?'

'Mrs MacDirk, my darling, told me she cannot wait to move out and get into that old folkerie. Remember, we visited it during the election.'

Charlotte remembered it well. Solid Tory from the stoker to oldest resident, it had been a dream to canvass and was certainly very comfortable with a view of the North Sea and its gales well shielded by plate glass. 'Can she afford it? I seem to remember it was terribly expensive.'

'Of course. The MacDirks are rolling in money, they're in newsprint and whisky. You've met some of them yourself.'

Charlotte had: the MacDirks all appeared to be big noises amongst the local Tories.

Robin's Volvo was a congratulatory present from Charlotte, a safe car that could come out on top, a car also for a family man. There would be a family; Charlotte had promised him that even if they had to adopt. In the mean time there was still hope, Robin was determined and nothing – no headache no lethargy or disinclination – would distract him from his purpose to procreate.

Sandhill was in the right place, rural but not remote, stone built and solid with a tiny walled garden, sheltered from, yet overlooking, the sea. Unlike many other houses nearby, Sandhill had not sprouted warts; no angular bay or rattling glass porch disturbed its clean square lines. Outbuildings that could convert to further accommodation had charming pointed windows and were built in the same pinkish grey stone of the main house.

Charlotte fell in love with it. The owner was forced to sell, his investments having taken a nasty plunge, but Ivy MacDirk, the tenant for the past twenty years, had kept the place in prime condition. The decoration was not to Charlotte's taste but she would not for the world have made derogatory comments and offended the frail old woman who smiled sweetly and confessed that it had all become too much for her. The sneers of the Markham Street buyers still rankled.

The Scottish method of using sealed bids to purchase property was explained. The sale was imminent: only one other bid had been received and though Charlotte knew she was offering well over the guide price she submitted a very high bid. She must have Sandhill. She adored it, wanted it, bid for it and got it. Here was a place she knew she could be happy.

Robin was pleased too. Life in the House was wonderful, he loved his importantly ringing little flat, and furthermore Godfrey Fable and Tam Begg had put him up for membership of the Carlton Club. Knowing Charlotte was nursing his constituency by using local labour to refurbish Sandhill was better still. He liked to think of Charlotte happy, and far away.

Florence Begg was guarded when Charlotte told her news. Maybe she was tired after a fortnight with five Irish granddaughters. 'I hope you haven't been rash' was all Florence would say on the subject of the Brands' new house. Even when Charlotte told her that old Mrs MacDirk was gleeful at the prospect of moving out to Heather Bank retirement home, Florence had replied that she wasn't so sure, and no good comes from crossing a MacDirk. Phil Fleet, timid as ever, said he wasn't at all sure either.

'My Lady.'

'Yes, Prime.'

Florence was watching her husband through binoculars. Sir Tam was aping his ancestors by wielding a savage scythe, though his victims were not rival clansmen but innocent bullrushes.

'My Lady, it is his Lordship.'

'What? No more postcards?'

'No, my Lady.'

*

62

The rain that fell on the day of the funeral was prodigious. Water flowed down the baronial façade of Auchenkirk and poured from the red-rimmed windows making a most impressive display of inanimate grief.

Within the great hall all was rather jolly. Despite enmity in earlier centuries rival clans mingled convivially over the contents of the Late Lord Begg's cellar. A lot of the wine was too old, but it got drunk anyway, as a mark of respect to its deceased owner's great age.

Charlotte and Robin, in mournful black, felt excluded.

'It is your imagination, darling,' said Robin as he pushed himself into an advantageous position from where he could be seen and admired by his constituents. 'Smile, Charlotte, exude honest concern, don't look so gloomy.'

'But it is a funeral, Robin. One doesn't grin at a funeral.'

'Everyone else is. Just do as I say.'

Charlotte smiled cheerfully and was rewarded only by glares. After a while even Robin began to suspect that something was wrong.

It was Hawkhill the Younger, a cadet of the clan Dirk, who took the Brands to task. Hawkhill had drunk a lot of the '29 and was much emboldened by that and family indignation.

'It was a dire day for Scotland when the likes of you got elected to the English Parliament. We will not be making that mistake again, mark my words.'

'I'm sorry to hear that,' said Robin with brow wrinkled in perplexed concern. 'Please tell me what I can do to make you change your mind.'

'Return your house to its rightful owner, and I will think about it.'

'I don't understand.'

'You understand fine.'

Hawkhill hauled his sporran to a more comfortable position beneath his paunch and took a gulp of the whisky which was in pursuit of the '29.

'I am sorry Mr Hawkhill, I don't understand.'

'Give a man his proper name, damn you. I'm H' you. I've not known anything more villainous in than you buying yon house.'

Various massacres and dismemberments suggested themselves but Robin was too wise to mention them in front of this cross Scot.

'Sandhill was bought perfectly legally with a sealed bid which was accepted by the vendor.'

'Aye, and we ken fine why that was.'

'It was probably the highest,' Robin answered, 'and the former owner needed the cash.'

'Aye he needed cash right enough, but not that much, not that vulgar great heap, not blood money.'

'I am sure my wife did not intend her bid to be seen as that.'

'A man who hides behind his wife is not worthy to be called a man. I spit on you as I would onny wee worm.'

Hawkhill had attracted quite a circle of supporting admirers who all now turned away from Robin and Charlotte and followed their weaving kinsman out of Auchenkirk like a posse of muttering Montagus.

Charlotte asked Phil Fleet to explain.

'It appears that you are being accused of evicting Ivy MacDirk.'

Charlotte repeated all she knew of Ivy's feelings.

'But you see the fees at Heather Bank are altogether too steep. All Mrs MacDirk's wealth is being spent on keeping her there, all the wealth that her family were hoping to inherit. Ivy could live for ages.'

'I hope she does, poor old stick,' Charlotte replied, 'but what has this to do with me?'

'The MacDirks made it known that theirs was to be the only bid for the house. They had clubbed together to raise the money so they could guard their expectations and have a fine house to sell when Ivy died. The owner needed the cash badly, and naturally when you put in a high bid he had to accept it.'

'Isn't that how business works?'

'Not if you are trying to get votes,' Phil replied sorrowfully.

In June a bomb exploded in Westminster Hall. Robin wasn't nearby; he wasn't in Scotland either. By chance Winifred Forth knew where he was. She didn't tell Fraser, he would have made such an issue of Charlotte's betrayal, and she wondered whether it was her duty to tell her daughter herself. In the end she did nothing and stored the information as ammunition for later, should she need any.

Sandhill was quite perfect, the refurbishment and redecoration all completed by August when Winifred and Fraser stayed there and watched Nixon's resignation on television.

'The lying, cheating toad,' Fraser announced. 'The bloody, conniving obscene politician. They're all the same, just a load of two-timing corrupt scum. I think the whole lot should resign and then be put down.'

Winifred was glad she had kept her knowledge to herself; she would have hated Fraser to die of apoplexy. Anyway, Robin and Charlotte appeared to be quite happy with each other that summer. Robin spent much of his holiday reading and Charlotte was so absorbed by her new house that all she lacked was a family to keep in it.

'If nothing happens by Christmas we are going to see about adopting, while we're still young enough to be considered.'

'Young enough! Of course you are young enough,' Winifred answered Charlotte. 'You are young enough to start all over again. You do know that, Charlotte, don't you?'

'Yes, Mum, I do.'

Before Christmas came there would be the second election of 1974 to fight.

October 1994

'Piers, will you swap cars with me?'

'Why?'

'I want to run away, I don't want to be followed. Will you lend me that baseball cap?'

'Sure. When will you be back?'

'When I have had a think.'

'You aren't going to do anything silly, are you, Mother?'

'No. Why?'

'Because that would be stupid.'

'I know, darling, I know.'

While Piers endeavoured to entice the press to the front of the house by pretending he was his mother in the throes of doing her hair with his head tied up in a towel, Charlotte slipped out the back wearing her son's jeans and sweater as well as his cap; she would adjust to the smell in time. She then drove his car to her mother's house to dump Zoe the dog.

'Of course I will look after her for you, my love, but what are you going to do, where are you going?'

'I'm going away to think. I don't know what I will do, but I will think before I do it. I promise.'

'Promise me, Charlotte, that it won't be anything silly.'

'Of course not. When have you ever known me do anything silly?'

Winifred looked at her daughter sorrowfully and said, 'Lots of times, darling. Maybe this time you will get things right.'

8

October 1974

ELECTIONEERING WITH MARTIN Fable wasn't nearly as dire as trailing in Robin's wake and smirking at his supporters. Charlotte almost relished the horror of canvassing works canteens and housing estates provided Martin was there with his excellent command of snappy repartee. When taunted with the inevitable insults he beamed and thanked his attackers for their valuable comments, which he would be relaying immediately to Mr Brand who would be delighted to know that he could always count on the votes of those in Ramsay MacDonald Close and Jarrow Dwellings. Charlotte smiled and agreed that things should be done about the scarcity of launderettes, the price of cigarettes and the weather.

'Sam, I'm all for loyalty but your husband isn't God, you know.'

'But he thinks he is,' Charlotte replied. 'I am going to put the whole of that last street down as "doubtful".'

'There's generous.'

'I'm feeling benevolent and anyway my father says you should always give benefit of the doubt; it saves both time and effort.'

The second election had been called to put the government on a firmer footing. It was a bore to have to repeat the rigmarole but Robin, at least, was confident of retaining his seat. It was kind of Martin to come and help and to keep Charlotte entertained. Robin was finding her presence increasingly superfluous. A politician's wife should be either sensationally intelligent, beautifully stunning or at least usefully and frumpishly devoted. Charlotte was none of these, nor did she have any children to trot about with and be sweet. Except when reflecting on his own shaky finances he was finding it hard to remember why she was needed at all. Her political acumen was negligible and though she was good at going round hospitals and homes for the infirm, there were not a lot of votes to be got from invalids.

At first he had been dubious about letting Charlotte visit Ivy MacDirk in Heather Bank. One is not encouraged to fraternise with those whom one injures on the roads so maybe chumminess with those one evicts is not a good idea either. However, Charlotte had talked him round and he concluded that there was probably no harm done by a bit of friendly dropping in with a pot plant. That awful kilted relative had been mightily bottled at Lord Begg's funeral. As it was, Charlotte's visit was too late: cancer had been discovered rampaging through poor Ivy, who was now in hospital and terminal decline.

Election fever was tepid. The nation was bored with having to vote once more and the initiating of enthusiasm or igniting fires in bellies was turgid work. Robin's was an anodyne campaign.

The early autumn was wonderfully golden and warm, and no time to spend making silly promises to people who would never vote Tory except for spite. Martin and Charlotte had done enough rallying, seen enough snot on the next decade's voters and heard enough moans from their mothers to justify an afternoon off.

'Where are we meant to be, Wallace?'

'I think little Phil thought it might be a good idea for us to take a turn in that Land Rover and trailer and do a spot of loud-hailing.'

'Do you mean the Beggs' horsebox, the one covered with pictures of Robin and lots of bunting?'

'Yes, that's the one. He thought it might be nice for us to drive it down to the cattle market and round to Peason's Pies.'

'Really? He must be mad.'

'Either that or a fifth columnist. He makes no jokes. Here, let me give you a slice of Peason's very choicest.'

'No thanks, Wallace, I feel a bit queasy.'

'What do they call it when they are feeling middling up here?'

'Peelie, Wally.'

'Poor Sam. What about some beer?'

'No thanks. I really only feel like soda water, I've got some in the car.'

'Are you pregnant?'

'Maybe. Oh Wallace, don't tell anyone, will you, please. It is far too early to know. I just feel a bit sick, it's happened before, lots of times.'

'Poor Sam.'

'Don't, Wallace, I can't stand it. I hate people being sorry for me.'

'I'm not sorry for you. I'm sorry for me.'

Charlotte knew what he meant, at least she thought she did and it was not something she felt able to face. Life was not as easy as that, there were fences, barriers and doors all firmly locking her into the paths of righteousness. The most inescapable cage had been constructed by her father. Fraser would have done anything for his daughter. He adored her, he wanted her to be happy and was convinced that the only way she could be so was in the care of her husband. He also adored his wife. He had enjoyed a happy life, his one regret being that his family was so small. Now it was too late for regrets. Now he had been told that he was unlikely to live much longer, he wanted to make sure that things were straight for Winifred and Charlotte when he was gone.

He had spoken to his daughter; he had not got the necessary strength to confide in his wife.

Charlotte had promised him she was happy, promised him she loved Robin and gave him her word that she would be standing by him whatever befell. She would have promised her father all manner of impossibilities just then. How could she have denied this dear dying man anything? Of course, of course, she reassured him, what else could she do to ease his mind? Fraser was quite unconcerned about his approaching death; his love was entirely selfless. His only worldly concerns were for the adequate provision for his dependants. By Charlotte's declaration of her devotion to her husband she had comforted her father with the thought that his wealth was not going to be squandered by the unworthy.

Martin and Charlotte sat on a rock and waited for the seals. The sea was mistily calm, quiet and still, so breezeless that to breathe seemed raucous.

'What are you thinking about, Sam?'

'About how lucky we are not to be at work in a linoleum factory.'

'Oh.'

'Sorry, that isn't very profound. I haven't got depths, so try not to look for them.'

'You are wrong.'

'I am used to that too.'

'You declare defeat before the battle. You would never have danced on the eve of Waterloo, you would have stitched your shroud.'

'Hebridean brides used to go to their husbands complete with shrouds, also preferably toothless and pregnant. It saved much bother later.'

'What about you? What did Robin get with you?'

'I used to think he got what he wanted, I'm not so sure now.'

'Sam. You're not happy, are you?'

Charlotte picked up a flat pebble and was about to skim it but the water was ironed silk, it would have been cruel to agitate it with ducks and drakes. She threw the stone at a collapsed breakwater and missed.

'Are you happy, Wallace?'

'No, but we are talking about you. I don't think Robin appreciates you.'

'It isn't easy for him having a rich wife. It isn't a doddle being one either.'

'Supposing you were poor.'

'If I were poor, Wallace, I wouldn't be married to Robin.'

'No, but you might be with me.'

'Look, there are the seals.'

'You are changing the subject.'

Charlotte noticed that Martin's hand was touching hers, so

to not appear rude she made a play of shifting her position to see the seals better. She was troubled and did not wish to make a fool of herself.

'Do you really just look on yourself as Robin's treasure chest?'

Charlotte chose not to answer. The two black domes bobbed in the calm water approaching the rocks. Florence Begg liked to entertain her local seals on the mouth organ but Charlotte used to sing for the ones swimming in the cove below Sandhill. 'Seals are very musical you know.' Charlotte stood up and sang:

> 'Lang will his lady
> Look owre the Castle Downe,
> Ere she sees the Earl of Moray,
> Come sounding through the town!'

These were not musical seals, they looked at Charlotte with disdain and puffed fishy breath through their flat nostrils.

'They say the Earl was killed on this coast. No, I've got it wrong, it was Sir Patrick Spens, or maybe Young Lochinvar, I can't remember. Anyway, it was some braw gallant or other.'

'Sam.'

'Yes, Wallace?'

'You wouldn't sing for me in New York.'

'You remember that?'

'Of course.'

'Oh dear.'

Looking up, Charlotte saw a faraway bird wheeling, no larger than a comma in the gauze sky. Being no ornithologist, she hoped it was an eagle. Away in the distance a string of fishing boats was making for the firth returning with a catch to delight the harbour gulls and to provide greater entertainment for the seals than sad ballads. On the horizon a minesweeper from Rosyth was setting out into the North Sea, a muffled roaring of distant aircraft broke the silence and yet Martin and Charlotte felt isolated and alone. The world where bombs were slaughtering the innocent, where life, food, votes and fame were being fought for was as remote as the moon.

'What is to be done, Sam?'

'Nothing, Wallace.'

'Look at me.'

Charlotte turned from the sea and looked; the copper sun was visible through the westerly haze. She knew then what she had feared and saw for sure what she had missed. Martin wasn't as tall as Robin, he was stockier and more shortsighted, he had no floppy locks or bedroom eyes, and yet every bit of him was a marvel. He held out his hand to her. 'What are you thinking, Sam?'

'I think you are beautiful.'

'Come here. Do you know what I want?'

'Yes, Martin. I think, I hope, I do.'

He drew her down beside him, kissed her below the ear and whispered, 'I hope you want it too.'

'Oh yes,' said Charlotte. 'I do.'

The bird above, whatever it was, soared away to play at thunderbolts elsewhere.

'Where is Martin?'

'Gone. He got a message asking him to help his father in Godleham,' Charlotte answered softly.

Robin thumped his fist on the office desk and sat down with his head in his hands. The campaign was going badly. 'That is all I need; my best man deserting me, the bloody rat.'

Charlotte could think of nothing to say. She knew that Martin must leave, he couldn't possibly have stayed now and the excuse of needing to help his father was very convenient; it had an air of authenticity about it, blood ties being what they are. Next week Martin would be out of the country, certainly for several years, maybe for ever. His new job was as South American correspondent for a press agency and he would start by living in Uruguay. He and Charlotte had agreed to part, to break immediately: there was no future for them as a pair now. Possibly later things might change, but probably not.

'Look.' Robin thrust the local paper over the desk towards Charlotte.

TORY BRAND EVICTS DYING PENSIONER.

The MacDirk newsprint had been put to good vengeful use. A vindictive article followed about how the Conservative member had scant regard for the well-being of his constituents and how he had behaved with supercilious insensitivity in throwing a pathetic widow out of her house and denying her the chance of ending her days in the home she loved. Ivy was now too ill to be interviewed but a miserable photograph of her looking distraught had been procured to illustrate the article as well as a shot of Robin and Charlotte standing smugly delighted on the steps of Sandhill. Empty words, false hopes, broken promises were all the constituents could reasonably expect from one so openly callous and selfish. 'Money, Mr Brand, does not buy the votes of honest Pittenfirth and Netherloch folk.'

Charlotte read with incredulity. Put like that it sounded dreadful. 'What are you going to do?' she asked.

'It is more a matter of what you are going to do,' Robin replied. 'You bought the place, you must take the blame. I had nothing to do with it. I'm getting Phil to get a press release ready just now.'

'What is in the release? Surely if you are going to have me publicly pilloried I am entitled to see what is being said about me.'

'You have done enough already. Just stay quiet and do what I say.'

'Christ, Robin, you are making me look like an imbecile.'

'Well?'

'Robin, you can't do this to me.'

'After what you have done to me, you're lucky that I am still your husband. Before you get any bright ideas of deserting me let me tell you some truths. If you leave me now I will sue you through every court in the land for maintenance; after all, your actions are likely to cost me my only job. Secondly, it will kill your father. Thirdly it will be the end of you in every way. No one will want anything to do with you.'

'Robin, you are being ridiculous. I have never heard such utter rubbish. I knew you were ambitious but I never thought you were stupid.'

Robin rose to his feet and came towards Charlotte. She couldn't believe what was about to happen: she stood her ground and shut her eyes, bracing herself for the blow. Of all the things she had anticipated in her marriage she had never thought that Robin would strike her. He could wound her pride, defeat her self-esteem, his tongue alone could humiliate and render her speechless with misery, but surely he would never harm her physically. He was too superior for that: he would not want the scars he inflicted to be visible.

'Are you calling me stupid?'

Charlotte winced but stood still and waited. 'Yes I am.'

The moment passed.

He held her by the forearms, gently not forcibly. He was defeated.

'Darling, I'm sorry. Open your eyes. Look at me, you are right.'

For the second time that day Charlotte looked into a man's eyes. This time it was different: no magic, just the infinite sadness of inextricable commitment.

'I'm sorry too,' she said.

Thanks to Florence the press release was just an innocuous expression of regret at Mrs MacDirk's poor health and a declaration that as far as Robin Brand was concerned there had been no coercion or force used to rid his new house of its sitting tenant.

'Remember the Garden of Eden,' said Florence. 'One out, all out. It did Adam no good at all to blame it on the wife. If you want to make it better you two must be seen all over the constituency being gooey and devoted. It is the only way to redeem yourself. Believe me, Robin, I have known these people since the groom used to take me and my nursemaid to the sands in a governess cart.'

Heartbroken Charlotte put on a good act; she was strong and resigned to playing her part. Once the pain was too much and she rang Peta in the hopes of getting news of Martin. She was too late – he had gone abroad early, leaving no address, leaving no message. He had vanished into the blue. She told herself that she must have meant less than nothing to him, and then she cried.

It was the eve of the election when Florence found her in tears. The older woman did her best to comfort Charlotte, patting her as one might an out-of-sorts bitch. She meant well and Charlotte was grateful but she needed her own mother and in reality the only person in the whole world who could end her misery was Martin. He evidently didn't care; she couldn't have meant anything to him after all.

'There, there, my dear, only another twenty-four hours and it will all be over.'

Please God, thought Charlotte. Let there not be too much shouting.

Ivy died. Her death was reported as the polling stations opened. No one really blamed Robin for the cancer that killed her but dark hints persisted in dogging him as to how the frail widow's condition had been accelerated by grief.

By two o'clock on the morning of 12 October Robin conceded defeat with the best grace he could muster, which wasn't very much. The victorious Liberal candidate was utterly overjoyed, it was a shame not to be able to share his delight. In Mireness Jake Cleaver's majority had trebled but disillusioned Roddy MacPhail had come within an inch of losing his deposit in Kirkbeggie. That was Robin's comfort, that and knowing that from now onwards till he died he had earned a place in *Who's Who*. So too, of course, had his brother-in-law. No job, no constituency and not much hope were tough facts for Robin to face.

Charlotte was comparatively happy. She decided to stay on at Sandhill and had been admitted to attend lectures and had permission to use the university library for her research. She encouraged Robin to do the same: between them they might get both 'The Great Reform Bill' and 'The Prime Brides' into publishable condition. But Robin fretted and instead of letting his flat to a more fortunate and elected individual he persisted in keeping it on, torturing himself by gazing at the disconnected bell and brooding on his future.

The enchantment had vanished. The adoring women had disappeared with his seat, he spent his time plotting and watching television and trying to bump into his former associates who seemed all to have forgotten him as quickly as they had taken him up in his time of triumph. It was no good, he must go out and start again: time was on his side, he needed freedom to develop a better plan. By returning to the law he could earn enough to keep himself, he was sure that he would be able to retain his flat, and the rest Charlotte could keep. He would be a gentleman. Also Uncle Ludlow Brand's will had been most kind. On Remembrance Sunday Robin stood beside Charlotte at the local memorial feeling foolish in his bowler hat while the new member for Pittenfirth and Netherloch took up a prominent position bare-headed in a friendly duffel coat.

There was no invitation to Sunday lunch for the Brands and no guests were coming to them; he and Charlotte were to eat alone before he caught the sleeper south. It seemed a good moment to talk.

'Charlotte, I've got something to tell you.'

'I've got something to tell you too.'

'Oh? Well, you see I have been thinking.'

'Yes I know what you are going to say.'

'You do?'

'Yes, it's about the adoption, isn't it?' Charlotte took Robin's hand in hers. 'We can't go through with it.'

'I agree.' With relief Robin thought that Charlotte was going to be thoroughly reasonable about the whole matter. A civilised divorce would be such a good idea, as well as being comparatively cheap.

'Robin, I have been busting to tell you. I know I am right this time. I'm pregnant.'

9

October 1994

IT HAD RAINED like this on the day of the funeral all of twenty years ago. Then the front door had been opened for the bearing out of the old laird and for the welcoming in of his mourners once the disposal was done with. Auchenkirk had been opened up again for Florence's Diamond Ball in 1975, and that was that. Ever after the only way in was round the back and past the numerous sculleries, pantries, boot rooms and still rooms with which the house had been equipped where now forgotten fuel, crippled bicycles and sporting equipment that knew nothing of carbon fibre and logos lay abandoned alongside heaps of mouldering leather suitcases full of junk. The east wing was deserted and dilapidated but the west wing showed faint signs of life.

Charlotte pulled the bell. The wire was bent and looked broken but far away she could hear that the mechanism still worked. Whether it would be answered was another matter. She tried again. It was incredibly dank and cold though winter was not yet arrived and the trees were flaming as Charlotte had heard they do in New England. The baseball cap gave no protection and once more she regretted that in her hurry she had forgotten to bring some warmer clothes. Even her serape was heavy with dampness and smelt of pungent wet wool. She heard someone approach and shuddered; not that she was frightened, merely exhausted from driving so far in Piers's tiny car, with only four hours' sleep at a motel on the way.

Prime opened the door. He was well past it, yet it would not do to take his name in jest.

'You are very late,' he said. 'Her Ladyship will be most put out when I tell her. However, here you are, you had better come in and get down to work. His Lordship is restless. Hurry up!'

Charlotte followed Prime obediently. She should have expected this: Auchenkirk had long since been famous for housing the demented.

'Where is her Ladyship?'

'Her Ladyship, as you will have been told, is gone through to Stranraer and over to Ireland and down to the baptism of her great-granddaughter in County Kerry. She will return on Tuesday first by which time you had better have his Lordship sorted. I fancy Lady Begg will be quite exhausted by then with all that driving up, over and through in just the couple of days.'

Prime chivvied Charlotte up some stairs covered with a carpet so worn that scarcely a tuft of pile remained and along a mustardy, musty corridor hung with greatly foxed sporting prints till, pulling aside a heavy curtain designed to insulate rather than decorate, he opened a fumed oak door and announced: 'My Lord, the nurse is here.'

'Hello Tam,' Charlotte said to the ancient man sitting in a loudly checked threadbare dressing gown beside the window watching some wild duck loitering on his loch.

Charlotte heard Prime hiss. 'He is your Lordship, my Lord or Lord Begg to you.'

Evidently she had been forgotten or else the years had harrowed her even more than she had first thought.

'Very well, Prime.'

'Mr Prime, if you please, Nurse.'

'Sister, to you, Mr Prime.'

What the hell, thought Charlotte, I'll play at nurses for the moment. At least it will give me time to be alone and think.

June 1975

In June when Charlotte was nearly too vast to fit behind the wheel of her car Florence had decided to throw a ball at Auchenkirk. It was to be a Diamond Ball: not that it celebrated any kind of jubilee but it was to be the last outing for the Begg diamonds before they got sold. All manner of things needed to

78

be done and the sale of the tiara and other impractical devices would do much to finance the rewiring and some of the grandchildren's schooling. The diamonds lived in the bank in Cupar, it was an awful palaver to get them out and in again, everyone would be happier with them gone. Florence would wear them all just once more at her ball then the suave fellow who dealt with these things would whisk them off to auction and the Beggs would be temporarily smothered in wealth for a change.

House parties and dinner parties were arranged; Henrietta and Roddy MacPhail were fixed up to stay at Sandhill with Charlotte and Robin. Roddy, like Robin, was near the top of the list for a constituency at Conservative Central Office, but unlike him had never yet been elected. However, his staunch apprenticeship at Kirkbeggie, which he had fought and lost on three occasions, was laudable and meant he would surely get a safer place to fight for next time. The next time would not be for quite a while, maybe even not until 1979.

Charlotte felt well despite the bulk and had enjoyed getting the house ready for visitors. She felt herself to be more a party to the life of other young married friends now that she too was to be a mother. Pregnancy had engulfed her entirely. The seventies was an earthy sort of decade when it was quite the trend to make bread, grow or rear most food and heat homes by stoking Scandinavian stoves with all sorts of combustibles from rubbish to straw bales. Charlotte could not rise to the rearing of lambs for the freezer, though she was mistress of a fine hen run. The hens were whimsical and intermittent layers, at one point she had calculated that each of the three eggs in her rustic basket had cost twenty-five pounds to produce. Here was happiness: domestic trivia kept any longings suppressed.

There had been a change in Robin too. He was almost too excited about the impending birth and his enthusiasm could be irritating. Despite continents overflowing with babies he behaved as if he alone of all mankind was able to go inseminating. Naturally Charlotte dreaded catastrophes but somehow Robin managed to imply that he bore all the burden of worry. No one felt so responsible and anxious as himself. He read books, consulted everyone and was most solicitous, not so much about his wife as for what was swelling up within her. When it was discovered that she carried twins, his consternation and amazement could not have been equalled had Charlotte been Mary the Virgin informing Joseph that her lump was God.

'There are no twins on our side of the family,' said Elizabeth on hearing the news from her son.

'Believe me, there are no mysteries either; we have got immaculate records of our antecedents,' she told Charlotte on the phone. 'However, don't think that we are not utterly thrilled for you both. It is such a relief to Robin.' She did not elaborate as to the nature of that relief but Charlotte assumed her mother-in-law was all for carrying spares.

Later, when talking to Winifred Forth her co-putative grand-mother, Elizabeth said that she supposed the Brands had many such quirks in their lineage but as their origins were so obscure it would be hard to quote instances. She was, she said, put in mind of Jacob and Esau. Winifred replied that there was small chance of either baby being hairy, considering the smoothness of their father.

Before the dance the MacDirks gave a dinner party. Grudgingly they asked Robin and Charlotte to come with Henrietta and Roddy MacPhail, who were old friends of the family and quite without stain. It would have been impossible to exclude the Brands as the MacPhails were staying with them, even if the manner of the purchase of Sandhill still grated. With Ivy MacDirk now well dead they were prepared to dig a grave for the hatchet, stopping short at burying it.

Robin's appeasement gestures, verbal grovelling and meta-phorical rump presentation were so well enacted that Ivor and Janet MacDirk were quite won over by his charm and even went so far as to admit that occasionally their cousin, Hawkhill the Younger, let loyalty to his in-laws' distillery cause him to get things out of proportion. It wouldn't do to be vile to Charlotte either, pregnancy being an excellent buffer against hostility.

However, Charlotte still didn't feel she belonged: not like Henrietta and Roddy who had been bred in Perth and Argyll and were thoroughly at home in forbidding castles, stuffy cottages and chilly manses, knowing instinctively which way to turn in a reel and never ever to complain of cold or to opt for indoor warmth and a good book when given the choice of that or a day in the open harassing fauna.

If it hadn't been for Florence Begg, Charlotte might never have met any of this new circle of friends. Apart from casual acquaintances she had met while attending lectures, she knew few local people of her own age. Once Robin had lost his seat no one bothered to be pleasant to the Brands but Florence had persisted and had been Charlotte's foster mother in her new country. She bolstered her throughout the east coast winter, and tried to help her understand the people. Some were dour to hide their shyness, others were dour as insurance against disappointment, but with a few the dourness was but a cheerful patina compared to the real intense dire depths beneath. For the most part Charlotte met with friendliness though she was unable to forget for a single minute that she was a foreigner. She had to learn never to give way to illness or weariness and to ignore all such shortcomings in others. Nerves, alcohol, debt, homosexuality, promiscuity and unusual preferences were accepted like the scenery, present and unalterable, too familiar to merit comment. Insiders only could pass remarks about the quirks of their own kind; outsiders could not. The Brands were outsiders. To be accepted as natives would take a while: a generation, say.

As Charlotte stood beneath the threatening antlers beside the joyless dinner gong all the old dread of being left partnerless surged back.

She longed yet again for Martin Fable to be there, to be her friend. She thought of him far too often and he had gone away never even sending a card at Christmas. Only Peta, being his stepmother, had given Charlotte any news of him. He was well. All the other guests seemed so self-assured, loved and beguiling; she was alone amongst waves of urbane chatterers and confident beautiful people eager and able to sparkle till the stars died at dawn.

Her dress had been made by Peterina in Pittenweem from a

length of silk brought home from Thailand by her parents on a Christmas-dodging outing. Saffron was the colour; a large white collar had been added to detract from the bulge beneath, to no effect. Charlotte was lady into pumpkin.

'Charlotte my dear, you look forlorn. Cheer up, chicken!' It was the hostess all aglitter in her doomed jewels. If Charlotte was the pumpkin Florence was a combination of Fairy Godmother and Ugly Sister.

'You look astounding,' Charlotte exclaimed. Florence had got a tiara perched on top of her greying hair, which had been most surprisingly set in corrugations long since considered old-fashioned. A large brooch dangled from the bodice of her dress which once she had worn to be presented at court. Florence had remained thin but her bosom had sunk towards her stomach and no longer filled the darted place originally devised for it. Once white, the frock had been streakily dyed a chocolate brown, the uneven colour stressing its resemblance to a sloppy mousse. More diamonds encircled her throat and wrists.

'Fine rocks, what?' Florence suggested.

'Formidable,' Charlotte replied. 'Won't you be very sorry to see them go?'

'Not at all, dear. Anyway, apart from the tiara, I have been told they're all paste. Tam's mama sold the real stuff in the twenties; gambling debts, you know.'

Florence treated this catastrophe as no more than a flat tyre on her wheelbarrow. 'Rewiring is such a shemozzle anyway and some of these public schools today are most unpleasant. Where is Robin?'

'Parking the car,' Charlotte replied.

Big Hammy, Wee Hammy and 'Bubbly' Jock were directing guests' cars to a distant damp meadow. Robin made his case known: he might, at any minute, have to dash his pregnant wife across the Tay to be delivered. He must be given priority parking. Naturally he got himself in the best spot beside the gate.

Bubbly tapped on his window. 'Are you all right, sir?' Despite his prize place Robin had stayed in the car for a further ten minutes after parking.

'Yes, I'm fine. I am just listening to the news.'

'Right you are, sir.'

Big Hammy confided in the other two that Robin was a washout and has-been with no conceivable need to be listening to any news. Big Hammy was wrong about that.

'Charlotte, go and get your coat. We are leaving.'

'Why, Robin? We've only just arrived.' Charlotte was getting over her initial shyness and had risked all with a glass of nerving champagne. Maybe not everyone was as hostile as the snarling masks of the hunting trophies.

'Do what I say and be quick.'

'Why? What has happened?'

'You are about to have a false alarm.'

'No I'm not. How do you know, anyway? Predicting false alarms is like announcing the beginning of the Hundred Years War.'

'Do what you are told. At once!'

Charlotte knew she had no fight in her. She would comply if only to avoid a scene.

'Here, take my arm, darling. You'll be as right as rain by the morning,' Robin declared for all to hear above the distant din of the band. He bustled her out, attempting to appear surreptitious. 'You are just overtired, darling, don't worry.'

Back in the car he drove her not across the silv'ry Tay but back to Sandhill where he dumped her with Aurea, the Mac-Phails' bemused Filipina nanny, and left.

'Where are you going, Robin?'

'You will understand in the morning.'

Charlotte didn't fall asleep for ages. The twins, now too cramped for strenuous games, no longer kicked but her head was full of churning music and heart-rending yearnings that had lain dormant for many months and were now rekindled.

The MacPhail children who were no respecters of late bedders, started caterwauling and rampaging at seven, well before the time when Charlotte usually got up. Aurea did her best to subdue her charges with whatever she could find in the fridge but nothing pleased Caspar or Leonora except a cold treacle tart destined for lunch, so they ate that. She then pushed them both out to play in the garden where they amused themselves with throwing balls against the wall, or rather against Charlotte's bedroom window. Roddy and Henrietta, who had returned from the ball at four-thirty, slept on regardless. Charlotte could not, so heaving herself over by bending her knees and pulling up on the brass rails of the bed head, she turned on the *Today* programme. After a hymn or two and a godly thought she realised that it was Sunday: no avuncular information from John Timpson today. However, there was news as usual at eight.

Apart from the West Indies winning the World Cup there was only one item of any moment: the sudden heart attack and death of Godfrey Fable.

The previous night Peta and Godfrey were to dine late with friends in Holland Park. It had been a beautiful summer day and, for once, they had spent the weekend in London instead of in the constituency. On leaving for the party Peta realised she had left her shawl in the house and returned to fetch it in case the night turned chilly. Godfrey had got into his Rover, started the engine, and that was that. The heart attack was massive; forgetfulness alone had prevented Peta from being with him. She found him slumped over the wheel with the engine still ticking over, his chest pressed to the horn alerting the world to his leaving of it.

Godfrey was dead. He had died blissfully happy.

It was to have been expected, friends and constituents concluded. Godfrey had not been built to withstand a strenuous middle age and a racy young wife to lead him astray. Peta would never be forgiven.

Transfixed with horror, Charlotte listened to the report and then she heard Robin. He had rushed to be a comfort as soon as he had heard of the tragedy on the late evening news bulletin. Nothing would prevent him from being on hand to comfort and uphold the grieving widow and try and do his best to cause all arrangements to run smoothly. He was privileged to be a spokesman, he had made sure of that.

There was nothing to do.

Charlotte felt she ought to speak to Peta but some officious minder answered the phone and refused to let her talk to her friend.

Taking Leonora and Caspar by the hand she went with them down to the sea to look for shells. Two seals bobbed beside distant rocks but the tide was out and there was much damp crinkled sand between the white soft beach and the sea's edge. Slowly they picked their way to where tiny waves were lapping, tiptoeing for fear of sharp stones or jellyfish which Leonora had learnt to dread on the Mull of Kintyre. The children's soft feet were hurt by the hard sandy ridges.

'Carry me!' Caspar stretched his plump arms up, waiting to be lifted.

'Why are you crying?' Leonora asked. 'I never cry.'

'I'm not crying,' Charlotte answered. She picked up Caspar, but she had no hip left to support him and had to carry him under her arm like a little piglet with blond curly hair. Leonora, tough and self-important, refused any help. She ran ahead despite the hateful lumpy bumps and splashed into the water, squealing with delight at the icy cold of the North Sea. The seals were still there.

'We must sing to them,' Charlotte said.

The seals rose obligingly and pretended to be intrigued by 'Baa Baa Black Sheep' and 'Three Blind Mice', which the children bawled out into the clear summer morning. Beyond, Charlotte saw a frigate sailing by, keeping the peace. No fishing boats today, it being Sunday. She tried to bend down to splash her face with more salt water, but her bulk made it impossible; she was crying for many reasons.

It was noon by the time they had clambered home through the dunes. Henrietta and Roddy were scavenging for black coffee.

'I'm sorry,' said Charlotte. 'I quite forgot about cooking anything. We will have to have cold cuts for lunch; it's much too late to roast anything now.'

'Where is Robin?' Henrietta asked.

'Oh my God! You haven't heard? Godfrey Fable has died suddenly. Robin has gone south.' Charlotte told them as much as she knew about what had happened.

'Christ, how awful!'

'He didn't even tell me,' Charlotte replied. 'The first thing I knew about it was the eight o'clock news. Robin was interviewed.'

'I bet he was,' said Roddy. 'Robin has a nose for a by-election.'

'Roddy! That is a dreadful thing to say,' Henrietta scolded. They all knew that Roddy was right.

'Look, Mummy. Look!' Leonora pointed with appalled incredulity at the puddle round Charlotte's feet.

Instead of having lunch, the MacPhails drove Charlotte to Dundee.

'How that poor girl will have a baby, let alone two, without even having gone to Betty Parsons I can't imagine,' said Henrietta to Roddy as they gulped at restorative gins in the Station Hotel once the dash to hospital was done.

'Oh darling, people do, you know, lots of them, all of the time,' Roddy replied. His mind was on other things, especially the Godleham constituency.

October 1994

'HIS LORDSHIP IS partial to a stanza or two of verse,' Prime told Charlotte as they lifted Tam protesting off the commode. 'Nurse Bristle even washed his hair last week while reciting *The Lays of Ancient Rome*. Are you acquainted with the works of Lord Macaulay yourself, Sister?'

'Alas no, Mr Prime.'

There had been a time when she could recite the whole of 'John Gilpin', the repeating of his adventures had taken her mind off the first stages of labour, but now, twenty years later, she could barely get beyond the bit about his sister, his sister's child, himself and children three. She never did Holloway monologues these days, she hadn't the heart. Tam was calm while she tried to get Gilpin from Edmonton to Ware, but snorted at her stumbling delivery. In desperation she resorted to 'Under a Toadstool Crept a Wee Elf'.

'Heroism is more in his Lordship's line.'

'I could read to him,' Charlotte suggested.

'I will bring you the newspapers directly.'

'Thank you, Mr Prime.'

Old people need chiropody; like cattle they do better with comfortable feet. Charlotte thought she could fix that, it shouldn't be difficult. Dressed in a white coat in which Tam once paraded his champion Angus steer at the Highland Show, her son's jeans belt around her waist, hair tied back with a huge white handkerchief, she felt and looked a bit more into her part. Having put on her glasses, she had read the labels on the array of medicines drawn up on the Gothic washstand and decided that caring for Lord Begg would not be too tough, given a reliable watch and average intelligence.

She proposed to let his feet soak in nicely warm soapy water to soften the horny old skin. Lifting the tartan rug that wrapped his lower half she found only one foot. The right was gone, amputated from below the knee. She was sure that Tam had had all his legs last time she had seen him. A thought struck her: maybe he was a diabetic. Diabetics needed injections – that she couldn't, wouldn't, do. A memory of Flapjack the pony galloping off with a needle stuck in his neck while she stumbled behind him, bruised and bleeding, brandishing a syringe remained vivid. Even if Tam neither bit nor kicked, she was not prepared to stick a needle into any part of him.

'The daily papers, Sister and the *Courier*. His Lordship is entertained by the fatstock prices.'

'Thank you.'

Charlotte looked at herself gazing up from the front page. It was a recent picture. She was (the headline announced) missing. Without saying anything Prime managed to convey that he was becoming a mite suspicious. It would not be long before he recognised her or she rumbled herself by being incompetent. Confession was essential, if only to avoid wielding a lethal needle.

Before anything could be said Prime left to answer the jangling doorbell.

Sir Robin Brand, disgraced member for Godleham and discredited spokesman for youth, was pictured waving from his front steps most cordially.

Charlotte read on. Listed like this her husband's supposed sins did seem gross. Bribed and sweetened he had allegedly fostered causes and asked questions to promote his paymasters. His regard for the truth had been most selective on several less than honest occasions – allegedly. Amongst all the allegations that were being slavered over by a drooling press there was one sin about which there was no speculation whatsoever.

SIR ROBIN 'FAMILY VALUES' BRAND, SHUNS LOVE CHILD.

A picture of Piers aged eight grinned endearingly from the

bottom of the page. Only it wasn't Piers – the snap was recent and the boy was called Merlin van Schumacher.

In addition to a vitriolic book citing all Robin's peccadilloes and vices Ms van Schumacher's lurid work had been joined on the bookstalls by an even grubbier book, written by one Ocean Bray.

Tam spoke, a rare event these days but his hearing remained sharp, his long-distance memory comparatively acute.

'That Brand fellow always was a confounded cad.'

A pause followed then he asked, 'What's the time?'

Charlotte told him.

'Try not to be silly.'

Prime returned with a large flustered nurse.

'My Lord, here is Nurse Garton who was unable to inform us of her delay due to our telephone being disconnected, her Ladyship's cheque having been mislaid.' Then without a flicker of discomposure Prime said, 'Lady Brand, may I introduce Nurse Garton.'

The two women looked at each other and recognised their younger selves beneath twenty years' worth of flab, grey hairs and wrinkles.

June 1975

When Charlotte had recovered sufficiently to be coherent she rang her mother and told her she was now grandmother to a pigeon pair: a girl, bright and bonny and a small puny boy. Winifred was overwhelmed, delighted she said, quite shattered. She would ring back once she was composed. Charlotte asked to speak to her father but Fraser was not available. Winifred said she would tell him the wonderful news just as soon as possible.

It never was possible. Fraser would never know about the birth of his grandchildren: his gradual decline had accelerated in the last week but he had insisted that Charlotte be left unaware of his worsening health for her own sake and that of her babies. Robin would break it gently to his wife. Robin hadn't thought fit to mention it. Fraser had died one hour before becoming a grandfather.

'My love, I will ring you back as soon as I can.' Winifred hung up, she could dam her tears no longer.

Even Charlotte was surprised. Winifred was forthright and pragmatic, not given to tearfulness.

Robin broke the news of Fraser's death to Charlotte when he flew north to inspect his sudden family.

'He had a good innings.'

'He was barely sixty.'

'He was older than Godfrey Fable and enjoyed a fine life. Now don't cry, there's a good girl, you have to get your strength back to look after your own children now.'

Robin was besotted with his babies. He had photographs taken and processed in a trice of their screwed-up little faces so that he could have them by him when he returned south to help at Godleham and keep his profile high. He was a family man.

'Robin, don't go. I need you here.'

'Nonsense, darling. You don't need me, you are in hospital surrounded by all the very best attention. I must go to where I can do some good. Incidentally, I think it might be a nice idea to call him Godfrey.'

'Call who Godfrey?'

'Our son, of course, after Godfrey Fable.'

'Why?'

'It seems appropriate. It could be wise.'

'What do you mean?'

'A mark of respect.'

'I would like him to be called Fraser, after my father, for the same reason.'

'If you do that, he might as well be called Cyril after my father, who is at least alive and able to appreciate the gesture. Anyway Fraser Brand sounds like an oatcake.'

Robin said that they would discuss the matter later when he returned from Godfrey's funeral. He conceded that Charlotte could name the little girl what she liked; he could (he hoped) rely on his wife not to call his daughter anything silly.

Charlotte called her daughter Coral. Her sparse fluff of hair was almost auburn and her face a rosy pink, like thrift that grows beside the sea.

Robin wondered whether Coral wasn't a bit off as a name for a Tory daughter; Caroline would surely have been a better choice. He had no plans to go to his father-in-law's cremation, which was to take place on the same day as Godfrey Fable's burial. Charlotte wanted desperately to go and be with Winifred who had no other children . . . but she was far from well. The labour had been long and difficult, she was filled with stitches, bleeding and in pain below and above where milk was engorging her breasts and depression swamping her spirit. She was in no state to travel or experience the formalities of grief.

Florence Begg was sitting beside Charlotte's bed when she awoke after a night of much disruption. The baby boy was in an incubator but Coral was hungry and as keen to be fed as Charlotte was to feed her, though their mutual desires seemed incompatible and hard to synchronise.

It was eleven o'clock, almost hospital lunchtime, also the time allotted to Winifred for her husband's cremation.

'Oh Florence, how kind of you to come,' said Charlotte as she hauled herself into a comfortable position upon her rubber ring designed to avoid the sensation of sitting on hedgehogs.

'It is the least I could do, you poor old thing.'

'What am I to do?'

'You need help.'

'My mother-in-law is coming up after Daddy's – '

'I know, my little chicken, I know.' Florence poured herself a glass of Lucozade: she too needed strength, her age had been against her when it had come to vanquishing her post-ball hangover. 'I said you needed help, not a mother-in-law. A mother maybe, but preferably a nurse with her head screwed on. Will you let me get one for you?'

'Oh yes please, Florence, I know I can't cope on my own.'

'Of course you can't. One day your man might see that too instead of ingratiating himself with selection committees.'

'He says that Peta Fable needs him to organise the funeral.'

'Nonsense. I happen to know that Godfrey's son is doing all that.'

'Martin?'

'Yes, a splendid chap. The sort of man I would have liked to have had as a son myself. He is home for a week, that is all the time he can be spared. Important fellow, I'd say, charming too.'

The door opened and a young girl, a houseman, came in.

'Mrs Brand?'

'Yes. Please call me Charlotte.'

She brought more bad news. The little boy was very poorly.

'Don't go, Florence, please stay,' Charlotte implored. 'I need you.'

'Of course. Now Doctor – I'm sorry, I can't read your name . . .'

'MacInlay, Kirsty MacInlay, Lady Begg.'

'Well then, tell us what is to be done. Is the wee chap unlikely to live?'

'It's hard to say.'

'I want him christened,' said Charlotte. 'If I can't go to my father's funeral at least I want my baby to be christened.'

Florence and Kirsty were godparents, the hospital chaplain baptised the baby with holy water in a kidney basin.

Florence chose the name.

She had no sons. Had she had one she would have called him Piers. She had often thought that Piers was just the ticket.

Piers did not die. He recovered slowly while he was fed intravenously; there was much hope. Unbaptised Coral grasped life with vigour and enthusiasm. Her mother cried most of the time. Motherhood was messy, dirty, smelly and agonisingly uncomfortable. Where were the cosy pink babies and tinkerbelling prettiness of little cherubs wrapped in softest shawls resting in arms of blessed serenity? Instead of marshmallow sweetness, Charlotte stank of stale spilt milk and stale blood seeping from her ripped body.

'Woe to the fatherless, woe to the womb that teemed and to the cracked nipple that does not satisfy.'

Years later she found this written in her diary and laughed at the pretentiousness.

Elizabeth Brand rushed north declaring that she had dropped

everything. She arrived two days after Fraser's funeral and set to work by antagonising Flora-Anne, Charlotte's stalwart if inefficient cleaning lady, by showing her the correct way to scour a bath and upbraiding her for thriftless use of soap, and dusty lintels. Elizabeth inspected the larder and freezer, saying she could not believe her eyes. Such wastage, such extravagance. Charlotte hadn't even made marmalade . . . what hope did those poor children have of a proper upbringing, she would like to know. However she decided, on her husband's advice, to hold her tongue: Charlotte was in no shape to rectify the lack of marmalade and the terms of Fraser's will might yet prove interesting, especially as Cyril Brand was now the senior partner in Price, Forth and Brand.

Robin, having done all he could in Godleham to appear splendid in every way, was due home on Tuesday when the twins would be eight days old. Piers was improving slowly, while Charlotte was beginning to feel human and hopeful once more, especially as Coral seemed to have learnt how to feed to their mutual satisfaction. Maybe they could be discharged by the end of the week even if it meant leaving Piers behind a bit longer.

Charlotte awoke on Monday afternoon, having slept deep and long since the morning feed, to find Elizabeth arranging an enormous and fresh bouquet of flowers. The earlier ones had wilted in the hospital heat.

'How lovely. Who are they from?'

'Godfrey Fable's son, my dear. Martin Fable.'

Charlotte felt her heart jump.

'How kind of him to send them,' she said, hoping to sound normally delighted. 'Is there a note with them?'

'He said to give you his love.'

'You mean he is here?'

'No, dear. Not any more. He had to go to get his plane connection back to somewhere most exotic – Bolivia, I believe. Anyway I said you were not to be disturbed; you need to build up your strength, you know. Not many mothers have the chance to recover as comfortably as this. You should take advantage of this spoiling.'

'Has Martin really gone?'

'Yes, it is a long step to Prestwick. As I said, I insisted that you should be left to sleep. After all, Robin comes back tomorrow, you must be fresh for him.'

Charlotte turned her face to the wall and wept.

'For goodness sake, pull yourself together. In my day we were not allowed to indulge in any of this post-natal depression nonsense.'

The next day Elizabeth returned clutching books on parent-craft and child care plus a useful magazine article on 'Getting Baby into a Routine'.

'Now then dear, how about cicumcision?' Elizabeth asked in a brisk way as if enquiring of ignorant cannibals how they liked their missionaries stewed.

'What about it?'

'I am sure you feel you owe it to your dear late father to have his grandson circumcised, and it is the eighth day, though I have been talking to the doctors and they say the poor little scrap is not fit, so please, my dear, do take care.'

'Robin isn't circumcised,' Charlotte replied. 'I can't see why we should put Piers through all that when it isn't necessary.'

'Not necessary maybe, but expected, like we have our babies christened.'

'Piers was christened last Friday. They weren't sure he would live.'

Tight-lipped, Elizabeth tweaked Martin's flowers into correct formation and, looking at Charlotte with contemptuous disbelief, said, 'The zeal of the converted is always excessive.'

Even Robin found his mother's wifely virtues intolerable and packed her back south once Charlotte and Coral had come home. Poor Winifred was coming to stay soon: rival mothers would turn his disrupted domestic life into the Somme.

Florence had found Pat Garton through an agency. Pat was capable, dumpy, skilled and very expensive. Charlotte could afford luxuries and in Robin's book a nurse for an inexperienced mother who had endured a protracted and difficult labour with twins born early, one of whom was delicate, was nothing but a frivolous indulgence. Still, what was money for? Meanwhile Robin waited patiently to know the terms of his father-in-law's will and the decision about who should fight the Godleham by-election for the Tories.

Peta, who had been utterly devastated by Godfrey's death, made a most beautifully tragic widow. Black did for her what it never does for ancient crones. Gaunt and pale from grief, she was poignantly irresistible. Miserable and bereft as she was, she still failed to gain the sympathy of the Godleham Conservative ladies. Not only had she poached the Tory women's most desirable widower; she had caused him to die of exhaustion. Had she not insisted on staying in London for a rigorous and dissipated weekend, their beloved member would still be alive and have been able to enjoy the local fund-raising *fête-champêtre*.

Peta had found Robin's cloying concern and busybody helpfulness irritating in the extreme. She had never liked him, and though she was no great practitioner of fidelity herself she despised him for his treatment of Charlotte, who, despite their different temperaments, remained her best friend. When the subject arose of Godfrey's successor as member for Godleham Peta made it known she would prefer Roddy MacPhail, which was why the committee chose Robin Brand.

II

October 1994

EVEN WHEN TWENTY years younger Pat Garton had been competent and confidence inspiring: she could move painful bodies, clean and dose them skilfully and persuade the most reticent to take food in or push it out. Kindly and gently she stood for no nonsense. These days she was substantially fatter than the dumpy girl Charlotte remembered, but her beautiful peachy skin still glowed on her plump cheeks beneath her little sparkly eyes, though the hair that had been wavy and black was now almost completely white.

Charlotte held out her hand. 'Hello Pat, remember me?'

July 1975

THAT LAST SUMMER in Sandhill held mixed memories. Happiness tinged with dread, for Charlotte knew that this time Robin would win a safe seat and that she would be asked to move once more. She hadn't made many friends in Scotland but she only needed a few. Her babies, her house and to a certain extent her own imagination were enough company for her solitary nature.

Winifred had come to stay for a fortnight and was planning to return home and face widowhood alone in the house in which she had spent all thirty years of her ridiculously happy marriage. She missed Fraser more each day, but she knew she must go back and start a new life on her own. Later maybe Charlotte might like her mother to live closer, but for now, both women needed to establish their own separate ways: Charlotte as a mother and Winifred as a widow. Charlotte's grief for her father grew as the summer faded. She kept her sadness private.

'Darling, I am not interfering but I do feel you should be prepared to get rid of the nurse.'

It was the day before Winifred was due to catch the day train south from Edinburgh. She and Charlotte had walked along the sands bordering the golf course; it was sultry and thundery. Small black flies had speckled all the nappies hung out to dry. The washing machine was in perpetual motion but Pat was quick and efficient, making the changing of a baby's dirty nappy look as easy as breathing. Pat's prompt action had even saved Piers's life.

'Why should I sack Pat? She has been wonderful. If it wasn't for her Piers would have died.'

'I know, my darling, it is just that – oh well never mind. I expect Robin will be off on some political junketing shortly. Forget I said anything.'

Mother and daughter walked on in silence. Doubts about Winifred pestered Charlotte. She seemed so troubled, the grief of the last two months must have triggered demented imaginings. Piers had been discharged from hospital at three weeks old. He had regained his birth weight a week before and was growing slowly, having been out of the incubator for fourteen days. He would need skilled nursing; Pat could give it.

For five days Charlotte struggled to feed him but he had become a bottle baby and rejected her nipple. He was also sick. The sickness was more than the messy up-chucking of a greedy infant, it was explosive. For a small weakling, his projectile vomiting was phenomenal.

The doctor was called. It was nothing . . . all babies are sick. It could be the change of air, the home routine, anxiety of the mother: all manner of things might cause infantile vomiting. Still Piers had thrown back almost everything he ate. He must be discouraged from bolting his food. Slowly does it. The milk continued to be gulped down quickly, the poor child was starving. After a couple of minutes in his tiny stomach every drop would spurt out and spatter the surroundings till everywhere smelt of cheese. True, it seemed that more stayed down when Pat held the bottle but there was no need for Robin to call Charlotte an incompetent mother when their son wrecked the suit he had put on for Sunday lunch with the Beggs.

The apple pie bought from the Co-op but served by Prime was just being handed round when Pat had driven up to Auchenkirk with both babies in Charlotte's car. The Auchenkirk telephone was often on the blink then too.

Robin looked furious at the nurse intruding on Lord Begg's lunch party, especially as he was hoping to share a joke with the shadow Secretary of State for Scotland.

Florence understood at once. 'It is my godson, isn't it? He is not right.'

'No, he is very ill. I don't care what that doctor says – he must go to hospital immediately and I will need to take Mrs Brand with me to feed Coral and to sign the consent form.'

'What consent form?' Charlotte asked in panic.

'Consent for the anaesthetic. He needs an operation immediately.'

'They can't operate on a baby as small as Piers.'

'They can and must, or he will die.'

Pat was right. She had felt the tumour through the lean skin of his little belly: he had been born with pyloric stenosis. The sickness had nothing to do with nerves, air or diet but was caused by a congenital blockage.

Ten days later Piers was home once more, pink and greedy, happy and contented, but scarred and stitched from above the diaphragm to below the navel.

The ideal of coping without Pat appalled Charlotte.

'Isn't that the cottage you rented with Robin last year?' Winifred asked as they neared the end of the strand.

'Yes, that is Links Cottage. It's haunted, you know.'

'It is horrid, but surely it is too modern to have developed a ghost.'

Charlotte told her mother about the torching of Torquil on that site. Even as they approached the building it seemed to take on a sinister aspect.

'Let's go home, sweetie,' said Winifred. 'This place gives me the willies, and I want to get packed.'

'I wish you would stay longer, Mum.'

'No, darling, I must go. I would only stay if you needed me to do something practical. My home is not here, you have your life. You will find this out when your babies are grown too.'

They got back to Sandhill just as the thunderstorm broke. Everything was neat and tidy: bottles prepared, nappies folded, buckets filled with Napisan and a note on the hall table. Robin was shut in his study while both babies slept happily in their cots. Pat Garton had gone.

The note offered no explanation. All she said was that it was not possible for her to stay any longer, something had come up and she wanted to leave at once. She asked for no reference, only requesting that her last week's wages be posted to her mother's address. Nothing more – no well-wishing, no regrets.

'Robin, do you know anything about this?' Charlotte gave him Pat's note to read.

'Well, it appears that once again you have proved to be no good at keeping staff,' he replied handing it back.

'What on earth did I do wrong?'

'Well if you don't know there is little point in my spelling it out to you.'

'Oh Robin, how can I manage? I don't know what to do.'

'So it would seem. Have you got a new cleaning lady yet? This place is filthy.'

'It wasn't my fault that Flora-Anne left. It was your mother who told her she was taking too long for tea breaks.'

'That was your job.'

'I loved chatting to Flora-Anne, she was great company.'

'You shouldn't fraternise.'

'You played backgammon with Pat,' Charlotte replied.

'And you treated her like dirt.'

'I didn't, Robin. I liked her a lot, she was marvellous. I told her so, many times.'

'Maybe. You'll learn.'

Charlotte loathed Robin when he was all superior and patronising, but she had no strength to argue; besides, Coral was calling for her tea. Charlotte detected her breasts responding to the baby's demand and felt like a cow conditioned to queue for milking on hearing the machinery being switched on. Remembering tales of witchcraft and folklore she trusted that the thunderstorm would not have turned her milk sour.

'I can't manage without some help,' Charlotte said quietly.

'Whyever not? Fenella employs nobody and she has three children.'

'Jake does some of the work.'

'Surely you don't want me to be like that beardie weirdie. Typical socialist. I bet you'll find that he is secretly drinking champagne and subscribing to BUPA and only pushes a pram when the media are about.'

'Robin, I need help.'

'Well get some, I'm not stopping you. Now please send your mother to me, there is something I want to say to her. Off you go.'

Robin always seemed to be telling people to go off. As his children grew, 'Off you go' was the most frequent phrase he addressed to them.

'Ah Winifred, come in. Take a seat.'

'Please don't get up for me,' Winifred replied.

Robin hadn't.

'What is the meaning of this ridiculous document?' he asked, picking up some thick white paper that had been bound with red strings. Beneath it on his desk Winifred could see that Robin had been looking at a copy of *Penthouse* which he quickly concealed with a letter bearing a portcullis insignia.

'It looks like a will to me, Robin.'

'Of course it is a will. Your husband's will, to be precise. My wife's father's will. I am his son-in-law, in case you had forgotten.'

'How could I forget that, dear?'

'Don't call me dear. I obviously mean less than dirt to you.'

'What makes you think that?'

'This,' he said brandishing the document dramatically, ribbons trailing as lightning forked to the distant rocks and thunder rolled.

Winifred rose and shut the window. 'All this is in rather bad taste, do you not think? One expects Dracula or at the very least the Torchers of Torquil to appear. Do calm down, Robin. I realise you can't control the elements but you can at least approach your grievance like an adult. After all, the children are well provided for, their education fully financed and your wife assured of an income and a roof.'

'Am I to be treated as no more than a watchdog? A watchdog without teeth or means forced to escort a wife whose money is to be kept in trust till she is fifty?'

'I am sorry you see it like that. Fraser thought that this way you could avoid the ignominy of being labelled a fortune hunter. Now it would seem he was wrong. Poor Charlotte.'

'Poor Charlotte be damned! She is cushioned and coddled, protected by a phalanx of trustees and advisers like some precious ward of court, shielded from adventurers.'

'While you are free to make the most of yourself by virtue of your own talents. Free to exploit your abilities and brains.'

'I am nothing more than a remittance man.'

'No you are not. After all, dear Fraser has bequeathed you all his cellar and Disraeli memorabilia. He had great regard for your discrimination and intellect. These things would be yours even if Charlotte was not.'

'I am everything to Charlotte and you know it,' Robin replied. 'Without me she would be a lost soul.'

'No Robin, Charlotte's soul is her own.'

Winifred renewed Selina the Sealyham's tenancy at the boarding kennels and stayed on. She had been both nurse and mother and could now come in handy to her daughter. Though she had been idle for years, inactivity had been her choice; she remained supremely capable, and was neither as decrepit nor ill as she often pretended.

Robin left. There were many unspecified things that he needed to do. The by-election was looming: he knew he was going to win and this time Charlotte conceded that he was probably right. The rest of the summer was a seamless succession of feeding, changing, washing and sleeping. A replacement for Pat was found, Winifred helped Charlotte with the selection of a strong and hairy middle-aged woman who liked to be called Nana. Charlotte did wonder whether she was anything to do with the dog in *Peter Pan*, or if the resemblance was purely coincidental. Winifred was adamant that Nana was the right choice, and never expanded on why she had declared all the jollier and young applicants highly unsuitable.

October 1994

Pat and Charlotte sat in the kitchen at Auchenkirk with a large teapot between them and some shortbread bought at the Leuchars sale of work. The newspapers were still full of the Brand scandal; it was Sunday and every tabloid and broadsheet had its own speculation and comment to make on the affair. Prime was enjoying the excitement and had bought the lot, much to the fascination of Wee Hammy's wife who worked at the Auchtertay newsagent.

LADY B FLEES IN DISGUISE.

Immaculata the hairdresser was milking the situation for all it was worth. Lady Brand's hair had been 'transformed', she claimed, implying that Charlotte was now masquerading as a raven-headed temptress or Monroe lookalike. Immaculata, still veiled but grinning broadly, had got herself photographed outside her shop. Charlotte hoped the publicity would bring her trade; it was a shame that Mahmood's bulk concealed the salon's name. From her family there was not much comment except that Robin was described as distraught.

'He looks quite chipper to me,' said Pat pointing a knitting needle at a picture of Robin scanning a map as if Charlotte's whereabouts might appear amongst its B roads, level crossings and public houses.

Piers said he had helped his mother flee but had no idea where she had gone, though as she had taken her passport and lots of cash he expected she might try and go abroad, maybe to Coral in Paris.

'Good boy,' said Charlotte. 'Good thinking. He knows perfectly well that I forgot my passport and I have hardly got a penny on me. He can't be so thick after all.'

'He has grown into a fine young man,' said Pat admiringly.

'The last time I saw him he was that wee he could have fitted into my knitting bag.'

Soppiness was not overlooked as a publicity ruse. Zoe the dotty spaniel had posed appealingly, large eyes melting with injured innocence: WAITING FAITHFULLY – LADY B'S ABANDONED FRIEND.

Evidently Winifred had refused to be photographed and had issued the press with a charming picture of her much younger self looking radiant in a silly Ascot hat.

'Your mum's a canny yin.'

'You remember her?'

'Of course.'

'You managed to disappear. What happened?'

'Och, it wasn't difficult.'

'But why did you go? I never did find out what I had done to make you go like that.'

'You did nothing. I was that sorry to leave you. It was nothing to do with you.'

'My husband said that my behaviour had driven you away.'

'He would.'

Pat's knitting was apricot coloured and destined for her niece's newest baby, a jaundiced wean according to Pat who was hoping little Mairi's complexion would tone with the wool.

'You never married, Pat?'

'No, I've nae husband, weans or parents to fret about.'

'Do you mind? Sorry, that is very nosy of me,' Charlotte asked.

'Mind? I don't mind in the least. I had my chances, I just didn't want to take the risk. I'm happy, and that is not one bit of a lie. Now, what am I doing blethering here with the old codger needing a jab? Lady Begg will be skinning me if I don't get a move on.'

'I can't think how you stand it,' said Charlotte.

'That's the two of us. I can't think how you have stood your kind of life for so long. I was that amazed to find you had stuck by himself for all these years. What are you, some kind of masochist?'

Charlotte couldn't explain the hold Robin had over her but replied, 'He has a very strong personality.'

'Sure, like toilet paper, completely disposable.'

'Why *did* you leave, Pat?'

'Why do you think?'

'I don't know, really I don't.'

'Och well let's say that I could also write a nasty wee tale about your husband. Maybe I will, next month in my nursing column of the St Ninian's Kirk magazine. It would make a change from incontinence.'

'He made a pass at you?'

'Some pass! There was no mistaking his plans, none at all, it was all quite clear, not one bit subtle. He seemed to have a notion that a wee homey body like me would be grateful, but he'd got the wrong idea there and no mistake.'

Charlotte could scarcely believe what she was hearing. Still, she was certain that Pat wouldn't make up such a tale.

'What did you do, Pat?'

'Och I just kneed him in the groin and told him I would rather be boiled in oil.'

'What happened then?'

'He got that cross. He said that no one had ever refused him before and that a common little girl like me should be flattered to be noticed by the likes of him.'

'He said that?'

'Every word, I can hear his drawling voice yet.'

'Why didn't you tell someone?'

Pat turned as she left the room and said, 'If I had told anyone it would have made life even worse for you and the babies. I left before the mess got impossible.'

October 1975

'May I say, Mrs Brand, how utterly delighted we are to have your husband in our team. Godleham have returned a splendid member.'

Charlotte mustered a keen smile and was relieved that she had not lost her head and curtsyed when introduced to the party leader.

'Are you very involved in Robin's work? Or do you have a career of your own?'

'I am quite busy; we have young twins.'

The icy smile made Charlotte despise herself and cringe at being such a pathetic specimen.

'We have twins too, you know. Splendid! I am sure you will be most supportive.'

The leader moved on through the crowd of sycophants that were Robin's new constituents, Charlotte felt leaden with regret behind the sunny grin.

Another move, back to England and into affluent, safe suburbia, convenient and Conservative Home County stronghold of smug privilege. She felt that she was about to be blotted up by tidy beamed houses, professional zeal, Sunday joints, summer tennis and afternoon bridge. It wasn't a bad prospect, just flat and endless, like Hell. She would live to die in Godleham having been a tireless committee member, staunch at church and most proficient on the school run.

The seals in the Zoo might enjoy her singing, but she wouldn't be singing for seals again, not for a long time.

The by-election victor is greeted by the Commons with far greater ceremony than the droves of those who have fought a general election. A procession, oath-taking and waved order papers accompany the event. Robin carried the affair off with his usual suavity. In earlier and more leisurely years he might have been quite a one to parade with dashing style in the Mall and Bath or ridden to advantage in Rotten Row, causing much fluttering amongst the spectators.

Jake Cleaver, showing no sign of envy or enmity, was amongst those who congratulated his brother-in-law. Robin accepted his good wishes with reasonable grace. He could afford to be pleasant now: Godleham was one of the safest Tory seats in existence, far more secure than Jake's Labour-held Mireness. Elizabeth Brand witnessed her son's second coming alone; Charlotte was quite unable to persuade Nana to change her day off and was swamped by unpacking from their recent move south. She had quite forgotten what it felt like not to be tired and worn out. Everything drained her; only her babies, now and again, gave her pleasure. It must be worth it – she forbade herself to think otherwise.

Friends of Godfrey Fable and some older members had their

doubts about Robin but only a few of the bold covertly called the new member 'The Hearse Chaser'.

12

December 1975

'THIS IS GENERALLY considered to be the best example of the work of James Gibbs. The porch is a direct copy of the temple at – you aren't listening, Charlotte.'

'Sorry darling, do go on.'

Charlotte watched the dust-laden December sunbeams slanting past the pulpit perched above its curved staircase while the organ played Bach. The little opaque windowpanes reminded her of sunny skies shining upon ice puddles; she wasn't paying much attention to Robin's commentary on the architecture of St-Martin-in-the-Fields. The interior of yellowing cream and the faded gilding had the tasteful opulence of a pensioner princess. No stained-glass gaudiness nor tawdry glitter jarred the serenity of the church. Even the Christmas tree was restrained.

Being prominent, even in this most illustrious congregation, the Brands were placed near the front, a place most suited to the man who had inherited the deceased's mantle. Peta Fable had chosen the day in Advent as suitable for Godfrey's memorial service. Though he had died almost six months before, only now did she feel able to give thanks for his life with appropriate cheerfulness, enough time having been spent in mournful gloom. Furthermore it was the only date possible for Martin, Godfrey's son and sole surviving blood relative, to be in the country.

Charlotte sat next to Robin, MP once more, confident and distinguished in dark overcoat carrying a bowler hat and furled umbrella, fulfilling every matron's fantasy of the upper-crust Conservative male. He was to read a lesson. Godfrey had not been much moved by poetry so only the Bible was used for telling passages; he would not have held with Desideratas, Nun's Prayers or Going not gentle into good nights, having put his hand into the hand of God. An ardent constituent, much gifted on the cello, had offered to play, which was just fine but Peta had vetoed the Godleham Glee Group, and engaged the Tamesis Chorale at enormous expense to sing *Panis Angelicus*. Charlotte had helped with the flowers but no amount of bustle kept her jitters quelled. Nana had been reluctant to look after the twins for a day and a half on her own but Charlotte had insisted and bribed her to consent with the promise of all of Christmas and New Year off.

She could hardly sleep for anxiety. Supposing Martin didn't come? Maybe he would ignore her, perhaps he had changed, he might have a lover – some South American enchantress. Peta had only said that her stepson hoped to be there.

Charlotte didn't look round. She kept her eyes on the altar and prayed, but not for poor Godfrey's soul.

Oh God, please may Martin come. Lord hear my prayer, and let my cry come unto thee.

There was really not much likelihood of God assisting the adulterer and whoremonger, but it was worth a go.

All the forward pews were taken up by Conservative politicians and middle-aged, middle-class, would-be gentry but Peta, the young widow, sat alone at the front with a vacant seat between her and Mrs Bray, her cousin who had brought her precocious daughter along for the experience. After all, Ocean had been a bridesmaid to the deceased and it is never too early to get acquainted with grief, especially in its more social form: an antidote to all that television violence, she told anyone looking disdainful.

Just before the service started a man, thin and filthy in a duffel coat and dirty trousers, shambled up the aisle and sat himself down beside Peta.

For just a second Charlotte thought she would faint. She breathed deeply and looked again. Thank God – the man was not only too lean but also far too tall. The tramp came to most functions at St Martin's, he used the crypt as a refuge and kept himself warm and entertained by attending services. You could meet all sorts that way.

'That man smells terrible.'

Ocean's mother tried to hush her child; the tramp gave a gap-toothed smile, stayed and sang with gusto. Like a church mouse he knew what to expect, and was much more up in the liturgy than many of society's goodies who surrounded him and were bawling out 'Jerusalem', with handkerchiefs held to their noses.

Robin read his bit, the cellist swayed with rapture as she bowed her way through Elgar's serial climaxes and a friendly Dean recalled Godfrey the man, while wishing well to Godfrey the soul, being utterly sure and certain of meeting the departed in celestial clubland come Judgment Day.

A few prayers were said and then there was to be a tenor solo before Franck's anthem.

'Comfort Ye My People!'

'Christ, Charlotte, it's my bloody brother-in-law! What the devil does that idiot Peta think she is doing?'

Jake Cleaver had the voice of an angel, having been a choir-boy in his Maidstone youth and studied music before taking to politics. His recreation was singing: it was written there for all to see in *Who's Who*.

'Hush, Robin. He sings beautifully.'

All the assembled ranks of Tories were stunned. Never before had a sitting member of the Labour Party sung at the obsequies of a dead Conservative.

Robin was aghast; his kinship with Jake Cleaver was something he preferred to conceal.

'Just because he is singing the words of that bloody agitator, the sodding man needn't look like John the Baptist.'

Later Peta swore that she had no idea Jake was the corner-stone of the Tamesis Chorale but somehow Charlotte did not believe her.

On the porch overlooking Trafalgar Square where the Christmas tree from Norway sparkled, Charlotte searched the faces of the departing congregation in mounting desperation. Once or twice she was sure she saw him, she was certain, then doubtful and finally so panic-struck she could no longer remember what Martin looked like.

She managed to get hold of Peta.

'Where is Martin?' she asked, trying to sound like one making a polite enquiry. Her voice was shaky, she was on the verge of tears.

'Martin is in hospital in Recife. Poor darling, his appendix blew up and they had to give him an emergency operation. A telex arrived this morning: he is all right but fed up. Apparently his belly looks more like the tube map than ever now. Oh Charlotte, don't cry. What is wrong?'

'Nothing, it is just, well you know, six months since my father died too.'

'Liar.'

Peta took Charlotte's arm and drew her to one side. Facing the statue of Edith Cavell she said, 'Listen, why don't you write to him? I will always act as a postbox for you. It is no use being a martyr, it isn't worth it.'

Gripping her nine-year-old daughter by the hand Mrs Bray approached Robin: 'You won't remember us, I'm sure.'

'Of course I do,' he replied gallantly. Pretending to recognise strangers was an acquired skill he used at all times, on all occasions. To snub a constituent would be a grave crime. Best be friends with all, just in case. One never knows who might prove seminal to a political future.

1976

'So nice to see you settled, Charlotte,' said Elizabeth on her Easter visit. 'I was not at all happy about you in Scotland. It wasn't right for you.'

'I loved it there,' said Charlotte.

'But Robin did not belong. It is most important for our family to belong, if you know what I mean.'

'I preferred being a stranger there to belonging here.'

'Ah well, that is what comes of being a wanderer. Flitter flitter, off to Egypt, off to Babylon, in and out of wildernesses across steppes and deserts, haring over to America, never still, your lot. The English, you see, just don't let themselves get persecuted. However, I can understand why you find it hard to put down roots.'

'I can't,' said Charlotte.

'You will, you will. I know, I am such a wise old woman.'

Elizabeth could make a chuckle sound patronising.

Charlotte hated being treated like a wilful child. 'We hope to go back to Scotland there for our holidays, especially now that Roddy MacPhail has been selected to fight Pittenfirth and Netherloch.'

Roddy and Henrietta had bought Sandhill. Charlotte wished they had gone somewhere else. She hated to lose the home she had loved so much: to see it belonging to friends had been far worse than selling the Markham Street house to sneering unknowns. But she braced herself to endure the MacPhails' good fortune and go to stay with them in the summer. Charlotte could tolerate a lot these days; she had her consolations, and she had her children.

'No, dear, you mustn't take the poor twins up there.' Elizabeth clutched Charlotte's arm in distress, reacting to the suggestion of a seaside holiday in Scotland as if her daughter-in-law had planned to ship her grandchildren to Siberia.

'Cornwall is much more suitable, Cornwall or – at a stretch – Frinton. Don't you agree, Nana?'

Nana agreed to everything. It mattered not to her: she was about to give notice.

When she did, Charlotte was relieved. Nana considered no task, however small, to be easy and any lapse in routine was a major catastrophe. She nursed grudges and remembered slights, taking every possible chance for time off and never going an extra inch to be helpful. She would shake her head and do much maddening tutting of the tongue at the state of everything: the house, the children, the weather, the world and, most especially, her wage packet.

Robin said he wasn't surprised. Charlotte was grounded: she had to give up her holiday to look after the children. What, in any case, would she have got out of a trip to Rome? He was going there to find facts; further facts would be sought in Venice, Naples, Milan and Nice. The Risorgomento, he explained dismissively, had much to offer the modern politician. To a young mother such places were irrelevant, he would take her and the babies to a family hotel somewhere coastal later. He promised.

Peta's horizontal activities didn't interrupt her friendship with Charlotte. She quite enjoyed a day of playing with babies provided they were a temporary recreation, but her maternal urges were quickly sated. She had loved Godfrey and knew that she would never feel the same about anyone else, but this didn't hinder her from enjoying love with others and life, while her appetites were yet sharp, was to be relished. Charlotte was different but Peta understood. She was the only one who did.

At first the letters had been polite and chattily full of news. They arrived intermittently but increased in frequency and intensity as the years went by. Charlotte lived for the letters: they kept her from despair and kept her patient. Martin wrote beautifully, funnily and lifted her spirits above the domestic trivia in which she mostly wallowed. Her letters to Martin were cathartic, and a chief delight to both of them. He chose not to return to England at all, there was only one thing for him there and that was not his. Charlotte was as unattainable as any locked-up lady of legend. Later maybe, not now. It wouldn't be right or possible: theirs was a courtly love.

'I think you are dotty,' said Peta. She was a most conscientious postbox.

In Spring 1979 the Labour government fell. Robin's joy was complete. Now he could rise and take his place alongside the great.

Roddy MacPhail was voted in at last.

Jake Cleaver clung to his seat tenuously, but not to his wife. Fenella and the three little Cleavers went back to Dorset, mother and home.

Laura Brand, Robin's other sister, embarked on an enlightened relationship with a man of the middle, a faceless character who hoped to speak up for the voice of reason. No one would vote for Guy Tooth: he and Laura went to Norfolk to live off the land. They kept bees and goats and grew their own clothes.

1980

Coral and Piers started school and suddenly Charlotte felt old and at a loss. It would only get worse: her babies were gone, were growing into a world in which she would become part of the elderly population. Her hair was still gold but nothing was bright for ever. Martin's letters became less frequent, less intimate and somehow less spontaneous.

The day the twins became five a letter from Martin got delivered via Peta who, as Coral's godmother, had come down to Godleham for a dose of family jollity. Enclosed with it was a photograph of Isabelita, an Argentinian beauty, a graduate with a tragic past and much spirit. Martin had met her while unravelling a sinister tale of political intrigues and mysterious abductions. One glance at the dark woman holding the hand of her fatherless son and the substance went out of Charlotte's life.

The birthday party was progressing well, the agonisingly short-lived games had been cleverly spun out till teatime and most of the guests had swooped on the sausages and crisps with vigour. The two cakes – one a train, the other a Womble – had been modestly popular. The only unpleasant incident had been when Coral found Piers to be too sluggish with his puff and had not only blown out the Womble cake's candles but had dealt with those on the train also.

Piers had cried with frustration and Robin had told him it served him right for not being alert. Then, in Charlotte's hearing, he called him a mummy's boy, saying the sooner he got sent to prep school the better. Robin liked to make sure that he attended all parties and any other public occasions involving the children. For vote-catching, fatherliness was a sterling ploy. His was an ideal family: the perfect mix of sexes, the optimum size with the advantage of compact timing. Sometimes Charlotte felt that Robin the dad was smug enough to have stepped straight out of a reading primer or the *Children's Hour* of her youth.

After tea was done, Charlotte was delighted and relieved to leave the rest to the entertainer.

'God, Charlotte, do these kids really think that awful man is funny?' Peta asked, blowing elegant clouds of smoke over the crumby teatime debris.

'Yes, they love him. He does all the parties round here, isn't he dreadful? Still, I suppose twenty-five years ago we thought that sort of thing all right too.'

'Twenty-five years ago I was too young to notice anything.'

For the second time that day Charlotte felt age attacking her. Peta was only a little bit older than her and already she had begun to lie about her age. This must be the start of decline. Martin's letter nagged her from her pocket. She was looking forward to a stiff drink.

'Nice letter?' Peta asked.

The friends were strolling in the garden. Charlotte hoped one day to take a serious delight in planning beds and devising a more flowing pattern of lawn, but the old gardener who had come with Cedar Lodge was set in his ways and easily offended. He voted Tory, as did his cronies, but if crossed he could soon cancel the loyal blue support of all Godleham's horticultural society.

'Martin has a girlfriend.'

'Good. What did you expect?'

'I don't know.'

'Listen, Charlotte, if he didn't run after women you'd be worried and you aren't really prepared to give all this up for him, are you?'

'There are times when I would leave without any regret.'

'But the children. You couldn't abandon the children.'

'No. Of course not.'

'Robin isn't the sort of father to give them up either, I fancy.'

'No. He would never do that, he looks on them as extensions of his own body. He would never consent to an amputation. Though I'm afraid he finds fatherhood a bit of a disappointment.'

'Coral isn't disappointing, surely?'

'Maybe not, though Robin did say he was surprised that his daughter wasn't prettier.'

'Oh come on, Charlotte, you make Coral sound like Quasimodo. She is lovely – beautiful hair and terribly bright.'

'That is the trouble. She has all the drive and Piers seems to be quite without fight. Robin is always trying to instill in him a manly urge to win, to be competitive and tough.'

'Poor mite.'

At the end of the garden there was a lane and the other side of that a paddock which the Brands, or rather Charlotte, had managed to buy and in which they were planning to keep ponies. Robin was particularly anxious for his children to ride and explained his own inability to do so by quoting a hitherto unmentioned allergy to horses. Charlotte suspected Robin was scared, but she had been moderately keen when young and could cope with ponies if necessary.

Cedar Lodge was terribly convenient: handy for everywhere and close to both city and country. That was its trouble. Charlotte felt Godleham to be staid and unadventurous: everything was well appointed, prudent and depressing, like installing grab rails round the bath when young in anticipation of infirm senility.

Back in the house, parents were beginning to assemble to reclaim their children who would refuse to leave without a bag of loot to add to their already sizeable haul of prizes and balloons. The front drive was packed with Volvos fitted with trailer hitches and containing fenced dogs.

The two Potter sons were quite swamped by their prizes awarded for crafty nimbleness of body and brain. They always won everything. Failing to be first meant that questions would be asked. Phyllis Potter pretended to be indifferent but everyone, including her little boys, knew that there would be much injured disappointment at the Potter home if they fell short in any game.

'Mrs Fable! How lovely to see you. How are you, my dear?'

Phyllis greeted Peta with her usual ferocity. One glance at Godleham's MP's widow in skin-tight jeans was enough. Phyllis represented that faction of Tory ladies who knew no wrong of a pleated skirt and held that flashy glamour was not at all the thing. Charlotte Brand was much more suitable as their member's wife, though her legs did give rise to *frissons* of envy amongst some. Phyllis was above such issues and though she pitied Charlotte for her second-class son she found nothing at all amiss in Robin. Now there was a man: her boys were well advised to look to Mr Brand as a template for successful manhood. Her own Herbert, while being conveniently malleable, had abdicated his ambitions in favour of his wife.

Winifred Forth's Sealyham had met a local mongrel and given birth to some strange puppies, one of which now belonged to Charlotte.

'What a quaint dog!' said Phyllis with ill-concealed disgust. Her dogs were pure in urge and breed. 'What is it?'

'This is Pan. He was a present from my mother. Sit, Pan!' Pan sat.

'Pam! Ah yes. Short for Palmerston, I expect. You politicians are all the same.' She twinkled at Robin, who beamed back, knowing better than to contradict.

'He is called Pan,' said Charlotte, pouring herself a second large sherry. 'Short for Pandemonium.'

After the party had been cleared away and the children, fractious and weary, had been safely tucked up, Robin poured Charlotte a further drink and told her to sit down.

'I want to talk to you about a very serious matter.'

Charlotte wondered whether Robin had detected her feelings for Martin and, emboldened by alcohol, decided that she wouldn't much mind if he had. No, evidently Robin was concerned about Winifred Forth, which was odd considering his coolness towards his mother-in-law since the disappointment of Fraser's will.

'What are you going to do about it?'

'About what?'

'About her and that man.'

'Nothing. He is lovely, just the person to cheer her up.'

'He is a fortune-hunter.'

'Surely not. I think he is charming. Mummy looks happier now than she has for years and isn't ill nearly so often.'

'I am going to speak to him.'

Robin looked at Charlotte on the sofa. Her eyes had shut; she wasn't listening. Her glass was empty. It was the fourth such glass he had found drained and abandoned that evening, all of them hers.

13

October 1994

ONCE THE WEEKEND was over Pat Garton would be relieved by Nurse Bristle on the Monday night. Florence was due back at Auchenkirk late on Tuesday, luck and ferries being favourable. As a young girl, Florence had been one of the first female drivers in the district and was determined to be the oldest. She certainly was the most terrifying.

Charlotte wondered whether she should stay till Florence's homecoming or if she should take herself away for a couple of days before returning to confide in and consult her dearest friend. For all the difference in age between them, Charlotte had always felt Florence to be the one person whose advice and opinion she valued and trusted.

Charlotte was close to her own mother but Winifred's loathing of Robin did not make for detached assessments. However rotten he had been as a husband she always felt a compunction to defend him against his mother-in-law's barbs of hatred. Robin and Winifred had pitched their battle lines either side of Charlotte, who stood in the middle brandishing a metaphorical white flag and imploring them to call a truce.

Charlotte's guilt was known only to Robin; she had revealed it to no one and knew that even the sacred confidentiality of the confessional would never have wrung her sin from her. It was secret and would remain so until she felt she could carry the burden no longer. Perhaps that time was now. Maybe this was the moment to relieve her mind of its load and brave the consequences. After all, she was no longer of importance to anyone. She was expendable, her confession would do no one any harm.

She wanted more time: a few more days added on to eight years would be of no significance.

Once Tam had been bedded down, washed, combed and sweet smelling like a baby, Pat suggested that they might have a restorative drink. Prime always kept adequate whisky to hand for all emergencies, medical or social. At night with the blinds drawn even the Auchenkirk kitchen could be cosy despite the harsh glare of lights shaded only by collars of filthy enamel tin.

'Will you not take a dram, my lady?'

'No thank you, Prime. I'm fine.'

'Och go on, hen,' said Pat. 'It will do you good.'

'I won't, thank you. I am an alcoholic.'

Spring 1980

It was when Elizabeth Brand, now the wife of the senior partner of Price, Forth and Brand, called on Winifred Forth one morning and found a man lurking in her conservatory that the great scare started. So distressed was Elizabeth at the prospect of Winifred making a fool of herself and losing her head and the family's expectations to a parvenu that she rang her son at the House of Commons at peak rate time.

Robin was most grateful. Alarm bells tolling the prospect of a squandered inheritance were ringing louder than his division bell. Things must be done, and with speed.

Charlotte had agreed, albeit while insensible. He had interpreted her falling asleep as tacit consent to his scheme to intervene and banish Winifred's elderly gigolo. He would confront his mother-in-law's suitor and get him to lay off. How much would it cost? Robin knew that in such a situation he would demand a lot. Charlotte would pay once a price had been negotiated; after all (Robin told himself) he was only doing this for her.

Elizabeth spied for her son.

'What was the name of that nice man I met here last week?'

Winifred was somewhat startled at the directness of the question but answered it at once, only pausing to wonder why Elizabeth had called in on her again. Normally once per quarter was enough for the two grandmothers to exchange news of their children and local gossip.

'Would that be Barns with an "e"?'

'No. Carter has no "e" on his Barns.'

'So he isn't related to the Barnes family in Sherborne?'

'No, Carter has a flat in London.'

'Ah, a townie. I suppose he drives himself out to the country for the weekends.'

'He doesn't drive himself.'

'Oh. Well I must be off. Lots to do, lots to do with all Fenella's dear little tribe to keep happy. Don't you envy me having grandchildren at home all the time?'

'Frankly Elizabeth, I don't.'

Over a chorus of childish shrieking and motherly shouting Elizabeth relayed the information to her son.

Robin got his secretary to track down Carter Barns and invite him to lunch at the House. That should scupper him. As an afterthought, he told her to include information about adjacent bus routes and tubes with the invitation.

The food was just passable but the wine was superb. Robin liked showing off. To talk down to Carter Barns was a delight. The man was an obvious poseur; his immaculate suit, handmade shoes, silk tie and linen hankerchief were mere tools of the confidence trickster's trade.

Robin came straight to the point. He explained that Winifred was a foolish and gullible widow but it was his intention to ensure that no adventurer took advantage of her silliness. He appreciated that she might be lonely and therefore prone to latch on to anyone showing a modicum of interest in her simple little life. However, deception was impossible with such a zealous one as Robin waiting to beat off invaders and ensure that his mother-in-law remained faithful to the memory of her late husband whilst keeping her fortune intact and ready for her descendants, come her demise.

With dread Robin saw Jake Cleaver approaching. He resented the intrusion, fearing his thread and impetus might be lost. Jake wanted to negotiate a pair with his ex-brother-in-law. The acrimony between the two men was, if anything, more intense since the divorce, but pairing was quite a civilised arrangement.

'Later, Jake, please. I'll speak to you after lunch.'

Jake's beard was trimmed and neat, no more the manifestation of seething interior political revolution but a blameless vanity. Carter rose and shook Jake's outstretched hand. Robin even resented that Jake had clean nails nowadays.

'How are you, my boy?'

'I'm fine, sir. It is very nice to see you. Are you keeping well?'

'Remarkably well, thank you. I tend to be a bit of a recluse, though. Are you still singing? It is a shame I can't bring myself to vote for you.'

'I sing when I can. Maybe one day you will vote for us.'

'Quite possibly, the way things are going.'

Jake left, saying he would see Robin later.

Carter Barns resumed his seat and his conversation with Robin continued from where it had been before Jake's interruption. 'What you tell me is very interesting, Mr Brand. I wonder how you intend to stop me seeing Mrs Forth.'

'I would, of course, be prepared to make your sacrifice worth while, Mr Barns.'

'Well, well. How utterly fascinating. They say one should experience everything just once. This is a new one for me.'

'Indeed?' said Robin raising an incredulous eyebrow.

'How much were you thinking of offering, Mr Brand? I would love to know.'

Just then Liam Blackway came up. Robin glowed with delight at being singled out by a party prefect. How wonderful that Carter Barns, ageing bounder that he was, should witness such convivial hob-nobbing with one so close to the Prime Minister.

'Barney, old chap! We don't see you here very often. What a treat. Come and have a drink when you have finished your business with young . . . er . . . Robert here. Better still, I've heard old Tam is down bumbling about in the Lords, we'll go through and take a glass off him, what do you think?'

'Excellent. In fact we have already finished our business. I'll come right away.' Carter rose from the table, and after waving cheerfully at Roddy MacPhail whose father, he explained, had been up at Cambridge with him before joining the Guards, took his leave of Robin.

'I say, Brand, be a good fellow and nip down and tell Hartless, my driver, not to wait for me but to pick me and your mother-in-law up from the ladies' side of Boodles at seven-fifteen. We are going to Covent Garden.' Leaving Robin and his half-eaten lunch the two old friends threaded their way to the door.

'You've got some odd young fish about these days, Liam. Hang on a second.' Carter returned to Robin's table and said, 'I've paid for the ballet tickets with my own money, don't you know.' Robin stared at the immaculate departing back, stunned.

'How did you know Carter Barns?' Robin asked Jake later in the corridor.

'Sir "Barney" Barns? Of course. Even us socialists admire him, he's one of the last genuine publicity-shunning philanthropists. When he was chairman, Amalgamated Rivets and Associated Fastenings, ARAF, were my constituency's best employers.'

'I see,' Robin replied.

When he got himself put up for membership of Boodles, Robin Brand, MP, was blackballed. The ignominy cost him many sleepless nights.

Charlotte had noticed a change in her mother, and her mother saw one in Charlotte. Only the change in her daughter was not for the better and cast a dark shadow over what was otherwise a delightful period of Winifred's late middle age.

Long ago Winifred had admitted to herself that any affection or admiration she had once professed for Robin was dead. She regretted and reproached herself for having been beguiled by his oily charm, she pitied her daughter and yet, on the surface, Charlotte did not appear to be distressed. If Winifred had endured such behaviour from her own husband she would have been devastated, her equanimity demolished. Charlotte survived, she put on flab, her complexion got puffy and her eyes seemed to be disappearing into their sockets, revealing nothing: no sadness or joy, just the indifference of an automaton which would function as required if kept well fuelled.

For the time being Coral and Piers were cared for adequately; the holidays were a bit of a strain but while they were at school they seemed to thrive. Coral was top and won prizes. Piers did not. Robin was proud of his daughter, ashamed of his son, blaming the failures on Charlotte and taking credit for Coral himself.

Charlotte could be efficiently busy, provided she knew that rescue was handy. A drink would revive whenever she felt prone to flag. By keeping herself topped up she never appeared to drink excessively in public and always managed to smile even if she was hazy as to what it was that amused her.

Meanwhile Winifred continued to enjoy the companionship of Barney Barns, not only for the fun of his friendship and taste in outings but for the exquisite delight of causing Robin embarrassment. Operas, ballets and being chauffeur driven helped to divert her from worrying about Charlotte. While Winifred appeared younger and happier, Charlotte aged frumpishly. Deep down, beyond the reach of any distraction, liquid or otherwise, she pined and longed for Martin. His letters were very rare now, quite chatty and always mentioning Isabelita and how well she was going on. Though Charlotte wrote back, she often destroyed several passionate letters before sending off a few pages of anodyne news.

Peta may have understood.

After Christmas at the bleak beginning of 1982 the two friends lunched at Etoile in Charlotte Street. Peta was meeting her current man later, a powerful figure in advertising.

'I am sure that we only really love one person absolutely completely and utterly in a lifetime. My love was Godfrey. He may have been old enough to have been my father but I did love him, really I did. The others were just games. Now all I have is games, but I do believe in playing as much as I can. You ought to try and find something to distract you, Charlotte. Believe me I do know how you feel, but you said yourself that it was hopeless.'

'I know. Maybe if I could see him, just once.'

'You two seem fated to miss each other. Last time he came

home you were skiing and the time before you had taken the children on some other holiday.'

'Yes, St Mawes with my in-laws, it was hell.'

'Charlotte, do try and get over it. You must find something or someone else to plug the gap. Here, how about some more wine?' Peta ordered a second bottle, having only had one glass out of the first which was now diving face down and empty in its ice bucket.

It would probably be quite a time before Martin could come home again. Much ill feeling was hatching into hostilities between Britain and Argentina. A South American correspondent would have no chance of leave for a while.

In April the Falkland Islands were invaded by Argentina. Charlotte was thirty-five.

Coral and Piers were seven, Robin was forty-one and Peta, who was stuck at twenty-nine, looked younger than that.

'I hate this war. I hate the way everyone is so stimulated and excited by it. The sinking of the *Belgrano* makes me feel terribly ashamed.'

'For God's sake, Charlotte, stop being so stupid. What on earth has it got to do with you anyway? You know nothing.' Robin had been home for the weekend. Dealing with constituency affairs as well as coping with family life always made him long for London. He generally returned there on Sunday night; Charlotte knew not to ring him at his flat. He always telephoned her to say he had arrived safely, but she was almost certain that he did not always do so from his own address or if he did, he was not alone.

'I think it is terrible to have sunk that ship full of young men when it was sailing away from the war zone. It was cowardly, not chivalrous, dishonourable; it was none of things we are meant to be.'

'Grow up, little girl. This is the real world now, not story books about knights of old.'

'It isn't fair play. I thought you were keen on fair play. Isn't that why you want to send the children off to boarding-school?'

'The children will go to boarding-school for a variety of reasons.'

'What? Name them.'

Robin chose not to reply.

One excellent reason was that Fraser Forth's will had caused a trust fund to be created specifically for the payment of his unborn grandchildren's education. By setting himself up as an unstinting example of parental self-sacrifice Robin wished to be seen buying what he hoped to be the very best for his children. No one need know that his self-denial was utterly painless.

'Charlotte, haven't you had enough to drink?'

'I'm not drunk. I'm upset.'

'Well, that is one reason why I want the children to go away. I don't want them to be upset by you being upset.'

'And me – doesn't it matter to you that I will be upset?'

'You'll get over it. Now let me hear no more of this pacifist nonsense from you, it is bad enough having my sister joining the Greenham women without you being disloyal too.'

'I'm not disloyal. I just feel entitled to have an opinion.'

'As my wife, you are loyal to me. You share my opinions.'

'And if I don't?'

'You let me down. I rely on your support. You are the perfect wife.'

Robin was masterful at inserting the effective barb of flattery. His tactics were faultless and his timing precise. Charlotte was not so stupid as to believe what he had just said but was trans-fixed by his charm like a snake's next meal.

'Come on, darling, come to bed.' He held out a hand to help her up. She staggered slightly and then steadied herself with purposeful determination as she walked towards the door but before she got there she tangled her feet and cut herself on a brassbound corner as she fell against the bookcase.

Gently he mopped her cut forehead, and bathed it with disinfectant. Tears had fallen with the blood. 'Poor love, you are in a bit of a mess.'

'Why are you being so nice to me?'

'Because I love you. You are my wife.'

Through the numb boozy sedation Charlotte heard Robin's

words and felt miserable, not knowing whether to take this as the truth, and if she did, whether to be happy or sad.

'I want another baby, Robin.'

'Babies aren't toys or hobbies to fill spare time.'

'I know.'

In the bath, after a lovely evening with only the television and a bottle for company, Charlotte wondered whether her coil was still *in situ*. Feeling a thread, she gave it a tug. Well I never. Fancy that. It didn't look much like a coil: coils were curly. The children had a coil that somersaulted downstairs, one's nerves when goaded were like coiled springs. This thing that she had found concealed about her person was more like a fish hook. What the hell, whatever it was probably would be better out than in. She chucked it in the waste-paper basket and put it and the bottles out for the bin men the following morning.

Accidents can happen. She promised God that she would stop drinking if He saw to it that she became pregnant. Robin was right: the baby she wanted was only a device to postpone middle age, and an excuse for leading an empty life. Other wives had jobs, or even worked with their husbands. Not so Charlotte. As Robin realised his ambitions she retreated into the background and only got aired when protocol demanded it.

One more year and another election. A victory election, the gung-ho voters, much delighted with having vanquished the tin-pot enemy, were gripped by passionate admiration for their own Iron Lady. A Tory victory was almost a certainty but then, it would be foolish to forget the débâcle of 1945. The campaign must be fought with vigour.

Robin campaigned and followed his leader to overwhelming victory; Charlotte fulfilled the traditional role of paying, packing and following her husband. Her opinions were not sought, her ideas were irrelevant, but Robin still felt that her presence as a wifely icon was vital to his victory. He was photographed kissing her and telling the world he owed his success to having been blessed with a happy family. Coral and Piers, dressed in blue, were stood in front of the harmonious pair. Robin's hand was placed with paternal pride on his grinning daughter's confident shoulder, but Piers scowled, arms folded as he tried to be bold about September when he would become a boarder at Salisbury Lodge.

14

Summer 1983

THE TREE FOR which Cedar Lodge was named had been an infant when the first brick was laid. It would have been an act of faith to have called a house after a sapling, so Cedar was not added to Lodge until the Edwardian era when all respectable houses had names to distinguish them from the numbered terraces of the labouring classes. The Lodge had stood square and plain since the Georgians, a butt of Victorian derision.

Charlotte saw with regret that silly starlings had indeed nested in a chimney: a chirping fireplace and a fall of soot had already raised her suspicions earlier in June.

'It is a lovely house, Sam.'

She started. She had expected no visitor, least of all Martin.

'Oh Wallace! Where did you come from? What a surprise!'

Charlotte was stilted and awkward. 'You are thinner . . . I'm not.'

'I'm older,' Martin replied, smiling at her confusion.

'We are all older – much, much older. Are you wiser?'

'I doubt it. You look sadder, Sam.'

'Oh but I'm so pleased to see you, Wallace.'

'You can't have got my message. I did ring. Are you really pleased to see me?'

'Of course. Of course. It has been so long.'

'Almost nine years, Sam.'

She had been given no warning. The children were fractious, the place in a heap and, worst of all, her hair was dirty.

He kissed her cheek. 'You smell of horse.'

'Wallace, please give me time, I must get tidy. I didn't want to meet you again like this.'

'I don't mind.'

'I do.'

Coral ran up. 'Mum, I want to go and ride now. Please will you catch Flapjack? Clemency won't help, she says she has got a call to make. Please.'

'Coral, say how do you do to Mr Fable.'

She held out a grubby hand stained with felt-tip pen and smiled. Like her mother, she had a long nose, and her adult teeth were too large for the child-sized face.

'Coral, you have your mother's eyes.'

'But I have Dad's brains,' she replied, glaring at Charlotte. Evidently the incident involving the new trainers was not forgotten.

'Where has Piers gone, darling?'

'I don't know.'

'Run and find him.'

'I said I don't know where he is, so how can I run and find him? I'm not a headless chicken.' This was a new expression, learnt from a neighbouring child who had already been at Lordstone for a year, the school at which Coral was to start in September. She could hardly wait till then for excitement.

'Well take Mr Fable down to see Flapjack. Get some nuts and see if you can catch him while I sort myself out.'

'Why?'

'Because I'm a mess.'

'But you are old, it doesn't matter what you look like any more, Clemency said so.'

'Your mummy is much younger than me,' said Martin.

'You are a man. That's different.'

'Did Clemency say that too?'

'Yes,' Coral replied. 'Come on, I'll show you Flapjack, and my rosettes.'

A rustling was heard coming from the branches above. A cone fell on the mossy ground in front of Martin, he looked up and saw a small boy with reddish hair gazing at him through round glasses. He recognised him at once: he found the truth came not as a shock but as confirmation of a fact long sought.

'Hello Piers.'

'Can I call you Wally, like Mum?'

'Of course, you both can. Are you going to come down and talk to me?'

'Yes, later.'

'Good, I'll look forward to that, Piers. Come on, Coral, let me see your pony while the others put themselves to rights.'

Clemency van Schumacher was twenty-three, a graduate, and as beautiful grown as she had been as a child when Charlotte had last met her in upstate New York in 1969. Christmas cards had kept the brief friendship alight between Charlotte and Clemency's parents, so when she got a letter asking if their daughter could have a holiday job with the Brands it seemed to be an answer to much. Only it wasn't.

From the moment Charlotte met Clemency at the airport she knew she was being despised. Despite being quite tall Charlotte felt squat and frowsty beside this young slender amazon. She knew she was stupid, uneducated, trite and pathetic without questioning the young girl's cold analytical gaze.

Clemency was there to assist with the children, to be part of the family and join in all the holiday activities as well as sharing the driving and helping to cook. Apart from the driving, Clemency did nothing except to talk to the twins about herself and her exciting life. She sowed discontent and mocked the domestic trivialities which kept the family going, neither giving nor lending a hand to any enterprise she considered beneath her. The children loved her. Robin was most smitten. He said he admired her intellect but her cleverness was not her only characteristic that kept him enthralled.

Charlotte was endeavouring to dry her ill-rinsed hair and paint some healthiness on to her insomniac drinker's complexion when Clemency walked into her bedroom without knocking, returning tweezers she had borrowed without asking.

'Clemency, why didn't you tell me that Martin Fable rang?'

'Didn't I? I guess I forgot.'

'You should have told me.'

'Come on. It's no big deal. I'll fix some coffee for him if

you like,' she said with enough resigned condescension to imply that she had consented to scrub the house throughout and by the look she gave Charlotte, conveying that all of the older woman's efforts to smarten herself were quite pointless. Had she shouted, she could not have been more eloquent. Charlotte was wasting her time, she was past it, there was no further use in trying.

Clemency, Martin and the children were all laughing when Charlotte entered the kitchen. *They are laughing with you not at you. You are looking at them, not them at you.* Charlotte recalled her mother's advice given to her during a particularly gauche phase of her childhood. The maxims brought not much more comfort now than they had then, when anxiety would make her sprout spots and splutter at the very thought of a party. In fact the joke that was causing so much amusement was at Martin's expense, and nothing to do with her. Martin had made a complete bungle of catching the pony and had had to be rescued by Coral, who showed him how such things were done and adored her new-found Uncle Wally for his charming incompetence. Piers had swapped Martin's glasses for his and the effect was startling. Clemency smiled secretively, her large smooth lips concealing her faultless teeth. Her mouth and legs were perfection and could only belong to an American.

'Hello Sam. Better?'

'Much, thank you, Wallace. Don't you want something stronger than coffee?'

'No thank you, do you?'

'Absolutely not,' Charlotte replied untruthfully with excessive vehemence. 'Why don't you and I take ourselves to the Anglers Arms for lunch? Clemency, could you possibly feed the children? I've made a shepherd's pie and there is jelly.'

'Clemency calls it jello.'

'OK, Coral clever-clogs, jello. Can you do that, Clemency?'

'No, I can't.'

'Oh dear, why not?'

'I have to drive to London. Robin rang: he wants me to take some papers up to him urgently.'

'My Robin?'

'Sure, your Robin.'

Clemency had put on a voice that would have done to humour a child. The insult bypassed Martin. He looked at Clemency with obvious admiration. 'How are your parents, Clemency?'

'You know Mom and Dad?'

'I introduced Charlotte to them when she was on honeymoon in New York. Robin had to go away on some business and had left his new bride alone so I took her out to stay with Mallow and Floyd for the weekend. You were there, I remember. Do you?'

'No, but it all figures.'

'What does?'

'Forget it.'

Charlotte had been called away to the phone in the study – some query concerning a whist drive – leaving Martin and Clemency in the kitchen with the dirty coffee cups which Clemency had no intention of clearing away. It wasn't a bad summer, good enough certainly for her to wear her jeans raggedly cut off and give her legs an airing and spectators a treat.

'Don't you like working here?'

'I don't need to play house. I majored in politics and figured I could get somewhere, learn something, contribute you know in a political household, not be a nanny to two repressed English kids and Mommy's little helper to a homebody lush.'

'I see. Anyway, you haven't told me about your family.'

'They're fine.' She bestowed another of her dazzling smiles on Martin.

Pandemonium jumped on the table and ate a couple of biscuits, licked the sugar lumps and departed. Clemency was well above such banal irritations.

Just before the picnic party set out Martin spoke to Charlotte while they were trying to find paper towels.

'Clemency is a lovely girl, isn't she?'

'She hates me,' Charlotte replied.

'That is strange; I would have thought she could have risen above jealousy.'

'According to her, she can rise above anything in which a rich worm, such as myself, is embroiled.'

'I'm sure you've got her all wrong,' said Martin.

'Maybe,' Charlotte replied. 'One can but hope.'

A bridle path ran through the woods beyond the paddock and led to a clearing where picnicking was encouraged by the provision of litter bins, rustic benches and instructions to behave. It never seemed to be quite right: it was too contrived and convenient for a real picnic, the genuine kind with sandy sausages, smoking fires, midges and loo spots plagued by prickly gorse. Nevertheless it was a compromise, and as the day was fine, Charlotte decided that she and Martin should go there with the children. Flapjack and Pandemonium could come too.

While talking to Phyllis Potter about the bothersome whist drive Charlotte had managed a quick shot of whisky for medicinal purposes and now felt far more human and able to cope.

'This basket weighs a ton. Are you sure we need two bottles of wine?'

'Better be safe,' Charlotte replied, adding a couple of cans of beer just in case, thanking God that this time at least she had remembered the corkscrew.

'I'm off,' said Clemency. Changed from the shorts into a fatally simple linen dress and carrying Robin's missing file under her arm, she was anxious to be gone. 'I need money for gas.'

Without daring to mention that the car was full of petrol Charlotte handed over enough money for a further tankful. 'Give my love to Robin.'

While not actually replying 'Whatever for?' Clemency pocketed the money and left. Martin watched her drive off in Charlotte's car, with the sunshine roof open, her blonde hair flying and her own music blaring.

The whisky saw to it that she felt more confident. The initial meeting had been stilted and awkward but somehow things were easier, less tense, in the presence of children, pets and alcohol. Charlotte even stopped worrying about how shocked Martin must be by the deterioration in her looks. Of course, without Clemency at hand to act as yardstick, things were bound to appear more cheerful.

'A picnic, what fun!'

'We don't want to go on a picnic, do we Piers?' said Coral.

'Oh you do, you do. You know you do.' Charlotte could get brisk when necessary. It was a characteristic that seemed to grow with motherhood, like worry lines.

Martin picked up the basket, gasped, put it down again and rubbed his hands with stylised gleeful heartiness.

'If you are going to be a textbook mummy, Sam, I'm going to become a jolly uncle. Come along young 'uns, let's go for a wizard ramble and see what wheezes nature has in store. Oh what capital fun!'

'It's going to rain,' said Coral looking hopefully at the cloudless sky.

'Better than ever. Nothing more spiffing than a downpour on a picnic unless of course you can get somebody to hold a modest massacre or minor insurrection.'

The party set out in single file along a path narrow and much clogged with venomous nettles. It was not normally a popular route which may explain why the Godleham cell of mountain bikers had picked it that day for a practice pedal. About a dozen cyclists crashed past buttocks aloft, helmeted heads at handlebar level.

On they pressed. Coral and Flapjack went first. The pony could and did defecate repeatedly, leaving a steaming trail for easy following, then came Charlotte carrying the bottles that were too heavy and precious for the basket, then Martin with the food and finally Piers, who received the brunt of all the nettles as they swung back and hit him after the adults had pushed them aside. Pandemonium got the most from the outing by scuttling up and down the line, buffeting his way between feet, entwining himself round legs and snapping at ankles.

Just before the picnic spot was reached four cross ramblers, aflame with their rights, approached from the opposite direction muttering about the villainy of letting horses clutter up bridleways. The cyclists made another pass, spattering the walkers with horse excrement and the bosky summer woodland reverberated with rage.

'Maybe we will get to have a massacre after all. Goody!' said Martin, who was becoming quite sweaty. 'One longs for the security of the Amazon jungle.'

They had the picnic area to themselves, but that was a brief joy. A minibus from Oak Court, a hospital for the long-term severely disabled, drew into the clearing and slowly and carefully eight or so patients were unloaded.

'Look, Mummy! That man has got no legs!'

'Don't stare, Coral. It's rude.'

'Poor sods,' said Martin. 'Bad enough being in that state without being forced out on a picnic.'

'Come on, Wallace. This is meant to be champion fun. Have a drink.'

Charlotte had already poured and drunk one glass of wine while Martin had been helping to tie Flapjack to a suitable tree. She then poured one for Martin and another for herself: that way it would look as if the bottle had only just been started. (If she wanted it thought that she had not been at the gin she had learnt how to top the bottle up with water so it appeared to remain at the same level. The trick was to turn it upside down, mark the level and then refill it to that mark once the slurp had been extracted.)

'Gracious me, Charlotte! You never said you were coming here for a picnic.' Phyllis Potter and her sons had strode into the clearing. She sat down at the bench without being asked and sent her obedient boys off to scavenge for interesting trophies for the Cub Scout Great Nature Trail Competition. The prize, she informed all, was as good as theirs.

Martin looked inside Piers's sandwich. 'Has someone eaten that already?' he asked.

'It's sandwich spread, his favourite,' Charlotte replied. Piers was giggling so much as he stuffed the white pappy bread into his mouth that he did the nose trick.

'I always insist on wholemeal bread,' said Phyllis. Half-heartedly Charlotte offered her one of the smoked salmon sandwiches she had made for her and Martin, but Phyllis had fed her family earlier. Charlotte's heart sank as she heard her accept some wine, especially as Martin poured her such a large drink into such a big beaker. Only one bottle remained.

Charlotte fantasised about Phyllis being struck by lightning or even by a thought that she might have left some gadget on and smouldering at home – anything to get rid of her. Eight years of longing, eight long years of daily yearning and the reunion had to be like this. If providence didn't come up with an exterminating device she might be forced to wring the Potter neck personally.

'Uncle Wally, will you look after Flapjack while I go and explore?'

'Of course, Coral. He doesn't savage people often, does he?'

'Ah! That explains it,' said Phyllis. 'The children's uncle. Of course, I should have spotted it at once.'

Coral went off to tell the limbless of her many achievements aboard her pony, and Piers, who loathed the Potter boys almost as much as Charlotte did their mother, went to explore the car park with Pandemonium. He was not the sort of child to be set alight by the spoor and turd of wildlife. However, he liked animals and hated to see them shut up and denied fun. He knew that the Labrador belonged to the Potters. She looked so mournful imprisoned in the back of the station wagon which bore the appropriate POT registration number. The car wasn't locked.

'Well I must be off. Thanks for the vino. Cooeee, boys! Oh dear, I expect they are so absorbed they have no ears open for their old ma!' Phyllis pounded off into the woods clad in clever co-ordinated cotton jersey which stretches accommodatingly, but unkindly.

Martin reached across the table and took Charlotte's hand in his. She squeezed it back and felt fit to die. 'It wasn't meant to be like this.'

'I know, I know. Poor Sam. You never did pick up your musket.'

'No, I didn't. And it is too late now.'

'No, it isn't,' Martin replied. 'But I do just wonder whether this is the way things have to turn out.'

'It seems to be the way they do. When do you go back to South America?'

'Never. I'm finished there. I am being sent to Russia instead.'

'But what about Isabelita?'

'Dead.'

'Dead? How? You never said, you never told me.'

'I couldn't, I didn't want to believe it, but it's true. She hanged herself. I might have been able to prevent her, but I didn't.'

Charlotte tried to stop herself being glad that Martin's love was dead. She must do her best.

'Why did she do it?'

'Depression, grief. Her son was killed, you know.'

'How terrible. I can't imagine how awful that must be. Was it an accident?'

'In a way, yes. He was drowned. He was in the army.'

'But he looked as if he was a child in that photograph you sent me.'

'He was only just sixteen, a conscript. He was on the *Belgrano*.'

'Oh Wallace. I am so sorry.'

She meant it.

Martin and Charlotte were still holding each other's hand for comfort when Piers came rushing into the clearing.

'Mummy Mummy, Pan is stuck to Mrs Potter's dog!'

'Quick, water! Someone get me a bucket of water,' Phyllis commanded. But there wasn't a bucket handy, which left her no choice but to douse the amorous dogs with anything liquid that came to hand, all the remains of the wine and beer included.

Phyllis roused to fury was a troubling sight. The patients from Oak Court looked on with fascination. Charlotte offered to pay for an aborting injection and was told it was the least she could do.

'Mummy, did Daddy stick to you when we were made?' Piers asked that night as he got into bed.

Martin had gone, but he had promised to write. Maybe he would. Charlotte was happy to have reason to watch the post, to keep cheered by secret anticipation. She forced herself to admit that Martin was bound to find someone else one day. All she could hope was that that day would not be soon.

15

October 1994

IT WAS KIND, albeit pointed, of Prime to rise early and make her a packed lunch. Refusing the greaseproof-papered parcel would have been churlish, though the thought of old baps filled with margarine and sandwich spread made her heave, like the idea of lobster in treacle.

Her presence was beginning to become irksome, she was an embarrassment. Fleeing women often are, especially when they are no longer young or romantic or being persecuted by spectacular tyrants. She would spend the day walking along the coast she had once loved so much, returning to Auchenkirk only to sleep. Charlotte still felt that Florence could put things right, wipe her tears and set her on the best route to recovery and the next phase of life. Florence would have to hear her confession.

The proprietors of the Auchtertay general stores and off-licence were named Patel; they opened at eight. With luck she would pass unnoticed, just one more late tourist buying a few provisions. It would have been daft to show her face in the other newsagent's, the one run by Mrs Wee Hammy. Charlotte had a craving for a bar of chocolate and the Patels stocked plenty. Parking Piers's car had been easy in Auchtertay: it was not a busy spot. Traffic passed through rather than visited to linger; like many another, Auchtertay was demanding a bypass.

She picked up a paper and noticed that her flight now only commanded a couple of meagre inches of the front page. Evidently she had been sighted in Strasbourg. Why Strasbourg, she wondered? While having nothing much against that city except sympathy for its geese, she could think of no reason why she should ever have chosen it as a refuge, unless she was in the unlikely state of liaising lustily with some Euro-mandarin. Coral in Paris was being besieged by the press and enjoying it greatly. She was pictured on an inner page in a man's dressing gown handing out tea and toast to all. The owner of the dressing gown was a glass-blower but, according to his landlady, extremely well brought up. Charlotte wondered what Granny Brand would think to all that. Not much, she imagined.

Clemency and her son featured everywhere. Merlin looked delightful but his mother's still beautiful face proclaimed her bitter spirit: confident youth had soured from too many ambitions denied and successes foundered. Life had not delivered its promise. Vengeance was her only comfort. Her career as such was taking her nowhere near the White House: scuppering Robin's bid for Downing Street would be a sweet revenge. Her sister harpy, Ocean Bray, was milking the scandal for all its worth and promoting her gimcrack book, *Branded in Blue* in highest gear. The ideal Christmas present, burbled her publishers. Well, it did make a change from the hand-wringing and tooth-gnashing of angst-ridden royalty.

A small man entered the shop. Charlotte turned and recognised him at once. With age, Phil Fleet had come to look like a meek mole grown grey with years and anxiety.

'Good morning, Mrs Patel.'

Mrs Patel greeted him by name and invited him to sign the bypass petition.

'An excellent scheme, Mrs Patel but not, alas, within the budget's scope right now I doubt.' Phil Fleet was to retire shortly from his job as Pittenfirth and Netherloch's Conservative agent.

Mrs Patel smiled. 'Maybe when the Labour government is voted in we will be getting much funding for better roads.'

'Oh dear, Mrs Patel, does this mean that you and your good man will no longer be supporting Mr MacPhail?'

'Worry not, Mr Fleet we will always be voting Conservative, even if we are the last ones to do so in Auchtertay.'

Charlotte was hiding behind a central fixture selecting her favourite caramel wafers which had never been available in Godleham and wondering what became of Cremola Foam when Phil peeped over from the paper stand. He caught a glimpse of Charlotte and gasped silently, a flash of confusion passing over his worried little features. As if bitten, he turned and went to the cash register where he realised he had bought nothing and snatched up the first thing that came to hand.

Mrs Patel had always assumed Phil to be totally celibate.

'Are you sure, Mr Fleet, that these are what you are meaning to purchase?'

'Yes, yes,' he said proffering a tenner.

'Your change, Mr Fleet.' Mrs Patel chased Phil out of the shop, waving grubby pound notes.

'Are you all right, Mr Fleet?'

'Yes, I'm fine, just in a hurry. So sorry, I'm much obliged. I must dash. No time to waste.'

Auchtertay lacked the bustle of Karachi but it was not without event.

The only traffic warden for miles about was booking the car. Auchtertay parked its cars on the left on Mondays, Wednesdays and Fridays and the right for the rest of the week, leaving only Sunday as a free-for-all. Piers's car was erroneously upon the right. Charlotte lingered in the shop till the paperwork was done and the warden gone. She didn't want to risk any more personal encounters.

Whilst waiting, she glanced through a glossy magazine which she could not afford and saw that both Piers and Coral had been photographed at Casper MacPhail's twenty-first. Caspar was a fine young man with a place secured in his grandfather's old regiment once he had completed his degree, and Leonora looked exactly like her mother had been when she and Charlotte had shared that subterranean flat in the late sixties. Henrietta and Roddy beamed from the pages, giving the lie to rumours circulating about their tottering marriage.

Passing Sandhill Charlotte saw that an agent's board was being erected announcing the house as being for sale: a prestigious, five-bedroomed family residence in a sought-after location affording an excellent outlook, standing in its own landscaped grounds. Early viewing was recommended. Perhaps the Mac-Phails really were parting, or maybe one or other of them had inherited something. Both Roddy and Henrietta had substantial expectations, and even if their marriage did collapse would still be able to grow uncomfortably old in separate castles. Charlotte wondered whether she dared go round Sandhill on the pretext of being a prospective buyer but decided against it. Whatever happened, she was resolved not to retrace her life. It would not be right to return, better a pleasant memory than an inadequate reality.

Never the less she did go down to the rocks where she had been with Martin on the day they had truanted from canvassing in October 1974, twenty years ago. The seals weren't about, no minesweeper nor fishing boat sailed by, but indiscriminate gulls wheeled and swooped on Charlotte's packed lunch. Despite the lateness of the season, thrift still flowered in a boulder's shelter.

August 1983

'Please Clemency would you look after the children for me on Thursday. I have to go to a funeral.'

'I've fixed to go out that day. I don't work Thursdays.'

Clemency didn't work Thursdays or any other day for that matter.

'Just this once Clemency, please. I am willing to pay you extra.'

'You reckon you can buy me too? No way.'

'Is it jealousy?'

'Is what jealousy?'

'I just wondered why you feel you have to be so hostile towards me in particular.'

'I'm sorry, it is just that you are so materialistic, so tied up with your possessions. I can't relate to someone who is no more than a charge account. It is so banal, so trivial. Go into analysis and what would you find? Zilch, just banknotes. You cannot buy soul or intelligence. I couldn't be jealous of you, we aren't the same species. I dare say you can't help it because you believe in rearing and conditioning. I don't. I am a free spirit and I can get to where you are without paying a cent. You would be no better than a bum on the sidewalk if you weren't so darn rich. What's with this funeral anyway, do you just want to get to wear that gross black coat? Maybe you should have the price tag on the outside, then everyone would know you're a walking bank vault.'

'I'm sorry Clemency, you can't be feeling well.'

'I'm not sick.'

'I take it you are not going to change your mind?'

'The dead person stays dead whether you go to their funeral or not.'

'He was a friend of my mother.'

'He was your mother's friend, then your mother goes to the funeral. Easy. No contest.'

'Very well, Clemency, as you are so unhappy I would like you to leave now.'

For someone so patently despising wealth Clemency presented a remarkably astute calculation of monies owed to her by Charlotte. 'Where will you go, Clemency?'

'What is that to you?'

'Your parents will worry.'

'So? They worry. I can handle that.'

'What shall I do with your mail?'

'Leave it, I'll call.'

Clemency got on the train without once looking back. She never did call. There was no post to forward and no more Christmas cards ever from the Van Schumachers.

When given the generous cheque Clemency had made a show of crunching it up, albeit carefully. The money left Charlotte's account that very day: the cheque was cashed in Victoria.

'Horrid Mummy to send Clemmie away,' said Coral the following weekend, the last of the holidays.

'Don't be difficult, Coral,' said Robin. 'Mummy can't help being bad at looking after people who work for her.'

Charlotte was too busy to let any threats uttered by a self-opinionated girl irritate her. It was quite a relief to find that Robin wasn't home much either as she got the children ready for their respective boarding-schools.

Protesting vigorously, Piers and Coral spent that contentious Thursday with the Potters while Charlotte accompanied her mother to Sir 'Barney' Barns's funeral.

Charlotte cried; Winifred was restrained. Her love for Fraser had never dwindled since his death; Carter Barns had just been a very pleasant friendship. She remembered him with affection and gratitude, he had remembered her with a minor and obscure Tissot called *The Rich Widow*. Though neither the leering, fawning chancer nor the middle-aged woman in lavish mourning bore any resemblance to either Carter or Winifred, the message was clear. Robin pretended ignorance of the irony. Strangely enough, a third figure, that of a slender girl whose charm alone had captured her admirer, looked disturbingly like Clemency van Schumacher.

Leaving the children, first Coral at Lordstone near Henley and then Piers at Salisbury Lodge ten miles further north, was undoubtedly the worst thing Charlotte had ever had to do. Robin came too, was brisk and efficient and impressed the staff at both schools with his upright reliability. To have gathered the children of such a rising star, as well as the young MacPhails, was honour indeed. Both Miss Beach and Mr Trader hoped to get either Robin or, at the very least, his wife, on to their respective boards of governors.

Coral was to sleep in a cosy room called Tiggywinkle. She knew two other girls there already and had been issued with a 'shadow' to show her where toothbrushes lived and how and where to find breakfast, boot lockers, classrooms and to acquaint her with the argot of the place. Leonora MacPhail had been head girl and was now at her mother's old school near Basingstoke. Coral looked fresh and happy in striped green and was almost hurtfully pleased to wave her parents goodbye and get on with showing photographs of Flapjack and Pandemonium to her new friends.

'I don't want you to go, Mum.'

Charlotte longed to tell Piers that she didn't want to go either.

'Come on, Old Man,' said Robin. 'Show us what you are made of. Charlotte, stop that!'

'I was only giving him a hug. Listen, Piers,' she whispered, 'I will be thinking of you all the time, so will Pandemonium. I will write to you lots and lots.'

'That isn't the same.'

'I know, darling but it is the next-best thing.'

'No, it isn't.'

Brown Three, a burly child, had been sent by Matron to make sure that Brand found his way to Mafeking, where he had been allocated an iron bed with dippy mattress, a locker and a hook of his own. Unpacking took place quickly: countless grey and navy garments got stacked in cupboards at the dormitory end, where each boy had the good fortune of possessing a labelled shelf and six inches of hanging rail.

'Excellent, excellent,' said Robin gleefully rubbing his hands. 'Goodbye, mate.' He thumped Piers mannishly between the shoulderblades, causing the child's glasses to quiver in front of eyes already dangerously brimming. 'Come on, Charlotte, don't let Piers down.'

Taking her hand he propelled her forcibly from Mafeking, and down the stone staircase to the waiting car that still retained the homely smell of Charlotte's banished babies. As they were leaving the dormitory Charlotte had observed two older boys approach Piers asking to see the contents of his tuck box. She prayed they would not find Blue Bunny.

Henrietta and Roddy were in the car park having just left Caspar who, as Prefect of Sebastopol, was lofty in Salisbury Lodge pecking order.

'Don't worry, Charlotte,' said Henrietta as she kissed her old flatmate. 'It gets better, and a lot of the staff are really nice. I've told Caspar to keep an eye on Piers, who is already quite a star for having nearly got born in our car! We must have lunch, now you've got more time. I'm often in London at the flat.'

'What do you do now, with the children gone?'

'You will find there's always masses to do. Never fret. Oh I must tell you, the garden at Sandhill is now superb, we made over five hundred pounds this summer when we opened it in aid of the nurses. Mind you, Mum did send Barr through to help and Roddy's mama is only at Baldunning and quite indefatigable. You must come to stay.'

'Did Henrietta tell you about the garden?' Roddy asked.

Charlotte said she had and that it sounded marvellous though deep inside she seethed with resentment at the thought of any alteration to Sandhill.

'Roddy is terribly supportive in the garden,' said Henrietta. 'Are you supportive in the garden, Robin?'

'Rather!' Robin replied.

Robin's sole contribution to the garden was to suggest that the cedar be felled to let more light into his study.

'Well goodbye, and don't worry. George Trader is a really good headmaster, I expect by the time we meet at the conference everyone will be as happy as sandboys. You are coming to the conference, aren't you? After all, you haven't got the little darlings as an excuse to stay at home this year.'

'I don't know. I've never been yet.'

'Robin will bring you. Won't you, Robin?'

'Of course.'

Later, as they drove home Charlotte remarked that she was quite looking forward to a trip to Blackpool, noted for fresh air and fun.

'You may come this time, provided you behave.'

'What do you mean?'

'You know what I mean. Just stay sober and keep your mouth shut.'

'I will, I promise.' Charlotte tried not to brood upon the reason why she was suddenly free to go junketing. She also told God that if she did get pregnant again not only would she give up drink but she would never let her next child be farmed out in the cause of social climbing.

Twinkly keen and agog with zeal the hearties of the party converged upon Blackpool, up to the gills with enthusiasm and self-approval. Ovations were expected to be long, loud and standing, applauding the architects of Britain's golden future where enterprise marched unflinching to the noonday sunshine of prosperity.

Charlotte had heard and seen enough to slake her thirst for group dynamics within half an hour of arriving at the conference.

Her other thirst was not so easy to quench. Parties, gatherings, *conversazione*, were scheduled for every hour when pressure groups, constituency worthies, women, the young, the pensioners all formed themselves into delegations to be heard the better in shoulder to shoulder formation. Tedium developed remarkably quickly but, with the help of as many glasses as she could grab, Charlotte put up with it staunchly. All this was better than doing nothing, nothing being yet worse than brooding or fretting.

The children's letters were not satisfactory. Coral and Piers had written laboriously to say that they were well and hoped their parents were likewise. Charlotte had good reports from Lordstone, which was a comfort. Matron at Salisbury Lodge had only meant to be kind by mentioning that bed-wetting was by no means unknown amongst new boys.

Major speeches were awaited breathlessly, then lavishly praised. The Home Secretary on Law and Order was particularly super. The Prime Minister herself would be greeted with the ecstasy of the blessed getting a preview of the Second Coming.

As official jollities go, the Conference Ball was no worse than any other contrived revel and a good excuse to air finery long left hanging and out of use. Charlotte danced with Robin, Robin's agent, Robin's chairman, his campaign manager and the local delegate from the Young Conservatives. The music was loud enough to eliminate conversation and of a bouncy beat that prevented intimate clinching, a good thing, considering the scarcity of attractive partners and the poor young Conservative's abundant spots and sopping hands. She marvelled at how silly other people could become so quickly on such meagre quantities of drink. She could and did drink three or four times as much as any others on her table, and still she smiled. Only at midnight when many had left did she begin to feel the warm, mellow tension of an appetite well supplied. She laughed at everyone's jokes, and wallowed in the surge of artificial happiness.

Charlotte and the Leader's consort agreed that theirs was a supporting role. Just then it looked as if they were supporting each other.

Not everything was solid upon the Golden Mile: the Fates had hazards stored up ready to ruin the feast. The glorious smooth and heaven-sent Secretary for Trade and Industry had a secret and soon the world would see that the well polished bespoke shoes and wrinkle-free socks concealed a pair of feet wrought of most tiresome clay. A scorned and much-infuriated mistress-with-child had been straightening records by revealing her troubles in *The Times*. Her woes thundered about the world. It was hard to imagine a man with such a straight parting in his shimmering hair throbbing and thrusting upon a lusty extra-marital bed, but throb and thrust he had, lots of times, partnered by his bright but trusting personal assistant. An immaculate tailor's dummy shafting an efficient chief monitor was a quaint thought made flesh. The baby was due in early 1984. George, if a boy, might be an apt name.

Men will be men. Who would not envy the energy of one so active and libidinal? Why should such a fine example of heterosexual dexterity resign, especially as he had chosen to stay with his wife and keep his tidy family all of a piece? This was the attitude of the Leader, whose position on peccadilloes and extraneous offspring was seemingly more detached than those nearer the body of the conference hall.

Robin agreed. He agreed with everybody, whatever their view. He kept his options forever flexible and firmly upon the high moral ground, wherever that was. Once he knew which way the wind would blow upon the tower he would add his shoulder's weight to hasten its tumble.

The Trade and Industry Secretary resigned, to be replaced later by another new man of the Right, an airline pilot and one-time trade union member. Whatever next? The party Methuselah snorted into his ante-penultimate nightcap Scotch and confided in Robin that a good horsewhipping all round was what was wanted. Robin agreed.

16

December 1983

MARTIN NEVER MENTIONED it, perhaps he didn't even know. The miraculous thought that she might not have lost him gave Charlotte hope. With hope came willpower, or at least enough of it for her to cut back drastically on the amount she drank each day. She was never free of alcohol but she took great pains to remain sober. She lost weight, partly because of the reduction in drink and also because she took up exercise to exhaust herself and to keep her mind off the next glass. Once a week she sang with the Godleham Glee Group and actually enjoyed herself, not minding the deprivation of an evening's sobriety. The Glee singers were abstemious and could have passed muster for the Band of Hope, taking themselves almost as seriously as the Godleham Bridge Club where no playful levity was tolerated ever.

Charlotte made herself finish a bottle before she opened the next. She stopped refilling bottles to deceive herself into thinking that she had drunk very little. She cleaned out her hiding places. It was difficult, but not impossible. Even anxiety about the children was blotted up by the unique joy she got from Martin's letters. They weren't love letters, but they meant more to her than passionate or sentimental prose. She was worth writing to, someone loved her, someone who was quite indifferent to her wealth. There were no snags or conditions in their mutual understanding.

'You look wonderful,' Peta said when Charlotte visited her Chelsea flat to collect more post. 'It can't just be relief at being without the children.'

'Peta you say the most awful things.'

'No I don't. I'm honest. If I were a mother I'd have my children suckled by wet nurses and reared by poor clergymen till they could be let out alone and guaranteed to hunt for rich spouses. You look wonderful because you are in love.'

Charlotte said nothing. Peta continued.

'Don't tell me anything. I don't want to know. I just like seeing you look happy. Robin isn't responsible for your transformation, I suppose? Don't answer that either.'

Peta lit a cigarette and offered one to Charlotte.

'I won't, thank you.'

'You must have it badly.'

'Have what badly?'

'Love.'

'Nothing will ever come of it,' said Charlotte. 'I'm just being stupid, I know.'

'Good,' said Peta. 'Why do we always want something to come of it anyway? What is the point? Founding dynasties only leads to unpleasantness. The world needs no more people. I'm always trying to be in love, but I never want any of that commitment that everyone keeps on about so much. Keep the appetite well stocked up and enjoy yourself. Sooner or later you find that all lovers can be squalid. The moment anyone uses the loo without shutting the door or goes into a pub and asks for their usual or expects me to cook Sunday lunch I know the magic is over. You don't know anything about Martin yet.'

'I know enough to love him.'

'Yes, and he is lovely. His father was lovely too, I loved him a lot, but I made certain he didn't go to bed in his vest.'

'Godfrey would never have done that.'

'I know, that is why I loved him. I still do.'

Godfrey Fable sleeping in a vest was as unlikely as the Pope in a kilt.

Elizabeth Brand, though wholly admirable, was not a jot more lovable for the joyous way in which she coped. She throve on martyrdom, treating each sacrifice as a prize. No raffle winner was as delighted, nor as smug. She invited and deserved admiration, getting it certainly, but grudgingly. She made such capital of her virtues that being utterly marvellous became for her a lifetime's career.

Fenella and Jake's little girls didn't like their grandmother much but had to tolerate her selfless ways. Elizabeth was well beyond child-rearing age when she had to welcome three grandchildren into her house. Fenella worked for Amnesty, was a keen feminist and part-time Greenham Common protestor, none of which she could have done without her mother's help. According to her daughter, Elizabeth was the apotheosis of the Extended Family and Kinship Group. That in itself was reward enough, Elizabeth told Winifred Forth.

Charlotte felt guilty. She often did, especially when Christmas neared. This year, because the children had gone to boarding-school she managed to convince everyone that staying in Godleham was the only kind option. Coral insisted on taking Flapjack to the Boxing Day meet and that was not something to crow about in front of her Aunty Fenella. A compromise was achieved by Charlotte organising a mammoth family outing to the theatre at the beginning of the holidays, thus excusing her from the Brand clan at Christmas. Robin would have preferred his mother-in-law to have been excluded too, but that was impossible especially since Winifred had moved to Godleham following the death of Carter Barns. No more suitors would be found loitering in her conservatory; the flat she bought was intensely luxurious but without nooks for lurking lovers. The Tissot hung in prominence, and Winifred even chose extravagant striped curtains to match the young girl's dress. Elizabeth was sorry that she had not been consulted: cutting down and causing old curtains to fit new windows is not such an arduous task, considering the economy to be made from such little diligence. Elizabeth's indulgence for 1983 had been to get her stair carpet shifted up half a step.

'Christmas isn't Christmas without *Peter Pan*!' Elizabeth announced with comfort and joy exuding from most pores. She and Fenella had brought her granddaughters up from Dorset. At the last minute Cyril Brand had ducked the jaunt. Pressure of work, he maintained, was keeping him from his dearest wish to go on this family outing. Charlotte said she understood. She imagined her father-in-law ecstatically grasping this unique chance to be alone at home.

'Christmas won't be Christmas without any presents,' Coral replied, wincing as her paternal grandmother gave her cheek a peck followed by a moist handkerchief dabbing an imagined smut.

'Coral, that isn't at all nice.'

'It is the beginning of a book we're reading at school.'

'Don't make it worse by telling lies. Ah here is my little Piers. Come and give your granny a kiss.'

'I'm afraid Piers is a bit off kissing,' said Charlotte, who respected her son's wishes despite her hurt feelings.

'Nonsense! He loves his granny.'

Elizabeth seized him and planted a moist horror on his puckered face. Without giving him a moment to retch, she asked how he liked his smart new school.

'I love it – '

'Good, good. You are a lucky boy to have a daddy who can send you to such a lovely place.'

'I've got my fingers crossed!' Piers shouted in triumph and his three older cousins giggled. Fenella's Julie, Anna and Pauline only came to London occasionally when the courts decreed that they visit their father and get walked about museums and the zoo.

'This isn't *Peter Pan*!' Elizabeth said as she tried to intervene in Charlotte's attempts to get everyone happily sat next to someone who wasn't their very worst enemy.

'No, Elizabeth, it is *Joseph and the Amazing Technicolor Dreamcoat*. I told you.'

'What a disappointment! I suppose you find this story more appropriate.'

'I took them to *Peter Pan* last year,' Winifred announced. Then, feeling mean for scoring points off her fellow grandmother, said, 'They hated it.'

'I liked the crocodile, Granny,' said Piers. 'That was cool. The rest was yuck.'

'What was that word, Piers?'

'Yuck, Granny, you know, to rhyme with that other rude word that you said Daddy would never use.'

'That is enough, Piers,' said Charlotte. 'Sit down.'

'Only he does, Grannie, I heard him. Oh look, there he is!'

Robin had entered the theatre at a moment of maximum impact. He apologised with charm to all for his late arrival due, he said, to having much demanded of him before the Christmas recess.

He smelt of pricey lunch.

Such a grafting chap was only to be praised for making time to entertain his family so lavishly. He kissed and waved and declared himself delighted, behaving with the geniality of well-honed royalty visiting an irksome institution.

Julie Cleaver asked whether Robin had seen her father before leaving for the theatre.

'Yes indeed,' Robin replied, beaming as he always did when faced with a poser. He had not been to the House that day, Jake's whereabouts were quite unknown to him but being both conscientious and nestless, it was possible that his sister's ex-husband was indeed taking advantage of winter Westminster's central heating.

'Don't bother Uncle Robin with silly questions about your father, Julie.'

'But they work together, Mum.'

'Uncle Robin isn't friendly with your father. He doesn't like him. Nobody does.'

'We like Daddy,' said Pauline, 'don't we, Anna?'

'Be quiet, all of you,' said Fenella. 'If I hear one more peep about your father out of any of you I will take you home and you won't see the show, or anything – no ice-creams, no Coke, nothing. Do you understand?'

'We understand,' said Julie.

Two seats remained vacant in their row, one for Cyril and the other for his younger daughter. Laura still lived in Norfolk and had become a belligerent vegetarian. December was no time for pleasure, with so many turkeys meeting their end. She and her newest man were mounting a vigil outside a Fakenham poultry farm and promoting their humane alternative to festive fare, a sort of loaf made from their own organic produce. Elizabeth had tried some and declared it delicious, provided one liked the flavour of compost.

'Darling, what a shame that you have been let down,' Winifred told Charlotte. 'It is too bad after you have spent such a lot for these seats.'

Elizabeth too was disappointed: she believed so much in the united family. Fenella and Robin had forgotten their political differences and, on the principle of their enemy's enemy being their friend, had united in mutual hatred of Jake Cleaver. Fenella's divorce from him had been civilised but since moving back to live with her parents the situation between her and her ex-husband had turned very sour.

'It is all right, Mother. Peta Fable is coming along with a young relative.'

Peta quite outshone Robin's arrival. Her trick of wearing black worked yet again as she stood alone among the fussy women of the matinée audience who had attempted to conceal their flawed shapes beneath loud patterns. She entered the auditorium late, just as the overture was starting. She was followed, not as Charlotte had expected by her young cousin Ocean Bray, but by her stepson.

Charlotte was pulverised. Mercifully the lights faded to dark.

'You two don't look like twins,' Julie Cleaver told her cousins during the interval.

'Yes we do. Look!' Coral had put on her brother's glasses. 'There!'

'Oh Lord, Charlotte,' Winifred whispered to her daughter. 'The words of that song are a bit near the bone, aren't they?'

'What the one about the Brethren?'

'No, the one about seeing for certain what I thought I knew. Look at Coral.'

Charlotte had ordered and paid for the interval refreshments and left Robin to distribute them, preferring to stay away from the bar.

'Sam.'

'Hello, Wallace.'

Though it would have been perfectly normal for two old friends to kiss on meeting he only took her hand, squeezing and holding it gently for as long as he dared.

'I didn't know you were home.'

'I only arrived this morning. All this has happened by chance. Peta didn't tell you in case you got in a state.'

'I am in a state.'

'You look wonderful.'

'You aren't wearing your glasses.'

'I saw what you looked like before I took them off. Are you happier?'

'Yes.'

The three Cleaver girls came to say that they were off to the Ladies. 'Right you are. Do you know the way? Don't be long, the second half will start in about five minutes.'

'Five minutes is all we've got, Charlotte, darling.' He had never called her that before. She was frightened.

'Can't we meet again?'

'I'm off to the States for Christmas and back here for a couple of days in early January. Any good?'

'No,' Charlotte replied. 'Robin got me to organise skiing.'

'He is a keen father.'

'Yes, he adores them, especially Coral, and she loves him to pieces. Are you coming to eat with us afterwards?'

'Robin did ask me, but I can't. Sorry, I better not.'

Poor Jacob mourned his favourite son. Joseph erred with Potiphar's brazen wife and Pharaoh, as Elvis, thrilled the audience, all except Elizabeth who was hating the whole irreverence of the show despite it being restricted to the Old Testament. The Bible may be lewd in bits but the Word is no joke.

'Where are Julie and the girls?' she asked Charlotte in a loud whisper.

'They went to the loo. They are probably standing at the back, there may have been a queue.'

The show ended. Winifred said she had never seen such a splendid specimen as Joseph, and Fenella put forward her unoriginal theory of man as sex object. Meanwhile her three daughters had vanished.

Martin and Peta endeavoured to keep the remains of the party calm.

'You are not parents, you don't understand,' Elizabeth shouted when they tried to offer comfort.

'Be reasonable, my dear,' Winifred implored. 'No one is going to abduct all three.'

'Just because you only had one child, there is no need to assume that having three makes them less precious.'

'I didn't mean that. I just think there is safety in numbers.'

'Aunty Fenella, I think I know where they are,' said Coral. 'Pauline said that Jacob looked like Uncle Jake. Then Anna said that she was sorry for Jacob when he lost Joseph so Julie said that they should go and look for their daddy, to make him happy.'

'It was that bloody beard,' said Fenella.

'I knew we should have gone to *Peter Pan*,' said Elizabeth.

Fenella was white with rage more than anxiety. 'I'll kill him. I'll make sure he never sees them again, ever.'

Robin had taken charge of the whole situation. He was magnificently efficient, establishing quite quickly that the little girls had walked from the Strand to the House of Commons in the rain and had arrived bedraggled but triumphant at the Palace of Westminster. A kind policeman had managed to help them find their father to give him the nicest surprise he was to get that Christmas.

Later, when Robin had done his smoothest best to calm his sister and mother, he posted them and the three little girls back to Dorset in a chauffeured limousine. The train seemed too risky after such upheavals. Robin promised to pay Charlotte back for the cost of the hire. He forgot, and so did she. Charlotte often preferred to let things slip her mind.

Peta and Martin had melted away once the situation had dwindled from national headlines to domestic unpleasantness. Once the Dorset contingent had gone Robin accompanied his own children, wife and mother-in-law to their station, whether to ensure that they caught the right train safely or to reassure himself of their actual departure wasn't clear.

At the station where good sorts were singing carols under a tree laden with empty parcels and some paper vendors sported red bobble hats Robin took Charlotte's arm and told her how sorry he felt for Jake. 'I don't think I could carry on if I lost the children.'

'But you aren't going to, Robin.'

'You promise?'

'Yes, Robin, I promise,' Charlotte replied. What she had seen that day convinced her that she would have to keep her word. To break it would be worse than murder.

A week later Robin gave Charlotte an eternity ring for Christmas. She was quite overcome and amazed. Robin never gave her expensive presents and this ring was no trinket.

'It is quite, quite beautiful, Robin. Thank you so much, I am terribly touched, but what have I done to deserve this?'

'It is to remind you of your promise about the children. You do remember?'

'Yes Robin, I won't forget. I can't.'

October 1994

SITTING ON A municipal bench made from green painted wood and porridge-mixture concrete Charlotte looked out across the golf links. The coming winter did nothing to stem the flow of players anxious to have a round or two at the birthplace of their favourite game. There must be something really special about whacking a ball about in all weathers till it plops into a hole. The thrill of it eluded Charlotte. She wondered what God made of golf: it must form part of His creation but it seemed such an absurd part like underarm hair and the flappy bits at the edge of dogs' ears. Some people in Japan play on courses constructed like multi-storey car parks, ancient Americans play till they drop into their caskets and far too many people talk of little else. It seemed such a daft thing to do. Yet playing golf was not what Piers and her mother had meant when they had implored her to do nothing silly. She had given her word. She would keep her promise, as usual.

Glancing down she looked at her familiar engagement and eternity rings. Money was getting short, but she was not so stretched yet as to have to sell anything. It was nice to know she had something saleable if things got bad. Unlike Florence Begg, Charlotte knew her diamonds were not paste.

Martin had given her one of those tatty souvenir Russian dolls the same year that Robin had surprised her with the eternity ring. She had hidden her babouska full of babies in the back of her desk with Martin's letters. She wondered whether anyone had discovered them yet.

A crumpled but clean copy of the *Scotsman* was poking out of a nearby litter bin. Feeling a mite sheepish and not unlike a bag lady, she fished it out to read. Edinburgh was full of entertainments despite the Festival being over. *Joseph and the Amazing Technicolor Dreamcoat* was playing to packed houses of both evening and matinée audiences. Some things do seem to last for eternity.

17

Summer 1984

CORAL AND PIERS spent the last few days of the 1984 summer holidays in bed with chickenpox. They only missed one week of term (which they thought a grievous swindle) but at least they had managed to get through most of the holidays in good order. Coral had camped with the Pony Club and had won a cup for enthusiasm, Piers played badly in several humiliating cricket matches, and the whole family, apart from Winifred and Laura, spent a tempestuous seaside fortnight incarcerated in a Cornish villa being argumentative and bored senseless by board games, except when beaten outside to be spotted playing beach rounders or striding the coastline in united family formation.

On their return home, Charlotte organised a match for Piers on the Little Godleham cricket pitch. His team of eleven, chosen for their affability rather than their skill, was trounced by the Potters' team of superboys. Robin umpired while Phyllis Potter kept the score. They didn't always agree about the game but were in perfect harmony as regards politics. Godleham Conservatives were thriving, their member had found high favour with the goddess of the party and was sky-rocketing to the top. The Conservatives were no longer an annexe of Eton's sixth form; clever men, products of the grammar schools, were rising above the old comrades. Robin had got himself a junior cabinet post, very junior indeed but more elevated than Roddy MacPhail, who was stuck, popularly rooted to the back benches.

Charlotte was in charge of tea and had made a heap of sandwiches to satisfy all quirks.

'What is wrong, Piers? Don't tell me you've gone off sandwich spread.'

'I'm not hungry, Mum.'

'I think I know someone who is not being very sporting,' said Phyllis.

Potter Minor had bowled Piers first ball. Robin, shocked and disappointed at his son's apparent lack of killer instinct, had made his feelings known to Piers when returning him the jersey that had been redundantly shed.

'Balls,' said Piers. 'I'm always bowled out, I couldn't give a fish's tit.'

Piers was sent to spend the rest of teatime in the car and disgrace.

'Mum,' said Coral. 'Piers isn't feeling well.'

'Rubbish, we'll soon see to that,' said Robin. He watched his daughter in rapt admiration as she let her pony graze upon some unpopular fruit cake and wondered why his twins had not been born identical in intellect and drive.

'He has come out in spots.'

The next day Coral was spotty too and within a week most of the cricketers had succumbed. Charlotte couldn't help gloating when Phyllis complained about how much school work was being missed by her team who should have been swotting for the Common Entrance. To be sure of winning, the Potter team had consisted of boys far too old to have been a fair match for the likes of Piers.

It wasn't just the loathsome business of returning the children to school that made Charlotte feel low. Spots and temperature developed on the lonely drive home, she would have welcomed death by the time she got to bed and didn't have the strength to ring Robin till the next day, by which time Winifred had volunteered and installed herself at Cedar Lodge, a nurse once more.

'Robin says I should have got over childhood diseases at the proper time, like he did.'

'That's rich, coming from him!' Winifred bustled about, loving the chance to prove her training had not been in vain. She even stood with her hands behind her back at the bed end when the doctor called, as if expecting Matron to commend her for irreproachable bed-making and blanket-bathing. Charlotte was hot, and often delirious. Winifred understood most of her daughter's ramblings. Robin didn't reappear till all the worst was over.

The conference was to be at Brighton. A double room at the Grand Hotel was booked for the Brands and Robin hoped fervently that his wife's spots would be less repulsive by October. While being nurse Winifred had commandeered the Cedar Lodge phone and got much done; she even invited Peta, who had wisely had chickenpox in infancy, to come to lunch once Charlotte was well enough to enjoy seeing her. Despite the considerable age gap, Peta and Winifred had always liked each other and got on well. They were honest about what they wanted and didn't dither or dabble with hypocrisy.

For the fortnight of her illness Charlotte had drunk no alcohol at all. It could have been a good time to stop altogether.

Martin and Charlotte had seen each other once at Easter but only in the company of the children. They had gone to a safari park, where monkeys had molested the car and a lion had peed backwards all over the bonnet. Coral and Piers loved that. A car drenched in urine with windscreen wipers dangling was an unsatisfactory but blameless place for a tryst. No more leave was due to Martin till October.

Things were easing up in Russia. Relations were friendlier betwixt East and West, glasnost and perestroika evolved into popular themes, it was an interesting time to be posted to Moscow. Now and again Martin's dispatches were transmitted on the radio, but never the television.

'Poor old Martin,' said Robin. 'He just hasn't got it.' Robin had appeared on the box several times; he had been taught how to project himself and was becoming a media darling.

'What hasn't Martin got?' Charlotte asked.

'Sex appeal,' Robin replied.

It was Wednesday morning, Charlotte had packed her predominantly blue smart suits and silk frocks for Brighton and was just about to run Pandemonium round to Winifred's flat when the telephone rang.

It was Winifred, sounding incredibly frail.

'Darling, I'm ill.'

'Don't worry Mother, I'm sure that Mrs Porter will have Pan instead.'

'No, you don't understand, I am ill, really ill. The doctor says so.'

'What is wrong? Quick tell me, what can I do?'

'He says it is shingles, darling. Complicated shingles.'

'How complicated?'

'Too complicated for me to be left alone. He says I must be kept very quiet, and you must have me to stay till I'm better.'

'I see. Well of course, Mother. I'll come for you at once.'

'No!' Winifred suddenly sounded her old brisk self. 'I've ordered a cab.'

'I'll see if I can find a nurse. Don't worry, Mother, you will be fine.'

'No, darling. You must stay behind, you can't leave me now. I might die.'

'Oh God, really?'

'Yes, really. Remember, I am a nurse, I know.'

Winifred arrived looking brisk, adopting a sickly crumbling stance only when Charlotte came to help her inside and upstairs to the spare room where a turned-down bed and hot-water bottle awaited the patient. For someone suddenly sick Winifred had done an excellent job of packing; it was almost as if she had kept a case in readiness like an expectant mother.

She also made a good show of extreme ill-health. Charlotte did what she could but was forbidden to touch the unpacking, probably because of the large amount of biscuits, paperbacks, tapestry and writing paper which Winifred had brought to sustain and entertain her during her battle with death.

Robin could have greeted the news of his wife's forced absence with greater regret and still retained his reputation for commendable stoicism. Despite the demands of normal manners he sent no messages of sympathy or well-wishing to his mother-in-law: he knew better than to expect much from either her survival or her death.

Charlotte put her good Tory wife's good outfits back in the

wardrobe and resigned herself to being a good daughter. It was not much of a sacrifice but she did wonder if it was entirely vital.

Once an hour she would visit her mother to find out if there was anything needed. Winifred needed nothing, just to be left to be ill, which she did by lying down, groaning quietly and looking like a sleeping beauty under a slapdash spell, shoddily enchanted and allowed to age. She wore a beautiful silk night-dress which bore no vestige of feverish sweatiness or terminal distress. Starve a fever, that was the way. Charlotte was sure that there were biscuit crumbs and an apple stalk beside the bed, not to mention a whiff of gin coming from her mother's glass of water, which she only just managed to sip unaided. Radio Four droned on till the sleepy lullaby ended and the broadcast-ing baton was handed to the World Service with a rousing selection of British tunes and 'Lillibullero'.

Charlotte slept well, but the next morning Winifred whim-pered that she had passed a hellish night and was no better. Indeed, she said, she was much, much worse.

'I am going to get the doctor.'

'No!'

Winifred sat up abruptly. There was absolutely no call for the doctor; he had seen the patient once, that was enough.

'But you say you are getting worse. I worry about you,' said Charlotte as she tried to plump up her mother's pillows under which she found a purple scrap of paper not unlike a Cadbury's wrapper.

'One gets worse before one gets better,' Winifred replied. 'Or not, as the case may be.'

Robin telephoned between morning meetings. He had been singled out for much adulation; there would be plenty of interest about him in the press. Charlotte said she was delighted and he replied that she should be proud of him. Robin was proud enough of himself. He would call again on Friday, but in the mean time he would be utterly swamped by busy appointments and rallying functions, she must wish him well. She did.

Henrietta MacPhail rang to say that Charlotte was missed and that much love was sent to her by all. Even if this was mere civilised good manners, Charlotte was cheered. Peta called too: she sent her very best wishes to Winifred and hoped Charlotte was not bored on her own.

'Mother, are you pretending to be ill to stop me going to Brighton?'

'Oh darling, whyever would I want to do that?' Winifred replied in a quavery voice. The glass beside her bed was empty yet again.

'I don't know. Maybe because you said I looked like an old soak when I got home from last year's conference.'

'Oh no. Only you can control how much you drink. That is not my affair. I'm ill, really ill. Now off you go. I thought you said you were going to wash your hair.'

The lustre had returned following the listless lankness that had made her hair look so vile during the chickenpox; most of the scars had gone too. Charlotte looked out on to her autumn garden as she blowed her hair dry and was so glad that she had persuaded Robin not to have the cedar felled. It was a noble tree, a wonderful shape and worth every watt burnt as a result of the dark shadow it cast over the study.

Just as it was getting dark Peta's distinctive car drove up to the front door. She must need company or be between boyfriends. Unlike Charlotte, Peta did get bored on her own. It was sweet of her to come out to the country again so soon. Mentally Charlotte scanned the deep freeze and larder for something celebratory for supper. She and Peta would gossip while they dined off tinned palm hearts, smoked salmon and scrambled eggs. It would be fun.

'Can I come in, Sam?'

'Oh my God!'

'No, it's me.'

'Oh Wallace, I can't believe this.'

Martin had brought champagne with him and some real Russian caviare. That evening was the best Charlotte had ever known and was to remain the best, probably for the rest of her life. Just then, for those few hours, heaven became an earthly possibility.

'I must go and check up on Mother. She is being ill upstairs.'

'I'll come with you.'

'She might be infectious, she says she has complications.'

'Your mother has a perfect imagination.'

'She is convinced she is ill; dying, even.'

'Sam, wait. I adore you, do you know why?'

'No, tell me.'

'Because you are so gullible.'

Later, when both bottles were empty and the fire they had lit was glowing low, Charlotte whispered in Martin's ear as they lay beside each other in the flickering light. 'Robin is wrong.'

'Of course he is. Most of the things he has done are wrong, you and I know that.'

'He is wrong about you.'

They were still holding each other when Charlotte woke with a start. She turned on a table lamp and looked at the clock. It was just after three, a few more hours yet till dawn. She fetched a rug from the sofa and put it over Martin, who was deep asleep. Then she knew why she had awoken so suddenly: her mother was banging on the door of her empty bedroom upstairs. It would have felt wrong to have slept together there; their spontaneity would have been wrecked by guilt. One day, perhaps but probably not, she and Martin might have a bed to really make their own.

Hastily flinging on her clothes Charlotte dashed to deal with the commotion.

Winifred had been unable to sleep and had heard the news on the World Service. The Grand Hotel at Brighton had been bombed.

To wish, to hope, to will someone to be dead is murder in all but deed. Charlotte tried to keep the thoughts away; she did what she could to remain calm and conceal her inmost longings even from herself. All prospects were terrifying, her own emotions being the most horrifying of all. What about the children, how would they manage? She hoped that they at least would stop her selfish desire to be a widow; she must do her utmost to comfort them. They would be devastated, she would have to act well.

Martin drove to Brighton and arrived at dawn. Delegates still in pyjamas were huddled in front of the Grand as stretchers were borne away from the ruins. Some of the hotel guests were dead, several injured and a handful as yet unaccounted for. Everyone who could, rang their families to reassure them. No call came for Charlotte from Robin.

Charlotte and Winifred sat in the kitchen. The shingles had gone. Doctors knew nothing. Winifred declared herself to be quite well enough to keep her daughter company during this vigil.

'Oh my darling, I am so sorry. I didn't mean this to happen.'

'Mother, surely you aren't suggesting that you planted a bomb?'

'Of course not. It is just that my plans have gone all wrong.'

'Was this sickness your ploy?'

'Your father was right, I shouldn't interfere.'

Neither of them dared say what was uppermost in their minds. Had Charlotte not been prevented from going to Brighton by her mother, she too might have been a bomb victim. She might have died. Robin possibly had. Charlotte knew that his room overlooked the front.

Martin rang at eight. When the rescuers had got to Robin's bedroom it was empty: his bed had not been used.

At nine Charlotte received a second call.

'May I speak with Mrs Brand.'

'This is Mrs Brand.'

Charlotte recognised the voice – American, female, probably young.

'Your husband has asked me to call you. He is busy right now but he wants you to know that he is just fine.'

'Thank you, I had heard that he had not slept in his room.'

'Right. Well maybe he will call you later.'

'Wait. Who are you? Who am I speaking to?'

'I am Robin's PA. He needs someone around, especially when you have to stay home to care for your mom.'

'Clemency, is that you?'

'Sure. Didn't Robin tell you? I have been doing research for him for quite some time.'

'Do Robin's parents know he is safe?'

'Of course. I rang them first.'

Robin's explanation for his absence from the Grand Hotel was corroborated by his personal assistant and researcher. He had been working late, become tired and because of commendable caution concerning the breathalyser, had spent the night at Bexhill with colleagues.

'Yes, Mrs Brand,' said Mr Trader, headmaster of Salisbury Lodge. 'I have already told your son that his father is safe. Mr Brand's secretary rang an hour ago.'

Coral's housemistress told Charlotte that everyone at Lordstone was greatly relieved; in fact Coral had even spoken with Miss Shoemaker herself.

'Miss Shoemaker?'

'Miss Shoemaker has been most efficient. She is going to drive Mr Brand here on Saturday to give Coral reassurance.'

Both schools were delighted to know that the MacPhails too were safe: they had been staying with old friends at Glynde.

Clemency van Schumacher's words resounded in Charlotte's ears. She could get to where she desired without paying a cent. There was nothing Charlotte kept with her wealth that Clemency couldn't freely take from her. Clemency could win the lot – husband, children, everything, if it pleased her so to do. Martin admired Clemency. Charlotte remembered how he hadn't believed her when she told him how Clemency hated her, how she professed to loathe and despise her wealth and stupidity. He had actually rebuked Charlotte for over-sensitivity saying that he could not imagine Clemency being unpleasant. Unpleasant! What an understatement. Clemency regarded Charlotte with phobic revulsion.

Martin was struck by Clemency's capability, her verve, her nerve. Charlotte's virtues were less strident: restrained aggression and gentler subtleties had endeared her to him. Power hunger and greed to conquer were hardly the stuff that Charlotte thought would matter to Martin, but Clemency was young and lovely, scheming, self-confident and ruthless. She was in a position of advantage and sure of getting what she wanted. Everything that was Charlotte's could be hers, it was just a question of time and skill. Clemency got people to fall in love with her while never giving an inch of ground herself. Life was brief and serious, all prizes were worth winning and Clemency never entered any competition in which she might be a loser.

The future might be interesting. Meanwhile life as Robin's personal assistant was proving to be sufficiently absorbing for the moment.

'Isn't it a bit early, darling, to be having a drink?'

'I need it, Mother.'

Martin rang later. Winifred took the call and told him Charlotte was unavailable: her daughter was asleep, the agitation had been too much for her. Was there a message?

'Yes, Mrs Forth. Please tell her I rang to say goodbye. I'll write.'

'I see. Is that all?'

'Yes, and thank you, Mrs Forth.'

'What for?'

'For trying.'

'It was a mistake, Martin, but well intended.'

'I know.'

Charlotte couldn't speak to Martin then because she had passed out, drunk.

18

October 1994

A THOUGHTFUL COMMITTEE, many years ago, had felt the place where the road between the sands and the golf course petered out should be enhanced with a public shelter. The building was square; recessed benches faced outward from its four sides so that the hardy could dodge the wind when it blew from any direction. From the circulating draughts it was impossible to hide, not that any of the views from there were worth the walk. Picnickers mostly ate in their sealed cars when they got to the road end, venturing out only to throw their litter in the vague direction of the bin that resembled an intergalactic intruder but was rotten at handling rubbish.

Charlotte parked the car and walked to the fringe of the beach. She sniffed the pungent saltiness of the sharp grass that grew in the dunes where few lovers ever enjoyed themselves amongst the tussocky undulations. An unusual amount of detritus got washed on to this section of shore; bloated sheep and festering seabirds mingled with mankind's rejections. Once a smallish and very dead whale had lain upon the sands waiting to be washed away on a tardy high tide. The dried leathery body thudded like a muffled drum when stones were thrown at it. After a while the novelty and stench both faded and the creature's stripped ribs, whitened by the wind, turned the corpse into a wrecked ghost boat.

A plaque below the stopped clock on the shelter's cupola stated that the structure had been erected by subscription in memory of Marion Begg. Nothing more, not even the late Marion's dates, gave a clue as to why subscribers had felt moved to remember her in this way at this forsaken place. Charlotte wondered if she had been any relation of Tam and Florence Begg. Poor Florence. Charlotte felt guiltier than ever about burdening her with her troubled conscience. No one else would understand, it would have been yet worse to have confessed to her own mother. Winifred had withstood enough and had supported her daughter staunchly but she was too close, too involved. Her sympathy would be selfless but her judgement flawed.

Once it was known, Charlotte wondered whether she would have to stand trial after all these years. The shame she would bring on her family would outstrip any of that induced by Robin's peccadilloes, stupid excesses and idiotic corruptions. She might even go to prison. She'd rather die. Perhaps Wally would rather have died too.

November 1984

Charlotte didn't give up drink when she became pregnant. She was seldom regular when in good health and with her sickness and subsequent depression a great lateness came as no surprise.

It was a very early miscarriage, so early as to hardly count. Once again Winifred acted as nurse; she had endured plenty of failed pregnancies herself and understood that it was more than physical loss that drained her daughter. By tacit agreement, Robin was never told the real reason for Charlotte's internal troubles. He was busy in London, enjoying greater cabinet promotion and much more besides.

Wives were apt to ail if they had empty lives. He was reminded of Nature's attitude to vacuums. Other women had careers or home-based children or did good by running things, raising funds and sitting on committees or the Bench. Charlotte was an adequate wife in that she was congenial and zealous at constituency functions and a conscientious mother in the school holidays but apart from that she was nothing on her own. She didn't even shop much. However, she did drink.

Martin had written. He had returned to Moscow and the letter didn't get delivered till Peta brought it with her to Cedar Lodge during Charlotte's convalescence.

It was over. He would always love her, he said, but together they were finished. Everything that had happened had been marvellous, she was not to get him wrong, but as a pair they were not right. They had lives that touched but would not knit. Had things been different, then maybe. If they could be lovers without being in love it might have been all right. They must not love each other any more.

From then onwards only the bottle could anaesthetise the blank despair. Every day and in every way Charlotte saw the evidence around her which confirmed that her only purpose in life was to be a blank cheque. Without her money she would not exist, she would evaporate; for her there would be no memorial unless she provided it herself in the form of funding others. To act the broken piggy-bank was to be her pleasure, her only pleasure apart from alcohol.

Winifred wept for Charlotte. She blamed herself in part: she had no business to try and engineer her daughter's happiness. As time passed she grew to dislike Robin more but she had to curb her feelings and rise above her own emotions. With Charlotte a psychological and physical casualty, someone strong had to keep the family steady.

Coral and Piers took themselves to their grandmother when life got puzzling or rough.

Martin left Moscow and got a job with a London-based independent television company. He had acquired quite a reputation for gimlet journalism, and even Robin admitted that age, contact lenses and a skilful barber had done much for his old friend. Martin, Robin maintained, would never be sexy but maturity made him more acceptable to the media, in a grotesque sort of way. To watch the news was exquisite torture for Charlotte. It was the only place she ever saw Martin now. Once, after many solitary gins she had kissed the dusty screen as he reported some miscarriage of justice. Only artificial crackling technology sparked between them.

Seeing their father and their Uncle Wally on the telly gave the twins quite a buzz. Apart from Jake Cleaver who had mellowed greatly, Martin had not, as yet, been seen questioning any mutual acquaintances. Winifred longed for the day when

Robin would be Martin's interviewee. The prospect excited her theatrical imagination.

Summer 1986

Term had ended before the Godleham Conservative fête and summer fayre took place, not as might be expected, at Cedar Lodge but in the grounds of Martin Fable's childhood home, now a comfortable refuge for the prosperous aged. Tam Begg, as one of the oldest peers – older even than many of the home's occupants – who was famed for having spent most of his commoner days as a Tory Member of Parliament, had consented to perform the opening ceremony. Actually he said very few words, all inconsequential and incoherent, before Florence swept forward, saved the platform party's confusion, declared the fête open and appeared thrilled to receive a potted begonia hastily presented by Coral, who had recently won a prize for initiative.

'You look a little distrait, my chicken,' said Florence to Charlotte. 'Much good can come from a dose of salts. Wonders can happen to the old liver with a timely slug of Alka Seltzer.'

'I'm fine, Florence, just tired.'

'Tired and emotional, isn't that it? Never mind, I am sure you have good reason to be one degree under, in fact many degrees under. I know your life isn't easy.'

After months of being brave Charlotte feared she might break down. 'I really am all right, Florence.'

'Just remember I'm always there. Any trouble you feel you can't tell your family can be spilled out to me. I'm pretty tough and awfully stupid but I have seen a lot of life's good and bad bits. You will remember?'

'Yes, Florence. I promise. I will, thank you.'

After several tours of the stalls the thrill of the affair palled. Coral went off to stay with a nearby schoolfriend, which left Piers feeling foolish and awkward bowling for pigs, guessing weights of cakes, numbers of sweets and names of dolls. All the time he longed for the beastly event to end so he could go home and shut himself in his room with a comic.

'Sweeping the board of prizes, are you, Piers?'

'No, Dad.'

'Here, let me show you how it's done.' Robin took the bowls from his son and swinging through hit the skittles square in the middle to win himself an enormous blue teddy bear. Robin feigned delight, pinned a blue rosette on the toy's breast and put his arm on his scowling son's shoulder. Too bad yet another photo opportunity was ruined by Piers.

'Don't look glum, chum!' Phyllis Potter felt she was doing such a good turn by being hearty. Piers winced as he heard the dread invitation to come home with her sons for an icy swim in their filthy pool, followed by a barbecue and a jolly night in the awful new tent they had pitched in the garden as a rehearsal for their sturdy lakeland holidays. Piers knew the Potter garden: it wasn't large and all of it was near their compost heap. This heap was alive with grass snakes, a cause for pride amongst the nature-loving Potters.

'How kind,' said Winifred. 'Piers would love that, wouldn't you Piers? I'll run him round myself. He has a spare pair of trunks and a sleeping bag in my flat.'

Winifred could see that Charlotte would be in no fit state for much that night, especially after winning the star prize on the bottle stall. Winifred herself was going out to supper; she had made several new friends since her move and was a popular bridge partner.

Cedar Lodge was clean and tidy, the holidays had only just started so the children were yet to overflow their rooms and invade downstairs, colonising as they went with their abandoned clothes and equipment. The kitchen was clean because Charlotte never cooked when she was alone, though she had been foresighted enough to restock the larder with tins – spaghetti hoops, baked beans, canned peaches – and fill the freezer with fish fingers and hamburgers, the children's favourite food. There was no point in making life difficult by introducing anything sophisticated, it just made for unpleasant arguments about gristle and greens.

Robin got fed on the readymade luxuries that saved the

non-labouring rich much labour. The cellar was locked and he kept the only key. Charlotte managed very well without access to his neatly stacked wines. She drank anything, and by the time the fête was over and they had returned to an empty house most of the prize bottle of advocaat was down her throat, circulating her body and assaulting her liver.

'I'm tired,' she said. 'I think I'll take a nap.'

Robin prepared himself for a solitary evening. He was seldom at home and a peaceful night there would be pleasant. He could watch *Pennies from Heaven* – that at least, might stir his loins.

Martin's voice woke Charlotte. She was used to hearing him coming over the air but after searching the darkening bedroom she realised that nothing that transmitted was switched on. The sound came from outside. He was standing on the front step – she could see him quite clearly despite the dusk. She felt hopeless joy surge through her bemused body. She loved him still: she adored him so much that even now, nearly two years after their last meeting, she still hoped he might come back. It appeared that he had been dropped in the front drive by a taxi; it had been his thanks and farewell to his departed driver that had made her wake up.

Robin opened the door, a few words were exchanged and Martin was invited in. Charlotte heard the men go into the study on the southwest side of the house, where the cedar cast long shadows while the red sun set.

She crept to the top of the stairs to listen. Except when Robin opened the door to fetch another bottle, their voices were indistinct. She managed to hear enough in that brief moment to set her befuddled mind racing and raise her saturated hopes beyond normal reason.

'The truth is, Robin, I can't. I'm not able to leave or forget her now. I know all about everything between you. That is your business, not mine. I just want to be honest with you about what has happened.'

'All very honourable I'm sure,' Robin replied from the drawing-room drink cupboard, in a voice of such cutting sarcasm that even Charlotte in her elated state was chilled.

Regretting all the Advocaat and most of that afternoon's

gin, Charlotte attacked herself with toothpaste, mouthwash and soap. She brushed her hair which had grown youthfully long and did her best to camouflage her blotchy face. A clean shirt and jeans, a bright smile and tidy hair might just disguise the degeneration beneath. A squirt of scent and she was ready. She would go downstairs and face the consequences. Her mind raced but did not contemplate difficulty or failure.

Mrs Potter was being brisk and managing. Never a one to stand for nonsense, she was dead keen on rearing the young to be tough.

'Now then, boys, look after Piers. Have you ever slept in a tent before, Piers?' Piers said of course he had, lots of times, which was a lie.

'Have fun, then. No ragging!'

'No what?' Piers asked.

'Ragging, Piers. You know, playing the fool, that sort of caper.' Phyllis went inside to join her husband, who was only a spear-carrier in the Potter family drama.

The three boys slept in separate canvas stalls of the new Potter tent. It boasted a double room, two singles, a lounge area and kitchen recess with nifty hanging larder. It was all tent to Piers, each room being indistinguishable from the rest, all equally musty and claustrophobic. Through the half-inflated air-bed and the waterproof flooring, the lawn felt as knobby as a coal tip.

'Do you like snakes, Piers?'

'Yes, I mean no, not really.'

'Oh what a pity.'

'Why?'

'There's one in your sleeping bag.'

Piers shrieked and jumped up, disentangling himself from the bag and stumbling over the bedroom threshold to collide with the hanging larder and spill all the enamel mugs and plates with maximum clatter.

'Oh dear. It wasn't a snake – just this bit of inner tube. I wonder how it got there? Wait, what's that I can hear?'

Hissssss.

'Look up!'

A slithery snake with green eyes was thrown over the canvas partition on to the place where Piers had made his bed. He screamed. Even when he realised that the clammy streak of whippy rubber was a joke-shop fake he was petrified. Sleep was impossible. The owls hooted and nocturnal rodents scrabbled about, a fox stalked over the lawn and then Piers could contain himself no longer. Too much Coke, he couldn't wait. He ran out of the tent and failed to get to the bushes before he had to pee on Mrs Potter's rosebed. He looked down and there it was, quite clear in the moonlight. No fake this time – long, dark and thick it squirmed away slithering into the denser growth, it went on for ever.

'Don't be silly. It's only a grass snake, it won't harm you. Much.'

Better to be murdered by footpads, abducted by perverts, anything would be preferable to spending a night in this nest of vipers. Piers put as many clothes on as he could find and set off for home.

Charlotte stood for a moment outside the study door. If this were a movie, she thought, the orchestra would be having an orgasm.

'Can I come in?'

'I thought you were sleeping it off, Charlotte.'

'I've woken up. Hello, Wallace.'

'Charlotte, hello.' Martin looked surprised, shocked even and far from delighted. 'I thought you weren't here . . .' He was confused and awkward before remembering his good manners and what would be expected of him. 'How nice to see you. You look well. How are the children?'

Manners and pleasantries, the ignominious trappings of cordial acquaintance, no more than that.

'Of course, you two are old friends,' said Robin. His voice was thick; he had drunk a lot very quickly. He was distressed.

'Martin has brought me some very interesting news.'

Charlotte looked from one man to the other. They were standing tense with anger, dogs with bristled hackles. Was she the hen in the middle that goads a pair of cocks to fight? Even through her addled brain she knew that all her stupid hopes, her drunk and fanciful imaginings, were rubbish. Neither man was fighting over her. Yet there was still a little hope, just.

'It seems that he has been poaching. He has been fiddling in other people's private business. Martin Fable, this clumsy homunculus, has come here to gloat. Congratulate him, my drunk darling.'

'Why?'

'Because he has stolen my woman.'

'Do you mean me?'

'God, no. No one would steal you, I couldn't even give you away not even if I threw in all your filthy lucre as a sweetener.'

'That isn't fair, Robin,' Martin interrupted. 'Charlotte is wonderful. I have always loved her dearly.'

'Had you not loved Clemency more.'

'Yes,' said Martin quietly. 'I'm sorry.'

'Please don't apologise to me,' said Robin.

'I wasn't,' Martin replied.

The sun was long gone. Where wallflowers had scented the late spring air, baby dahlias had been bedded, there was no colour anywhere as Charlotte looked out over the flagged path through the darkness to where she could just distinguish the sloping stones the cedar roots had raised into a pitfall. Coral had fallen from her first bicycle there and cracked her head. Charlotte tried to concentrate on the memory to eliminate the present. She must not cry, she must not.

Robin went to pour more drink. Before Charlotte saw Martin's reflection in the window she knew he was behind her. She recognised the smell of him. Funny that, she thought, he doesn't smell of anything definable, not sweat or nervous salesman's aftershave or smoke or port; Martin smells of nothing but himself, unique and magic. He put his hand upon her elbow. Charlotte whispered.

'Not Clemency, Wallace please. Not her, anyone but her.'

'I'm sorry, Sam. It happened. It has happened, it is too late.'

'You can't love Clemency. It isn't possible.'

Robin had joined them by the window. Staggering from treading on one of Pandemonium's discarded bones he saved himself by clutching at Charlotte's other arm. Robin had several smells; this evening it was whisky.

'Why can't he love Clemency?' Robin asked.

'She hates me,' Charlotte answered.

'Don't flatter yourself, Charlotte. She hardly notices you exist.'

Martin followed Charlotte to the kitchen where she opened the larder and poured herself a tumbler of cooking brandy. This couldn't be true, this dream wasn't really a nightmare, it was a joke, a tease. She gulped down the brandy and turned her swimming eyes towards Martin. The room seemed to be riding at anchor and a distant engine buzzed in her head. She shut her eyes and still the world revolved.

'I'm sorry, Sam. You do understand, I hope?'

'I don't understand anything. Why have you come here?'

'Clemency thought I should get things straight with Robin. She told me you were away.'

'She knew full well I was here, Martin. She has orchestrated all this, she is using you.'

'No, that is not true, she says she loves me.'

'And you, Martin? What about you? No, don't answer, please. Just remember, you loved me for being gullible.'

'I do remember.'

'Well remember this now. I love you always, I never lied to you.'

'I did love you, Sam, but it is too late.'

'It always was.'

Robin came in. He had just answered the phone: an irate neighbour who kept sheep in his orchard had found Pandemonium loafing about his property snarling at his lambs. He threatened to shoot if the dog were not removed. He was, he said, within his rights even if the dog were half the size of the lambs and twice as scared.

'Your bloody dog is going to get shot,' Robin told Charlotte with delight. 'And a bloody good thing too.'

Charlotte screamed. 'Oh no, quick, we must get him back. No! I can't bear it, I can't lose him too.'

'Why, what else have you lost apart from your marbles?'

'He is the only thing that loves me.'

'I wouldn't count on it.'

Martin intervened. He offered to go and fetch

Pandemonium; he knew the area well, after all, having been brought up nearby. Then he said he would call a taxi to take him back to the station.

'I'll drive you.'

'No Robin, you are drunk.'

'Not drunk enough, you shit. God, women are a load of crap. The very idea of you and that bitch together makes me sick.'

'Which bitch?' Charlotte asked. She had drunk another tumbler in a matter of seconds.

'Not you,' Robin replied. 'No man would even drop his trousers for you.'

'Come on, let's go and get the dog,' said Martin.

'Car keys, please,' said Robin abruptly.

'They are in it. I'll drive,' Charlotte replied. She couldn't even see the door clearly but she knew that she had left the keys in the ignition.

'Don't drive, Sam, please,' said Martin. 'Let me, then you can hold the dog. Come on Sam, don't be silly. I don't want to remember you like this.'

Robin shouted: 'Stop fucking about. Get in the bloody car.'

Apart from a petrified haunting scream, those were the last words she remembered before coming to in the scrub beside the old quarry. Pandemonium must have been found; he was licking the blood and vomit from her face. She heard a hiss, a scrambling and then a bang before flames shot through the wreckage further down the pit. She felt the heat from the fire and saw the bushes glowing orange as a belch of stenching black smoke smothered the moonlit treetops. Robin was leaning over her; another shape was silhouetted, slumped and distorted a few yards away.

'Martin is dead. Do you understand? Martin is dead.'

Winifred woke early. It was her age that kept her from lying in. Besides, she liked the gentle chirpiness of the suburban dawn before the morning migration got under way and every car in the district started its daily dance. Songbirds got on better in the land of little mansions than in the real country in which she had lived most of her life. She liked to keep her bird table stocked and bought a toy catapult with which to scare marauding cats. Hers was a garden flat.

Piers was huddled on her step, scared witless, too frightened to ring her bell and quite incapable of explaining anything.

'My darling. My little one, come in, come in. Tell your old granny what it is.' She spoke comfortingly to him as if he were much younger than eleven.

'I want Mummy.'

'Of course you do. We will go and find her just as soon as we have had breakfast.'

'I don't know where she is.'

The police came before Winifred had begun coaxing her grandson to eat his eggs and soldiers. Charlotte was in hospital, out of danger but pretty poorly.

19

July 1986

FOR HEROISM AND bravery, heedless of danger to himself, there were few to rival Robin Brand. Everybody said so. His extreme valour was widely reported.

Robin had dragged his friend and his wife from the wreckage seconds before the car had exploded into flames. Nothing recognisable remained, every wheel and cog was charred and buckled. No one would have survived that inferno. Lives had been saved, thanks only to Robin's selfless act.

'It was nothing,' he said. 'Anyone would have done the same.'

The story, as reported, was straightforward. The local paper's headlines had never been so huge.

Conservative MP Robin Brand (45) and wife Charlotte (39), mother of twins Coral and Piers (11) had been celebrating a successful fête with a bottle of wine when they received a call to say that the family dog, Pandemonium was straying a mile or so away. A family friend, journalist and television reporter Martin Fable (41), was visiting the Brands' luxury home and volunteered to drive the family car to fetch the mischievous pooch. Tragedy struck when the car skidded and left the road at accident black spot Gravel Pit Corner plummeting down the bank before exploding into a fireball. The flames were seen as far away as Godleham on the Hill. Domestic assistant, Mrs Mavis Porter (58) said something ought to be done, it was a disgrace, Gravel Pit Corner had been an accident waiting to happen.

'Is Uncle Wally dead, Mum?'

'No, but he is very, very ill.'

'Will he get better, Mum?'

'No, they don't think so, not completely.'

'Mum?'

'Yes, Piers.'

'Is it murder if Uncle Wally dies?'

'No. Uncle Wally was driving. Remember Daddy told you Uncle Wally drove us both to fetch Pandemonium.'

'Why?'

'Because he had run away.'

'No, not the dog. Why did Dad say Uncle Wally drove your car?'

'Because I had drunk too much. Dad had drunk a lot too, but not as much as me. I am never going to drink again, I promise. You will keep me to that, won't you?'

'If someone drove a car when they were drunk and someone got hurt would the driver go to prison?'

'It depends really on how badly they hurt someone.'

'If they were as bad as Uncle Wally, say?'

'Oh yes. Certainly. I expect so. Why?'

'Nothing, I just wondered.'

Robin visited Charlotte in hospital every day. She was able to go home after about three weeks and was on crutches till Christmas. Martin remained in intensive car until his condition stabilised.

He would possibly survive for many years but most of his brain had already died. Robin was meticulous at establishing exactly what could be expected from his old friend. Very little, was the truth. Martin was never going to be much more than a vegetable.

Clemency van Schumacher returned to the States. She had a life to lead in which vegetables were irrelevant.

Robin had never believed that it was possible for her to prefer Martin to him and now he had his proof. Martin must have been sadly deluded. Still, to have experienced the humiliation of being jilted was a new departure for Robin and not one he was prepared to repeat. He must be the one to do the sacking, he made this clear: he had no further use for Clemency van Schumacher. He had made alternative arrangements and so must she.

Robin needed to be adored. He liked power and the nearer he got to fifty the younger he liked his female company. Silly, fluffy and deadly, sweet and twenty was just the thing.

'I want Martin to have the best care ever. I want him to be kept as comfortable as possible,' Charlotte said.

'Oh yes, Florence Nightingale, how are you going to do that?'

'I can pay.'

'Conscience money?' Robin suggested.

'Yes, in a way. After all, none of this would have happened if Pandemonium hadn't run away and if we hadn't had too much to drink.'

'Speak for yourself.'

'I am, but you had drunk a lot too, Robin. Remember?'

'Yes I can remember. You can't.'

'No, I can't. It is all a blank after we left the kitchen.'

'Just as well, really, don't you think, Charlotte? Just as well considering what really happened.'

'What do you mean?'

'If it wasn't for me, my darling, you would be on your way to Holloway by now.'

'Why? How?'

'You were driving, my sweet.'

Charlotte gasped. She could remember nothing. How could she know what she had done? She was as guilty of blighting Martin's life as if she had gone at him with an axe. Martin, the only man she had ever felt she loved and whom she would have loved for ever even if he had no longer felt anything for her. She would always love him, now, before and to the end. Martin felt nothing for anyone now and it was all her fault.

Robin held Charlotte's elbow in a vice grip. 'Now, before you start confessing remember this: I have lied to save you. If that gets out, I'm finished too. You must keep quiet about this for ever for my sake, and for the children.'

October 1994

Charlotte bore no visible scars of the accident. Her physical recovery had been complete except for a slight stiffness in her left hip which might, after all, just be a precursor of age, considering she was now in her late forties. Externally she looked in fine fettle; internally her life was a ruin. She had kept her word about the drink, that was a cause for pride; she had also kept faith with Robin, up until now.

Leaving the car she walked across the end of the golf course by way of the back path leading to Links Cottage. It was a nasty spot anyway without seasoning its distastefulness with the ghoulish story of poor torched Torquil. Marion Begg may have met her end there too along with all those washed up and decaying birds and beasts. No harm would come of going to see what had happened to her first Scottish home, it would be reassuring to find it occupied and buzzing with family life.

The cottage had not changed. Stark pebbledash stood out against the scrappy rough on the golf course fringe. Sightless windows, some with ill-hung and dirty curtains, stared towards the sea, the empty washing line still stretched forlorn from the kitchen door to the solitary pole that grew from a concrete base central to the untended garden and withstood all gales as its hollow metal interior hummed reverberating with the wind. Some evidence of life remained. Junk mail was protruding from the letterbox. The postman must call if only to deliver the absent occupier gripping news of mail-order prize draws and special offers in financial advice.

Autumn 1987

Robin made a great deal of money in the eighties. He wasn't alone: there was much evidence of prosperity on all sides till late in 1987 when the boom got rocky. He became a member of Lloyd's, and would in due course become far richer when his cheques came in.

'I could murder your father,' he told Charlotte.

'He has been dead for twelve years, Robin, remember?'

'Don't be facetious. You know what I mean. If you could

get your hands on your money without having to creep to the "gang of four" things would be far better.'

'I presume you mean the trustees.'

'Yes. Being wed to you is worse than consorting a juvenile ward. If you joined Lloyd's too we'd become seriously rich.'

'We have enough,' Charlotte replied. 'More than enough.'

Robin scoffed. 'You do. I don't.'

'You will, at least that's what you keep telling me. Then you can leave.'

Charlotte heard him mutter to the effect that he wished that day would roll on. Robin did not leave her: he had reasons to stay and counted on his hitherto exemplary reputation as a man of old-fashioned value and loyalty to get on in the world. His honourable behaviour would be repaid with honours. Irregularities in his home life might scupper his chances. Lucky Charlotte would become a lady, vicariously elevated for Robin's sycophantic loyalty to an iron lady.

More importantly, Elizabeth's son would be Sir Robin and she would fairly pop with pride while pretending such awards were mere fripperies. She said that she hoped what her son had done for his wife was appreciated. Charlotte replied that indeed it was.

The cedar tree was blown down in the great October 1987 gale. Light flooded into Robin's study now as his finances leaked away with every disaster that his syndicate underwrote. It seemed that there was a jinx upon his investments. Boats sank, fires engulfed, rockets misfired, oil spilt, diseases struck: everything that could founder did so while supported by Robin's wealth. Instead of cheques coming in he was pressed to pay out everything he had. He was, once more, entirely dependent on his wife.

He never admitted that the 'gang of four' had prevented the Brand losses becoming total.

Robin's knighthood only came after he had manned the barricades for his toppling leader, who appreciated and repaid his loyalty with this prize. Assessing correctly the way the world was to wag and having got what he could from being loyal to the status quo Robin transferred his total allegiance to the new leadership. He was still climbing upwards and needed those of the hierarchy to provide him with a steady ladder. His day would come. Charlotte would look fine in Number Ten now that she had stopped drinking. He tried not to worry about potential snares of his own setting.

Despite well-founded fears to the contrary he managed to retain his seat in April 1992 as the Tories, backed by the tabloids and aided by a ditheringly led feeble opposition, entered their fourth consecutive term of office.

Like a clever parasite or a bug up in symbiosis, Robin had succeeded in transferring himself from old to new leader without detriment to his integrity. The Prime Minister who had sponsored his rise was now promoting her memoirs from the sidelines; her replacement had yet to prove himself and Robin was there should he falter.

November 1992

Windsor Castle was burning. The Queen, so dutiful and so badly disappointed, stood helpless, a forlorn figure watching as treasures frizzled and stately apartments dissolved in flames, impotent while her family props perished. The vulnerability of a monarch in a mackintosh was touching, wrong, like specs worn with the crown, and royal weddings dwindling into vulgar theatre signifying nothing beyond mass entertainment. The legend and mystery turned tawdry. In the end jewels are mere mucked-up minerals.

'Lady Brand, I wonder if you would give me an interview. I am trying to make my way as a freelance journalist and I'm doing a bit on the homes of cabinet ministers.'

Normally Ocean Bray was a rude little person. Charlotte had met her once or twice since she had grown up and into a sharp young woman. She even suspected her of having replaced Clemency in Robin's affections and almost certainly in his bed.

'Aren't you working in the Commons?'

'Yes of course,' she answered briskly. 'I am only doing a bit of journalism on the side, I'm just a beginner. Please will you see me? It would mean such a lot.'

'When do you want to come, Ocean?' Charlotte asked, fishing her diary out of her dump of a bag.

'I'm calling from the car, I'm in Godleham now. See you in a couple of minutes, OK?'

Of course it wasn't OK but the line had gone dead. There was no point in hiding; nothing else was pressing. Grudgingly she turned off the television and waited. Ocean was not to have the satisfaction of knowing Charlotte was flustered. She would give the interview as she was, shoddy and un-preened.

Ocean was neat, dark, as malevolent as a magpie and just as beautiful. There had been no time to ring Robin about the interview; anyway Charlotte had a feeling that today he was finding facts in Hull. Something was awry in the world of fish. Robin was on an environmental and agricultural rung in November 1992.

'What do you want to see, Ocean? I can give you a tour of the house. It is not at all exciting, neither castle nor hovel, there are no secret passages, ghosts or sauna suites to grip your readers.'

Ocean came straight to the point. 'How much does your husband's career mean to you?'

'It means a lot to him. Robin has ambitions.'

'Do you want him to succeed?'

'Of course. Ocean, tell me what exactly is all this about?'

'How much is his job worth, Lady Brand?'

'Enough, I imagine. I am sure you can find out how much he is paid. Look it up, I don't know. I've never asked.'

'So you wouldn't mind if he was suddenly forced to "spend more time with his family," as the saying goes?'

'No, but he would.'

'Do you share the same bedroom?'

'What has that got to do with anything?'

'Can you fulfil your husband's needs?'

'We are comfortably off, if that is what you mean,' Charlotte answered.

'Can you satisfy his appetites?' Ocean asked with a sickeningly sweet smile.

Equally innocently Charlotte answered, 'Well, I must admit he has always been what is known as a good doer. Never a dirty plate left in this house. Lucky fellow, he eats like a horse and never puts on an ounce.' This was not strictly true; of late Robin had undoubtedly got a touch of flab about the middle. Recently his jawline had blurred as his chin had become less acute in its jutting.

'That is not what I meant, Lady Brand.'

'I didn't think it was, Ocean. You had better call me Charlotte, I am sure you don't call my husband Sir Robin.'

'You see, I am writing a book.'

'Clever you. Is this another new line like the journalism? What kind of book?'

'That depends.'

'On what?'

'On how much I get paid. I could write a novel, if it was worth my while, or I could write a true and factual account. It is really up to you.'

'Well Ocean, I suggest you do exactly as you like. Now please go, I have nothing to tell you that you cannot hear tonight at the meeting of Godleham Ladies Guild. I am giving them a talk about my alcoholism. My life, you see, is public property.'

'I will ask you once again: how much does your husband's job mean to you?'

'You know perfectly well what it means to him. Now please go.' Charlotte took Ocean's elbow and led her firmly to the door and out on to the step.

'I've left my briefcase behind,' said Ocean, wriggling free.

'Wait there, I'll get it.' Charlotte put the chain on the door. 'Excuse me,' she said through the crack, 'the dog, you know. One has to be careful.'

The case was on the sofa pointing towards where Charlotte had been sitting. It wasn't locked and the tape was running.

'Here it is, Ocean,' said Charlotte as she unchained the door. 'Oh dear, butterfingers! I still get the shakes . . . never mind, I am sure no harm will have come to your papers.' The case had opened as it tumbled down the steps, scattering its contents. The recorder, Charlotte saw with delight, had landed in a puddle.

★

Charlotte met Robin in the House. He couldn't dine with her but had a moment spare, before some official function, to give her a drink in the Pugin Bar. Later she and Peta were going to *Porgy and Bess*.

A plateload of canapés accompanied the mineral water that both Brands were drinking. Robin had to keep the clearest of heads while so many items in his life needed to be juggled.

'I have arranged for you to employ a researcher, Charlotte.'

'Whatever do I need a researcher for, Robin?'

'For your book, the one on prime ministerial wives.'

'Oh that. Don't be crazy. I don't want anyone helping me. Doing my own research is the best bit.'

'You are to have a researcher, Charlotte, it is all fixed. Please arrange to have Ocean Bray paid on a monthly basis. I will give you a note of the figures.'

'No, Robin, I will not connive with blackmail. She tried that trick on me and I sent her packing.'

'I know, and made her very angry.'

'The woman scorned, Robin, there is nothing new in that, you should know. Does she know everything?'

'No, Charlotte. Only I know everything.'

'Well then, what is there to fuss about? I have supported you in every way and helped where I can but I will not pay to keep your tarts quiet about activities I prefer to know nothing about.'

'Not so loud, you fool.' Robin smiled at her benignly, patting her hand for colleagues to see. 'If I fall, I am taking you with me. Remember that.'

'I will, Robin. Sometimes I feel that being jumped on by lesbians in Holloway or playing Scrabble with Myra Hindley in Cookham Wood would be preferable to living with this awful guilt.'

'You aren't going to confess or anything stupid, are you? Think of me, think of the children.'

'I do, Robin, all the time. Now I must go. I won't tell but I won't pay. You must use your money to fix little Ocean up with a flat, a car and a salary so she can make her name as a novelist rather than ruin yours by being a biographer. That is your affair.'

Charlotte gave Robin a most affectionate goodbye kiss and

blew another to Roddy MacPhail, who was entertaining some turgid constituents to sweet sherry in a murky corner.

She almost collided with Jake Cleaver in the corridor.

'Hello Charlotte. You seem to be in a hurry.'

'I am, Jake, I've got tickets for *Porgy and Bess*, I must rush.'

'Lucky you. It's brilliant.'

'You've seen it?'

'Yes, at Glyndebourne.'

'How heavenly.'

Jake's beard was peppered grey, a great improvement. 'I suppose you are going to say I have turned into a Bollinger Bolshevik.'

'If I can't be original, I'd rather stay quiet.'

'Things are more original when run by women.'

'What, like Catherine de Medici or that rotten princess in *Turandot*?'

'Life isn't dull with women in charge.'

'But we are, Jake, we are, only sometimes we keep quiet about it.'

October 1994

Curiosity was a compulsive thing. Charlotte had always wanted to climb up ridges to see beyond and hated to turn back before corners. Sometimes she walked for miles just in case the next view was better or she would find fairyland. Closed cupboards could be full of joys. With age she had learnt much and expected little but still she reproached herself for not going the extra distance just in case that made the difference. Having got to Links Cottage it would be silly not to have a look round. Of course, if the door were locked then she would have to be content with peeping through windows.

It was stiff, swollen and warped but not locked, at least not securely. One heave of her shoulder and the door swung in suddenly, hurtling her over the threshold into the cottage's main room. Having neither hall nor vestibule had kept the place forever chilled as the central light swung in the draught making shadows on the ceiling. Charlotte recognised the parchment lampshade and its charred mark where once it had been burnt by an over-powerful bulb.

The smell of damp and cold was bad, worse now even than it had been in February 1974 when Robin had his first election victory. The olive green and maroon rag rug had faded to uniform brown; its tufts now resembled massed scraps of filthy stockings. The grate surrounded by yellow glazed tiles contained hundreds of butt ends and no fuel apart from crisp and cigarette packets. Charlotte tried a switch. Nothing happened; by the fading sunshine she could see amongst the piles of mailshots that a hostile electricity board had wearied of waiting for its bill to be paid and cut off the juice. The telephone was dead too. She tried a tap in the kitchen: it spluttered out a gill of rusty water then panted dry air. A busty lady much trussed in black leather and evidently having a wonderful time smirking coyly draped over a wheelbarrow must have been a favourite with the former occupant who had kept his calendar for ever at May 1982. Charlotte thought the model's antics highly unlikely, having never extracted either fun or gratification from any wheelbarrow. Time at Links Cottage was stuck at the month of the *Belgrano*'s sinking. The damp stain the landlord had once attempted to disguise with a coat of emulsion was concealed by a ragged poster of a knicker-free tennis player polishing a ball on her bottom. Somehow she didn't seem entirely wholesome, not quite the sort to delight John Betjeman.

Charlotte remembered losing her sheepskin coat and wondered if she could have left it behind in the flurry of moving to more congenial accommodation. The coat had been badly cured and stank too strongly to be hung in any wardrobe, so she had kept it in the cupboard beneath the stairs along with the firelighters and the coalite. The chances of it being there were remote: twenty-odd years had passed but she had always felt guilty about losing Robin's present, even if wearing it had been a test of endurance and effective defence against molestation. No coat dangled there. Just as well, she thought, for it was bound to have festered repulsively before disintegrating. A bag hung from the hook instead. Embroidered with lazy daisies and the word 'Pegs', it was the sort of thing to get snapped up at sales of work and given to relatives. The pegs it contained were not for drying clothes. Two flat half-bottles of Scotch nestled in the canvas hideaway. They were the right shape for carrying in pockets: one for offering and one to conceal. Charlotte understood the mind of the squirrel. She assumed, because of Miss May 1982, that the former occupant had been male, though secret drinkers come in all sexes. She shut the cupboard door and went upstairs.

Only the two bedrooms, one no more than a damp-ceilinged cubbyhole, were up there. It had always been a test of nerve and endurance braving the chilling stairs to visit the bathroom during the night. Charlotte remembered lying in bed half awake and very uncomfortable, not wishing to move but knowing she must, and falling asleep to dream she had made the dreaded journey only to wake with a shudder and find that she still had to get out of the cosiness and creep down to the icy bathroom to utilise Shank's vitreous china then crank the clanking, unwilling chain that made the building gurgle.

The same bed with the same plastic-padded bedhead embossed with fleur-de-lys stood there and the hideous candlewick bedspread carelessly thrown over the scratchy cream blankets left folded upon the grubby ticking of the mattress was also familiar. She lay upon the bed and looked up at the reflected shadows of sunset.

Even a pleated nylon lampshade looks better when viewed from a new angle. Charlotte would imagine herself a ballerina dancing on the ceiling's bare expanse beneath the inverted central pendant. She could remove herself from the urgent pounding that was happening on the bed below and dance with grace and ecstasy far removed from Robin's anxious attentions.

'Relax!' he would shout. She could hear him still, she could even recall her own moans and groans of fake rapture. 'There now, that should do the trick!' Robin had a way of making their coupling sound like dentistry. Once done, they would sleep, cuddled for warmth and reassurance but not for love.

Charlotte slept now.

For an instant she couldn't remember where she was. It was dark outside and a wan moon was shining reticently through travelling clouds. The beat of rain against the pane had awoken her from a dream of improbable peace. It might be a wild night, she must get away quickly, this was no place to be alone – the old dreads returned with every rattle of the window-frame.

She groped her way to the stair head and felt the wooden rail as she probed the darkness with her foot, searching for the top step. A sudden moonbeam through the skylight lit the stairs. A figure was standing at the bottom.

'Who are you?'

No answer.

Charlotte asked again and still received no reply. The moon was once more covered by clouds and everything went dark.

There was no option – she must run for it, raise the alarm, make a noise, shriek, scream and hope that someone might hear. No one but a pervert or an unquiet spirit would be within earshot.

This might be her end.

She rushed headlong down the stairs, missed her footing, stumbled, tumbling to the bottom and colliding with the coat-stand she had mistaken for an intruder. She attempted to break her fall with her arm before the solid stand toppled over, bruising her temple with a brass hook as it collapsed.

She was pinioned beneath the coat-stand and could feel an egg throbbing above her right eye while the agony of the broken wrist seared through her like a hot knife. After recovering consciousness she managed to extricate herself and stagger to the hearthrug where she lay writhing with pain and terrified misery.

The terrors increased as the pain numbed. There was no question of leaving the cottage now before light, not in this state. The Devil would be coming for her shortly, there was little to do but wait. In her befuddled state Charlotte was convinced that she was about to die. Death would cheat her of a chance to confess, she would go to Hell unshriven. She wished the end would hurry: all eternity could not be quite as bad as this.

After an hour she began to feel foolish; people didn't just die of broken wrists and glancing blows to the head. She was hardly bleeding at all, she was a rational being, foolish certainly but capable, just, of reason. Daylight would come. It always did, even to the condemned. Outrages and hostilities were happening the world over, people were being tortured, terrified, maltreated, abused and murdered while she waited under shelter, neither starving nor mortally wounded, indulging in self-pity, bloody petrified of something that might not exist.

She could sing. No song came, not even a hymn. A carol perhaps? 'Silent night, Holy night.' It sounded ridiculous. Last year when the Glee group had performed *Ruddigore* she had tried a chorus or two of the 'Ghosts' High Noon'. Not a happy choice. She sang of bad baronets and false fiddles, but all she could really remember was the patter song that ended with 'I'm going to die tomorrow, so it really doesn't matter.'

Well it didn't matter. She was finished in every way and meant little to anyone. No one would miss her, she was good for nothing. How many, she wondered, would turn out to bury her? Not a lot. Perhaps she should make her peace with God. He had an all-hearing ear as well as an all-seeing eye focused on his fickle flock. 'I have left undone those things I ought to have done, I have done those things I ought not to have done.' 'Oh Christ!' she exclaimed out loud and clenched her fists in anguish, crying out as the pain in her wrist was triggered. She had forgotten to leave money for the piano tuner, who was due to call on Thursday. The plants in the conservatory would be dead by now, more dog food was needed, the washing-up liquid was low. I have indeed left much undone, she thought.

Last cigarettes, hearty breakfasts and final requests were given to convicted prisoners. If she were for the drop she would ask for a drink. What's the point of self-denial if there was shortly to be no self left to deny? Once again she told herself that she was not dying, the dark watches would melt into daylight. She must wrap herself in the filthy rug and wait while the world revolved. But she did want a drink. More than anything she needed that whisky. She could face everything, even eternal damnation, with a warming slug of blessed spirits inside. She mustn't. She had promised Piers she would never drink again, not after that accident. She had kept her word, it had been hard. But this was the end. Even if she survived the night, tomorrow the world would know she was the inebriated bitch who had forced Martin Fable into limbo and arrested his brilliant life by driving down a defunct quarry when drunk.

Charlotte's mind was made up: she would have that whisky, she would drink the lot. No one should be denied anaesthetic. Jesus had refused to be drugged with gall, but then He was God. Everything had gone quiet. No rattling frames or beating rain disturbed the absolute silence and total calm of the night in which the moon now beamed clearly upon a transfixed landscape. The shuffle of her feet as she tried to get upright sounded loud, like a weight tugged over concrete.

The figure outside the window was outlined clearly. This time there was no mistake. This time her scream was heard.

20

October 1994

PHIL FLEET GRAPPLED with the dilemma for a while. He was not sure what he should do. Was it his business to inform the police? Was it their business to pursue runaway wives? Had the woman lurking behind Patel's island unit really been the missing Lady Brand? How was he going to live down his imprudent purchase of strawberry-flavoured condoms? Oh my, such worries, he normally only got this flustered at election time. He took an aspirin, drank some tea and tossed a coin. Heads it was, and heads meant he must act as sneak. He rang Cedar Lodge and spoke to Piers.

Robin was at home, busy formulating his own rescue and reinstatement. He craved support.

'Where are you going, Piers?'

'Out, just out,' Piers answered. So saying he ran off to Winifred, borrowed money, ordered a cab and flew north on the next shuttle. Robin did not actually miss him till teatime.

Phil adored Inspectors Morse and Taggart, relishing vicarious excitement through these screen heroes. Playing real detective was a great thrill. Piers was anguished by the old agent's meanderingly slow driving, but appreciated his local knowledge as Phil directed his ponderous duo-tone Morris Traveller down short-cuts like a cumbersome tin badger. Fleet by name but not by nature. Phil found Piers too grimy as his sergeant and too squalid to be an MP's son, albeit one who seemed to spend much time bringing disgrace on the party, and who had been required to relinquish his cabinet post once his corruptions and sexual excesses had been revealed by disgruntled females with doubtful morals.

Was it his place, he wondered, to warn Piers that smoking could damage his health? How difficult it was to know where one's duty lay with the young. In the end he decided to stay quiet but to indicate his disapproval by keeping the car windows ostentatiously open and wafting his hands about if Piers puffed in his direction.

'Her Ladyship is not at home,' Prime told Phil and Piers when they called at Auchenkirk. He was a blueprint for discretion, letting on nil without actually lying.

'Has Lady Brand been here at all, Mr Prime?'

Prime, whose personal idol was television's arch-villain Francis Urquhart, announced that Mr Fleet might think what he liked but he himself couldn't possibly comment.

'Your integrity does you credit, Mr Prime.'

'Thank you, Mr Fleet.'

'Is Lady Begg at home, Mr Prime?'

'Her Ladyship is not here at present, Mr Fleet.'

'Which ladyship would that be?'

'Neither, Mr Fleet.'

'Thank you, Mr Prime. I am much obliged.'

'A pleasure, Mr Fleet.'

Prime had looked on Piers with suspicion despite being told his name and that he was Lady Begg's godson. However, he did say that if he and Mr Fleet wished to call again tomorrow forenoon then his godmother might easily be at home and prepared to meet him. On other matters he was in no position to speculate: he had been told nothing and could therefore say nothing.

By four-thirty both Piers and Phil were heartily fed up with each other and had got nowhere by trawling about searching for Piers's car which, like so many student vehicles, was small, dirty, bashed and adorned with several generations of sticker. They had visited Sandhill and looked out across the firths of Forth and Tay then had a quick and very late lunch in the Victoria Café where they both felt excluded and awkward amongst the students. It was hopeless, and Phil was getting agitated at the prospect of having to ask Piers to sleep the night in his immaculate house where only his widowed sister had ever been a guest before. Such gossip would circulate – young men, strawberry condoms, how would it end? He could foresee himself forced to retire elsewhere under an assumed name. If only people kept themselves celibate and apart, most of the world's tough problems would evaporate. Phil Fleet believed life would be much improved by widespread sterilisation and bromide in the water supply.

Coral had several friends at the university but Piers knew none well enough to beg a place on their floor. Besides, he always became tongue-tied and gauche in the company of self-confident intellect.

At the edge of the town was a dreary, dire guesthouse with reasonable rates and wholly understandable vacancies. Despite Phil's polite but half-hearted protestations Piers elected to stay the night at Green Villa, if only to have a rest from his companion's obsequious caution until the next morning when they could return to Auchenkirk. Miss Moncrief did breakfasts; she did not do teas, high or low, and certainly did not encourage lingerers, though her guests could pay to watch her television till the end of *News at Ten* and have the use of the kettle for a modest charge.

It was an hour before sunset. Piers decided to take a walk. He would walk until he was tired and then go to some anonymous pub, unpopular with students, till it was time for bed. Miss Moncrief gave out keys on receipt of a deposit.

He walked head down into the icy wind. Salty foam flecks flew off the breakers queuing up to die upon the soaking sand beyond the ridge of stranded bladderwrack. Donkeys, kiosks and holidaymakers were all gone home, stowed for the winter; only a few returning golfers passed by. Piers didn't walk for pleasure, he did it to fill in time. The harsh weather kept his mind from gloom. He walked, as he lived, without a purpose. The journey back would be accomplished in a trice, unless the wind changed.

After fifty minutes of tramping he reached Marion Begg's shelter at the road end.

He recognised his car at once. Instinctively, without reading the number, he knew it was his. Joy gave way to dread. Piers only prayed in desperate times; he prayed now. He implored that no hose would be connected to the exhaust; he begged that his mother's corpse was not inside. His prayer was answered: the car was empty except for a grip, a couple of newspapers and a half-finished bar of chocolate. It was locked and the keys weren't there. Nor was there a note: it looked as if the driver would be returning any minute. Surely, he told himself, anyone wishing to walk to death in the sea wouldn't bother to lock the car or take the keys. He reassured himself with the thought that it would take ages to get deep enough to drown; frostbite might strike before a suicide waded to a covering depth. It was a pity about the locks, he could be doing with the chocolate and the car looked far more comfortable as a place to wait than the hard draughty seats of the shelter. Still, his mother would surely not be long: the sun was well away and a watery moon was dodging behind the rainy clouds.

An hour passed, there was no sign of Charlotte. Reluctantly Piers knew he must contact the police. He must. The time for amateur pursuit was over. The shore looked menacing and smelt of marine mortality. Then it began to rain. Behind him the lights of the town shone sparsely through the thick mistiness. Ahead of him there was a track of recent wheel marks. Once the rain stopped he would see if the ruts led to a cottage with a telephone to borrow.

A while later the storm was over, the shore became quiet, still and icy, the moon shone upon silent hostility. Piers had no idea of the time. His watch, like the shelter's clock, had stopped. He had been too idle to get a new battery: there was little point in knowing the time without any vital appointments to keep. He knew anyway that it must be getting really late.

The track was easy to follow and soon he found the silhouette of a whitish cottage looming up some fifty yards beyond where he stood. He thought he saw a light inside and there were certainly wires leading to the building; it would be worth a try, he hadn't much to lose.

He stood outside, undecided. The place was empty after all.

He recognised the scream. He had heard it before, eight years ago.

Charlotte heard the words. The same words, but shouted in the deep voice of a grown man.

'Mum! Mum! It's me!'

'Piers, darling. Is it really you? Oh thank God.'

'Of course it is me. Oh Mum, you said you weren't going to do anything stupid.'

'I haven't, darling. I promise you I haven't.'

'I knew it. Even when he was a sick babe I could tell that my godson was a good thing.'

Florence Begg, early back from Ireland and showing no signs of fatigue, had been at Charlotte's bedside when she came round from having her wrist set in the same hospital where nineteen years ago she had given birth to the twins. This time she could be discharged just as soon as the anaesthetic wore off. Florence insisted on having both Charlotte and Piers to stay at Auchenkirk.

The doctor who had stood proxy at Pier's hasty baptism was no longer there; she had become a specialist in Edinburgh but the sister on the maternity ward kindly said she remembered the drama of his earliest days and was proud now to be associated with his brief celebrity. The press was making much of the story, much more than Charlotte thought necessary though she was profoundly grateful and quite astonished by her son's initiative in finding her.

Robin sounded quite curt on the telephone. His voice betrayed his feelings; his words belied his tone.

'Oh my love, I am so relieved that you are all right. I have been worried to death about you. Come home quickly, I need you, we must have a talk.'

"You aren't alone, I can tell.'

Charlotte heard a whispered conversation at the other end and then the sound of a door being shut.

'That was William, my researcher. He has gone now.'

'A man! That should make a change. Anyway he has heard you speaking the correct lines. What do you really want to say, Robin?'

'Please Charlotte. Don't be like that. Just come home. Like I say, we need to talk this through. You do realise I knew nothing of Clemency's child up until now.'

'His name is Merlin, I believe. Are you saying you never knew Ocean Bray either?'

'That book is fiction.'

'Founded on fact.'

'Most things are. Now, please come home.'

'All right, but not until I have talked to Florence.'

'About what?'

'Me, my troubles, my conscience and what is to be done.'

Robin's voice became hard and furiously agitated.

'Don't even think about it. Don't you dare start unburdening yourself to Florence.'

'I must tell someone, I can bear it no longer.'

'Go and find a priest if you must. Don't inflict Florence – '

'She is very understanding.'

'And very honest. Can't you see what knowing your secret would do to her? It would wreck her, she does not deserve to be troubled like that. You would palm off your guilt on to her and she wouldn't know what to do.'

'I don't know what to do.'

'Do nothing, do you understand. Nothing. Be at home tomorrow afternoon. Make sure you look clean and cheerful, or I will be forced to say you are mad.'

'I think I am.'

'Will you be there?'

'Yes, if Piers can get his car to survive the journey.'

'It will, it must. Now go and get Florence, I want to speak to her.'

'Why?'

'Do what you are told. If I don't speak to her now I will go on ringing till I do.'

Charlotte was sitting on the windowseat next to Tam's chair when Florence returned. Piers was having a bath, which Prime had most pointedly drawn for him before confiscating the baseball boots and attacking them with pre-war Blanco. Tam hovered between being awake and asleep, possibly between life and death; either way he was calm and appeared happy and relieved to have Florence home again. Quite a crowd of ducks had settled on the loch; a coot speedboated past them trailing a rippling wake.

'It appears, Charlotte dear, that your husband thinks you are mad and suffering from delusions. He mentioned your age, the swine.'

'What did you say to him, Florence?'

'I said of course you were mad. No one but a madwoman would have put up with him all these years.'

Charlotte smiled. Florence was right as usual.

'I also gave him a piece of my mind,' Florence added. 'I told him I had read that ridiculous penny dreadful written by that floozie with the foolish name.'

'I'm told it is meant to be fiction,' Charlotte replied. 'Though Ocean Bray is her real name. She was a horrid child.'

'And an even more horrid adult, with a vile mind and rotten grammar. Don't read it Charlotte, it is junk.'

'The steamy parts are said to be accurate, only the names have been changed, slightly.'

'If that is what people get up to now, I'm glad I'm old. So blush-making, so terribly silly and so jolly uncomfortable but what is worse, nobody seems to even like anyone any more. It is all sex, not romantic heavenly loving stuff, the kind of thing that used to make me blub in the cinema, just self-indulgent smut and greed. I wouldn't give you tuppence for all those silly antics. That sort of thing went on amongst the unfortunate in special establishments when we were young, not all over the shop as written by Miss Bray. We had wars to worry us and give us a real sense of danger, and sports to blot up our aggression; the rest of the time we got on with making do and doing our bit, not having a bit and making asses of ourselves.'

'I am going back to him Florence, tomorrow.'

'Are you not going to tell me why you came to see me?'

'No, Florence, I'm not.'

The last of Scotland: 'Haste Ye Back' the kindly motorway notice read as Piers drove into England, carrying his mother home. They should get there by five, all being well, having made an early start. Florence, in mothy dressing gown and sheepskin mules, had waved them off. Prime did not start work till eight these days so he was not about to be affronted by Lady Begg's deshabille.

They had late breakfast at the service station outside Carlisle. Piers insisted that they both wore dark glasses and that Charlotte kept her plastered arm concealed beneath her serape. It was a dull day.

'We look like a couple of gangsters, darling.'

'Shut up, Mother. Have you seen the paper-stand? Your face is all over everywhere.'

The child Merlin was greatly featured too. How, in this day and age, columnists demanded, did an intelligent man like former Minister for Youth Sir Robin Brand, expect the nation to believe he knew nothing of his long-term mistress's baby? How could such a man expect others to support their children when he ignored his responsibilities? An outraged nation clamoured for the truth. Once more photographs of Merlin and Piers at the same age were juxtaposed. This time both boys were stripped for swimming; almost identical vertical scars were highlighted on their abdomens. An eminent doctor had outlined some features of pyloric stenosis and its congenital characteristics.

'Poor kid,' said Piers. 'Fancy wanting to have Dad as his father.'

'Oh Piers, it isn't all Dad's fault. I don't want you to take sides.'

'Mother, get a life! Coral and I took your side years ago.'

'Not Coral surely?'

'Honestly, you are a nerd, Mum.'

'Am I? Oh look at that view!' The had breasted Shap summit and were descending between the mighty Cumbrian hills into the lesser lumps of Lancashire. The westward landscape undulated towards the distant Lake District, an ancient countryside to illustrate a story book.

'Don't change the subject, Mother. Neither of us can stand Dad.'

'Are you sure?'

'Yes. Ask Coral if you don't believe me.'

'I thought she adored him.'

'You never listened, did you? Coral has gone off to get away from him, not to get away from you.'

'I thought she was just being grown up. I never thought she

was trying to get away from either of us. Why, what has he done?'

'What do you think?'

'I don't know, you tell me.'

'No. Ask Coral, ask any of her friends, the pretty ones. Ask his three little nieces. Dad is a fumbler, a dirty old man if you like, he chases every girl he sees.'

Charlotte hadn't wanted to know this. Children had appalling things to face these days: hitherto taboos were rampant everywhere, small wonder their imaginations got lurid. When they were small the twins would become ecstatic at the sight of Lancaster's 'pimple'; likewise Leyland, Charnock Richard, the long viaduct and that magic sign – Birmingham 100 miles. Each landmark passed meant another sweet to suck. Now the prizes were cigarettes. Piers was running out of them and petrol. They would need to stop soon.

The restaurant was quite empty. They lunched off pie and chips which Piers had to cut up for Charlotte so she could eat it with a fork in her good hand.

'It must be awful to have other people doing everything for you all the time,' said Piers. 'Like Uncle Wally.'

Charlotte felt the familiar grip of guilt take a stranglehold. Yes, she agreed, it must be utterly terrible.

'Mum?'

'Yes, Piers?'

'You do know that Uncle Wally wasn't driving when you all had that accident?'

'Yes, I do,' she replied quietly. 'Who told you?'

'Nobody, I saw it. I was there. I had run away from the Potters and was trying to get home when your car came round the corner. Afterwards, when it was over I went to Granny. She found me on her doorstep the next morning.'

'Oh God, how terrible for you. My poor child. Oh Christ, I'm so sorry. That makes it even worse. What made you keep quiet?'

'Fear, loyalty, all that sort of thing. I was scared.'

'Of course you were. Now perhaps you will understand why I wanted to go and talk to Lady Begg. I thought she might understand and be able to help me. I don't expect to be forgiven, ever, I just needed someone to talk to. Guilt is a dreadful thing, it never leaves you.'

'It wasn't your fault.'

'My darling it was. I was drunk, so drunk that I remember nothing except someone screaming, I think it was me, and another person shouting. I suppose that must have been you, I can hear it still, a child yelling for Mum.'

'That's right. I saw it all, though after the crash I was too frightened to make a sound. I even saw Dad set light to the wrecked car.'

'He did it all to protect me. Now can you understand?'

'Why was he protecting you?'

'Because I was drunk, I was a criminal, I would have probably gone to gaol. He risked his career by lying for me.'

Piers put down his fork and pushed his plate away. He looked at Charlotte, who hadn't touched a morsel of her food.

'Dad told no lies for you, Mum.'

'He did, Piers. He said that Uncle Wally was driving my car, not me.'

'But you weren't driving, you were sitting in the back. I saw you as you passed. Your face looked terrible, twisted and terrified, I will never forget it.'

'What are you telling me, Piers?'

'I'm telling you that neither you nor Uncle Wally drove that night. I promise. I swear you were sitting behind him on the passenger side.'

'Piers, what do you mean?'

'You know what I mean, Mother.'

'Oh my God, I do.'

21

THIS WAS MOMENTOUS, this was the beginning of a life that was not yet at an end. A reprieve or a waterproof, gilt-edged guarantee that heaven did exist and was indeed heavenly could not have given Charlotte more joy. Every cloud seemed to vanish, silver linings and bright sides were hereafter redundant. She was not guilty.

She thought about Robin and wondered how he could exist, knowing what he did. Sensitivity is relative, and the power to obliterate or deny must be one of his greatest skills, along with that of being able to conquer with charm and convince humanity of his integrity.

The last time she had seen him in action had been at a cocktail party at Number Ten. Strange to think all that was just a week ago, during the mopping-up period before the new session. The theme of the evening was 'Youth', Robin's province. Both Brands had been invited, which was appropriate now that research had disclosed the astounding fact that 'Youth' is best experienced with a brace of parents in tow. The survey that had discovered this had been quite costly; several nettled persons had muttered that its findings were far from novel and could have been had for free.

Charlotte had looked nice in her discreet frock; the Prime Minister's wife had also looked nice in hers. Clever, younger women were more competitively dressed and vied with each other to excel in all fields.

The Prime Minister was also very nice. Charlotte tried to picture that long upper lip enhanced with a luxurious moustache. Poor man, his face was a hundred years too late. His pleasant greyness contrasted delightfully with the pushy jostling and attention-seeking vivacity of his colleagues. Charlotte could see a bit of the Brutus in many, Robin especially. She wasn't the only one to detect the presence of conspirators.

Roddy MacPhail was there alone. 'Are you measuring the place for curtains, Charlotte?'

She laughed. 'No, not me.'

'Robin looks as if he is at home here already.'

'Nonsense, Roddy. What about you? Where is Henrietta?'

He was noncommittal about his wife, saying she was fine and promising to relay Charlotte's love to her. 'I am a born and bred backbencher. I will never get my bum nearer the front. In fact I'm thinking of packing it all in next election and returning home to farm.' He told Charlotte that Sandhill was on the market; he was going to make do with a flat in the constituency from now onwards. It all seemed very sad. Roddy and Henrietta had appeared to be the ideal couple. Perhaps they still were.

'You and Robin have done really well to stick together,' he said. 'It isn't easy.'

A waitress and a tray of canapés was approaching. Charlotte said to Roddy, 'Here, have one of these. Don't they look wonderful?' Smiling at the waitress she helped herself to something pink and fishy. 'Now I don't drink alcohol these bits and pieces matter lots.' Charlotte didn't dare say she was cured of alcoholism, because she knew that would never be true. The battle was waged daily, only victory was easier now than in the early days following the accident. She hadn't touched a drop for eight years, not even at Holy Communion. Christ's blood had been shed for her and for many but her sins would have to get remitted another way. A whiff of the stuff could trigger the addiction all over again.

Roddy finished his mouthful and said, 'At least it is nice to know that the cornets of smoked salmon have been filled by a blameless hand, and the olives stuffed only by the innocent. The bloody press got the rumour about the P.M. and the cook wrong, thank God. One seems to lurch from scandal to scandal these days. What next, one wonders – the Queen Mother as call-girl?'

Robin had floated, insinuated and manoeuvred himself

between the distinguished guests, all there because of their lofty posts associated with youth.

Charlotte was good at rescuing the floundering. She approached a man in a well-pressed suit who looked uncomfortable, and confided in him that the best thing about youth is that it does not endure. 'After all,' she said, 'you don't get many joy riders over fifty.' The well-pressed suit agreed but added that youth, like the poor, were always with us, which was just as well, seeing he was governor of a Young Offenders' Institution and did not want to be out of a job.

'My son needs a job,' she said.

'Everybody needs a job,' he replied, 'though it looks as if some young men will never have one, ever.'

'What we want is a good war,' said the well-pressed one's floral wife.

'Oh no,' said Charlotte, 'I couldn't bear that. I could never be one of those "Women of Britain" who say "Go"!'

'It's the only answer,' said the floral one. 'The world today is full of drones. If we were a hive the worker bees would rip off their wings and throw them out to die.'

'Do you have many sons?' Charlotte asked.

'No, we weren't able to have children.'

Charlotte wished she had kept quiet. She smiled at a jolly bishop, and introduced him to her new acquaintances. His Lordship had told her earlier that he had great plans for inner city workshop facilities for the young and unemployed of his diocese. He and the floral one should find much to talk about with their contrasting schemes for youth disposal.

The media representatives looked somewhat seedy and past it, dafter far than the audience for which they catered.

Charlotte's research into prime ministers' wives had stalled at Mrs Gladstone. She wondered whether she would ever get as far as the present incumbent, who approached her now.

'I loved your book,' Charlotte said. 'I too have become an opera enthusiast.'

'Do you sing yourself?'

'A bit.'

Singing had been a salvation for her and for Jake Cleaver. As one of the likeliest old lads of the Labour movement he was trusted and admired by politicians and pundits alike. Charlotte had been admitted to a London choir and had met Jake again in the spring of 1994 while rehearsing Britten's *War Requiem* which had been a giant production to mark D Day's fiftieth anniversary. None of her family or of his had come to the performance.

They had found somewhere anonymous off Queensway and revived themselves with portion-controlled, centrally devised platters as illustrated on the laminated menu. This cavernous satellite of a restaurant chain was quite without character; no one would recognise either the shadow minister or the minister's wife in such a hole.

Jake's job concerned Employment and he was a keen campaigner for the reform of the ailing Child Support Agency.

'You know, Charlotte, sometimes I feel I am the antithesis of a mistress. All responsibility and no power. I provided for the girls but had no say in their upbringing once Fenella left me.'

'Poor Jake. They loved you a lot, you know. Remember that time they ran away to find you? They often talked about you when Fenella and Elizabeth weren't around.'

'Did they?'

'Yes, Jake, they did. I wish I had told you. I'm sorry.'

'I would have liked that.'

'I understand they are all doing really well now, what with Pauline nursing and Anna's languages. Coral saw quite a lot of Julie at Oxford, they are good friends.'

'They're great girls, I just wish I had been able to watch them grow up. They are free to make their own way now.'

'You never thought of starting again. With a family, I mean, with someone new?'

'To be honest, Charlotte, I've never met anyone I felt I could ask to become a politician's wife, not an old politician like me.'

Charlotte replied: 'You'll need a wife if you are to make it to the top, Jake. That is my only vital role in life: being Robin's bit of essential kit.'

The car had skimmed Birmingham like a bird over troubled sea and made good time past Banbury and Bicester.

'Mother.'

'Yes, Piers?'

'Stop singing.'

'Sorry.'

Charlotte could sympathise; singing parents are ghastly. She recalled the excruciating time when Winifred had sung 'Camptown Races' at the village concert with her face covered in cocoa. Charlotte must have been about twelve, she thought she would never recover from that horror. She had, but the memory was still distressing.

'Mother.'

'Yes, darling. I won't sing again, I promise.'

'Do you mind if I say something a bit sort of personal?'

'No, of course not.'

Charlotte braced herself for further truths, though now she felt there was little left to surprise her and nothing that could hurt.

'You look rough.'

She did, very. Something salvaged from the *Hesperus*, or a scrofulous scapegoat would have been better kempt.

'You are right. I'm not going home like this, take me to Granny's flat first.'

'OK, but we'll be late.'

'Yes. So we will.'

'Mother, there is another thing.'

'What, more?'

'Yes. I want to get educated. I want to go to university.'

'Why this sudden conversion? Why now? Of course you can if you can get the right grades, I just thought you despised all that sort of stuff.'

'I'm fed up with being called a stupid bastard. I want to be a clever bastard. Another clever bastard like Coral and that little bastard Merlin.'

'You aren't stupid, Piers.'

'Yes I am, but I can do something about that.'

'I'm delighted.'

'I'll always be a bastard though, won't I?'

Charlotte didn't answer. They were making swift progress and were already climbing through the sliced hillside near High

Wycombe. Godleham would be reached well before five. There would be time to put on a brave face and make a good show. Piers took her silence for assent, and continued: 'I don't mind, I like being a bastard.'

'Poor Coral,' said Charlotte.

'Coral won't care. Her only hassle now will be knowing she is a legitimate target.'

It seemed better to let that subject drop. There were other things to plan and new facts were cluttering Charlotte's thoughts.

Having raided her mother's wardrobe and make-up (Winifred had never dressed her age) Charlotte then got Piers to drive her to Immaculata, who concentrated all her talents on transforming her best client from tramp to lady. Charlotte looked good even with her plastered arm strapped up inside Winifred's most huge, red and extravagant cashmere sweater. Charlotte could choose to be Red Riding Hood, Scarlet Woman, Whore of Babylon or Mary Stuart at the block.

'You are late,' said Robin. 'I want to brief you before we meet the press. Are you listening?'

'Of course.'

Zoe the dog's character had not been improved by her stay with Winifred. She squatted on the doormat and re-established territorial rights at her earliest convenience.

'Firstly and most importantly, you are to say nothing. Just smile, hold my hand and agree with everything I say. Have you got that?' Robin said. He had a checklist and was ticking items off as he spoke. Perhaps, as a result of popular demand, Central Office provided a kit with guidelines for the proper conduct of these events.

Charlotte nodded.

'Secondly I want Piers to stand with us, he can have that dog on its lead. I want to present a united happy family.'

'Where is Coral?' Charlotte asked. 'I thought you said you had sent her the fare and told her to come over.'

'Leave Coral out of this, she is being ridiculous.'

'Why?'

'She sent a stupid fax this morning. It doesn't matter.'

'Can I see it? She is my daughter.'

'Not now, you silly woman. You have caused enough trouble. Go and change that sweater, it isn't suitable.'

Charlotte recalled all the forgiving family scenes she had watched being staged for the press. The docile and supportive wife always seemed to choose a stygian Greek widow's outfit and worthy woolly to accompany her vital grin, a vital rictus grin if that wasn't a contradiction in terms. She had no intention of changing; anyway it was too late, the front garden was filled with cameras and reporters. Robin opened the door and ushered Charlotte out upon the steps followed by Piers with Zoe snarling stupidly at everyone.

'Lady Brand, How are you?'

'She's fine,' Robin answered. 'Just a little tired.'

'Lady Brand, what are you going to do now?' one of the reporters persisted as cameras flashed and whirred.

The excitement was too much for Zoe, who flung herself down the steps dragging Piers behind her. Boy and dog disappeared into the crowd, abandoning their supporting roles.

'We are just going to get on with living our family life,' Robin replied.

'Lady Brand, have you anything to say about your husband's son by Clemency van Schumacher?'

'His alleged son, don't you mean?' Charlotte replied.

Robin's grip tightened on her good hand and he whispered, 'I thought I told you to keep quiet.'

'Did you? Sorry, I forgot,' she replied quite loudly.

'What have you to say about his alleged son, then?'

'I think he looks a charming boy,' Charlotte replied. 'And if Ms van Schumacher is in need of money, she only has to ask, I would be delighted to help her. I should hate to think that the little boy did not enjoy the advantages of my two children.'

'Shut up, you bitch,' Robin hissed, and then in a louder voice said, 'My wife has not been well, that is why she went away for a rest. She is overwrought.'

'Lady Brand, are you still feeling ill?'

'Apart from the broken arm I have never felt better in my entire life,' Charlotte replied.

'Where did you go and why?'

'I went to Scotland to visit friends and I have come home now because the piano tuner is calling tomorrow and needs to be paid on the spot.' Charlotte smiled beatifically at the assembly, perfectly composed and in charge.

'Lady Brand. Are you going to stand by your husband?'

'Of course,' said Robin. 'You know she will. She is a wonderful wife and mother.'

'Can we have that from you, Lady Brand?'

'No you can't I'm afraid,' Charlotte replied.

There was a buzz of incomprehension. 'Lady Brand, are you prepared to forgive Sir Robin?'

'Possibly not,' said Charlotte.

'What are you saying?' Robin tried to keep his rage suppressed as he talked to her through clenched teeth. His sweaty hand was holding hers so tightly that she feared for the circulation. She shook it free.

'Can you tell us anything more?'

'Only that I am starting divorce proceedings directly and my husband will be moving out of this house tonight. As you can see, he is still quite healthy and attractive. I'm sure he will find someone of my daughter's age to keep him.'

'And you, Lady Brand. What will you do?'

'Live happily ever after, I expect. Good evening.'

She turned and gave the press a cheerful wave before going inside, bolting the front door and leaving Robin to parry the questions all alone, locked out on the doorstep.

Spring 1995

'Isn't it awful? He is no better than that bad vicar who joined a freak show and sat in a barrel.'

'Oh, I don't know,' Charlotte replied. 'I gather he has quite a fan club. Those greying wings of hair and sincere, injured eyes make putty of Mrs Middle Class. The hero wounded by his own charisma, the victim of passion cheers up droves of bored menopausal housewives.'

'Like us?' Peta enquired.

'No, Peta, not us. I'm not bored, you will never be meno-pausal and we have both quit housewifery.'

Charlotte was sitting in Peta's flat watching Robin on daytime television. He was host on an inferior chat show called *Brand Tub*. He interviewed nonentities and questioned the aggrieved between bouts of anodyne music and silly games in front of a bussed-in studio audience.

'Do you mind seeing him like this?'

'Not in the least,' Charlotte replied. 'In fact the more I see the more delighted I am to be rid of him. Unlike the other one.'

'You mean Martin.'

'Yes, watching him was both joy and agony. I used to torment myself and pretend he could see me, but he couldn't. Anyway I was generally drunk.'

Charlotte was being taken to a concert later. Peta had a different evening planned.

'How is the work going?'

'Brilliantly,' Charlotte replied. 'I got masses done in the London Library this morning and I think I may have got a publisher interested. Put one up for me, won't you.'

'Of course. How far have you got? Still on that poor Lloyd George woman?'

'No I'm way past her, in fact I am about to start on the blessed Mary Wilson. The book is on prime ministers' wives, I can't quite make up my mind what to do about Denis.'

'You can't leave him out, he will have to be an honorary wife.'

'That will make the book even longer. Still I've got time, it has only taken me twenty-five years so far!'

'Is it going to end with you?'

'Maybe. That is a thought.'

A week later, just as the daffodil spears were dropping into flower, Martin Fable's condition deteriorated. He couldn't breathe for long unaided, there was nothing left, it was time for his soul to go. The body was just a mass of organs kept functioning by exterior stimuli.

His eldest son gave permission. The machinery stopped.

Piers left Charlotte alone, sitting with Martin till the end. She held his hand and felt the pulse become a thread, she saw blue shadow grow upon his lips and heard the staggered breaths. His open eyes saw nothing, maybe he heard what she told him and died knowing how much he had been truly loved. A white wave swept over, then there was nothing.

She kissed him. As death took hold his leonine features became smooth like a wax effigy. She shut his eyes for ever.

Sister came and suggested tea. There were things that needed to be done. Charlotte could come back later.

'No,' she said. 'I will remember him as he is now. He never did grow old. He will always be beautiful.'

Charlotte stood among the rocks above the creeping sea. This place may not have meant much, or anything, to Martin. She would never know. A gentle breeze was blowing off the shore, enough to ruffle the water and carry the ashes away. The wind and the sea could take him anywhere, everywhere, wherever. As she scattered the urn's contents on the shallows a solitary seal appeared beyond the rocky outcrop, watching placidly, sorrowful or indifferent, before swimming off silently into the Firth of Forth.

Jake Cleaver squeezed her hand as she got back into his car. He didn't mind her tears. They wouldn't talk about them, it was not necessary, he understood.

'I think the Bonny Earl of Moray died near here,' said Charlotte.

Jake still had the voice of an angel.

> 'Lang will his lady
> Look owre the Castle Downe,
> Ere she sees the Earl of Moray,
> Come sounding through the town.'

Also by Amanda MacAndrew and available in Arrow

PASSING PLACES

'You will be a leader when you grow up', Ishbel promised her daughter. Her father told her she would be a great beauty.

In between something went wrong – hormones, thick ankles, spots – and with them arrived the realization that parents were not God. At fourteen, Andrea knew with sickening certainty that growing up was going to be a rocky business. Particularly in the small world of Scotland during the Sixties when sex, drugs and rock'n'roll were the merest dots on the horizon, frocks were worn to parties and the Gay Gordons was still an innocent frolic.

Nevertheless, anarchy is never far from the surface even in the most civilised of cities and beneath Edinburgh's grey Georgian face, simmered lust, duplicity and black-edged comedy.

Amanda MacAndrew's novel traces a riotous, razor sharp and poignant story of Andrea's rite of passage to adulthood.

'A poignantly comic evocation of adolescence'
Marika Cobbold, author of *Guppies For Tea*

'Amanda MacAndrew displays gentle wit and perception, razor-sharp characterization, a keen ear for natural speech cadences, with just a taste of Joanna Trollope, Mary Wesley and Barbara Pym (and just a hint, sometimes, of the Townsend farce)'
Polly Toynbee, *The Times*

There follows Chapter One of

THE ANNIVERSARY by Ann Swinfen

available in Arrow from August 1st. If you
enjoy it, we invite you to take up the offer at
the back of this book.

THE ANNIVERSARY
Ann Swinfen

The most evocative and compelling family novel since Rosamunde Pilcher's *The Shellseekers*, *The Anniversary* sweeps the reader into the fabric of a family, a community and an era.

It is June 11th 1994 in the depths of Herefordshire and Natasha Devereux's family and two hundred guests gather together to celebrate the fiftieth anniversary of St. Martins. From the vision of one woman who fled Bolshevik Russia and opened her doors to artists, musicians, writers and refugees from war-torn Europe it has become a sanctuary for five generations of a family who – over the course of one day – face marital crisis, impending birth, teenage trauma, a father's roving eye into forbidden territory, momentous news from the past, communal financial crisis, and a lost love from the summer of '57.

As the evening shadows spread-eagle across the lawn to the rambling house and the great old copper beech, Natasha comes to the fruition of her life's work. The kaleidoscope of memory has been shaken, decisions have been taken. There has been a birth, and a death, but above all a celebration.

'. . . weaves an absorbing and intricate tapestry of family history and private memories . . . warm, generous, healing and hopeful'
Victoria Glendinning

Chapter 1

THE WATERCOLOUR OF St Martins on the wall above the telephone table had been painted by Frances Kilworth's younger son Tony just before he left art school, and given to her four years ago on her fiftieth birthday. She looked pensively at it as she spoke.

'Yes, of course I'll be there, Natasha.' She raised her voice slightly. At ninety-four her grandmother's hearing was remarkable, but she had never been at ease on the telephone.

'I'm driving down very early, before the traffic builds up on the M4. Giles still isn't quite sure whether he can make it. Rehearsal in the morning. They're filming a second series of his sitcom – the one that's doing so well.'

Natasha Devereux gave a snort down the telephone, which might have been a suppressed laugh. Probably not a favourable one.

'Can we expect him later, then, doushenka?'

'He's going to try to come down after lunch. That would mean he could manage most of the day.' Frances recognised a familiar note in her voice, at once apologetic and pleading. It often surfaced when she spoke of her husband to Natasha. She despised herself for it.

'Drive carefully,' said Natasha automatically before ringing off, as if Frances were still a teenager, dashing about the Herefordshire lanes in her beloved soft-top MG. Frances sighed. Gone. Long gone. Vanished with that younger self, who now seemed as remote as a stranger.

Frances stood for a moment with her hand still on the telephone. The watercolour constantly filled her afresh with delight. Tony had managed to catch the endearing atmosphere of the place – the jumble of styles, from the mediaeval tower and the half-timbered sixteenth-century main house to the elegant Georgian frontage and orangery (now dilapidated), added when the family had aspired to gentility in the mid-eighteenth century. By showing it from an unusual angle he had been able to reveal its haphazard chronology. The horseshoe formed by the house and stableyard was flung round like the rough embrace of the military cloak St Martin himself had wrapped around the shivering beggar. In the right foreground (slightly shifted by artistic licence, she thought) was the great copper beech, planted in 1790 and recorded in the estate book of the period. Its partner, mirroring it across the lawn, had begun to rot in the sixties and had come down in a storm seven years ago. The surviving tree was the first they had learned to climb, she and her brother Hugh, soon after their mother had brought them to St Martins to escape the blitz.

* * *

Hugh will never find me here, thinks Frances, crouching under the rhododendrons. She holds her breath. He is ranging about the lawn, poking at shrubs with a stick, peering down the well that Mummy is always so fussed about. Then he seems to lose interest. He throws down his stick and starts to climb the copper beech. He jumps and catches hold of one of the lower branches, then walks his feet up the trunk and claws at the branch until he gets his tummy over it. Soon she can see nothing of him but the shaking of the branches. Furious, she crawls out from under the rhododendrons and runs across the lawn.

'You're supposed to be finding me!' she wails.

He drops neatly from the tree beside her, and grabs her arm. 'Got you!'

'It's not fair!'

She hits him.

Soon they are rolling over and over amongst the dead leaves under the tree, punching each other until they are tired.

Later, when they are lying on their backs, gazing up through the branches at the patchwork of purple leaves and blue sky, she complains again.

'You are a beast. It wasn't fair.'

He rolls over on to his stomach and grins to himself.

★ ★ ★

The morning of Saturday, 11 June, 1994, dawned milky white as Frances joined the M4 at Junction 10. The road stretched westwards ahead of her, almost empty. In three hours' time the tarmac would be hot with the friction of the hundreds of tyres rolling over it, the trees in the adjacent fields shaking with the thunder of lorries pounding to and from London.

Now she could see a kestrel hovering lazily overhead – not three miles from Reading. She reached up and wound back the sunroof, then pressed the buttons to open both front windows fully. Her sensible Cavalier hatchback could never rival the excitement of her old MG, but she still drove in a wild tangle of air when she was alone. Giles objected peevishly when he travelled with her, closing windows, hunching down with his coat collar turned up when she refused to turn on the heating, ostentatiously coughing into his handkerchief with unspoken reproach: My voice has to be cherished, I need to be cosseted, my looks and my voice are my fortune.

She shook herself in irritation. No need to think about Giles just yet. She would reach St Martins in time for breakfast. Probably before the children had even woken up. Yesterday afternoon Tony had collected Katya after school, on his way from London, and driven her down to Herefordshire; Lisa and Paul had planned to drive over from Worcester during the evening. It was only a month till the baby was due, but Lisa had insisted that she could not possibly miss the party.

'Not come to St Martins' fiftieth anniversary, Mum? I wouldn't miss it for the world. Anyway, Natasha would never forgive me.'

Frances had made protesting noises down the phone.

'If anything disastrous should happen,' Lisa said stoutly, 'Paul can always run me into the hospital in Hereford. It only takes twenty minutes. But I'm fine, really. Never felt better.'

This was not strictly true, but for Lisa Fenway the birth of her first child and Natasha's party for the fiftieth anniversary of the St Martins community had become somehow entangled in her mind. She had an odd, superstitious belief – which she would have admitted to no one, not even Paul – that if she did not go to the party something dreadful would happen to the baby. Which was idiotic of her, as she knew very well.

*   *   *

Frances switched on the car radio, tuning in to Classic FM. It offended her by playing only fragments, never completing a piece, but it provided an agreeable and undemanding background to the drive. She had always preferred driving alone, but since her marriage it was a pleasure she had rarely been able to enjoy. For years there had been the demands of others, creating tensions, making the metal and glass box into a prison. First Giles. In those days (before he had lost his licence) insisting on driving, though he was not nearly as good a driver as she was. Then Anya, fretting in her carrycot, the back seat around her wedged with carrier bags full of nappies and baby powder and made-up bottles of formula. Then Nicholas and Tony and Lisa. All of them quarrelling, wanting to stop, demanding to be sick or to go to the loo, and being pacified with chocolate by Giles, who laughed at Frances's rules about no sweets between meals.

Then, much later, when Anya and Nicholas were almost grown-up and Tony and Lisa were bored and aggressive teenagers, it started all over again with Katya.

I'm too old for this, Frances had thought, assembling a new set of baby paraphernalia, alien in design and purpose from the objects that had cluttered her early motherhood.

Tony and Lisa had complained and bickered about the space in the car being encroached upon by the new baby. Who – then – had been angelic. Quiet and good, with a smile to melt hearts. But her brother and sister had been unmoved.

'Honestly,' she had overheard Lisa saying to Tony. 'At *their* age. I think it's disgusting.'

4

Tony had snickered. 'Just Dad trying to prove he's still virile. Or Mum trying to stop him straying.'

* * *

Giles cried, that time, in the autumn of 1980. Tears, of course, came easily to him. They were one of his professional skills. No more to be trusted than his charm, once so enchanting.

'I swear to you, Frances,' he said brokenly, burying his face in her breast. 'You are the only woman I love. That little bint who's been in the Noel Coward with me – honestly, I was just giving the kid a bit of fun, showing her the sights, introducing her to some useful people.'

He heaved himself up, glowering. Frances noticed that he was beginning to thicken about the waist.

'How dare she ring you up like that! Who does she think she is?' he demanded crossly.

Ah yes, this is the real Giles. His sense of dignity is offended. Little Ms Bootsie Fabersham (what a ridiculous name) is finished. She has not played the game by his rules. She has invaded his bolt-hole, his private place, my home.

Her eye was caught briefly by a cool still life painted by Natasha and hanging on the bedroom wall. It was a study in yellows and greens, with a shaft of sunlight falling diagonally across a table.

He kissed her hair, stroked her.

Why don't I have the strength to throw him out of my bed, out of my life? Frances asked herself resentfully, knowing that she would not, feeling herself melt. Pitying him, with his injured pride.

She had not taken the pill for months. Until now there had been no need. She was not really worried. After all, she told herself, I am forty. Nothing can possibly happen after just once. But it did. And the result was Katya. A beautiful baby. Perfect in every way.

And three months before her birth, Giles was photographed with his latest girlfriend, attending the première of a film in which he had played a minor role.

* * *

In the bedroom she liked best at St Martins — a queer, lopsided space up under the mediaeval roof beams — Katya Kilworth stirred and pushed back the duvet, but did not wake. Her clothes were scattered all over the floor, a heap of black — skirts and sleeveless tunics and baggy jeans and boy's football boots. In bed she wore a grandad woollen vest with buttoned neck and long sleeves. It sported a wartime utility label in the back, which was currently considered by Katya's peers to be cool. She had bought it in the local Oxfam shop for 50p. After she had worn it for an hour or so, it developed a curious smell — reminiscent of wet dog. It was scratchy and too hot, but she had bought it to annoy her mother and so felt obliged to wear it.

Irritably she half woke, threw the duvet off the bed entirely, then stripped off the woollen vest and flung it across the room. The pale light of early morning fell on her from the uncurtained window, and she looked at herself in disgust, loathing her body. She threw herself on to her face, clutching a pillow in her arms and remembering, as she drifted back into sleep, her balding teddy bear. She kept it hidden at St Martins, to avoid the shame of Mum turning it up in Reading. Tomorrow she would rescue Ted and bring him back to her bed. No one disturbed your privacy at St Martins. Which was odd, really.

* * *

Two floors below, Natasha Devereux lay awake on her high, severe, four-poster bed. She slept very little these days. Not profound sleep. On the other hand, she dozed frequently. During the day, sitting in her favourite high-backed chair in the window bay of the drawing room, she would be dozing and yet at the same time aware, in some part of her mind, that she was still present in the room. So that Irina or Mabel, coming in to urge unwanted cups of tea on her, would start to tiptoe out again — only to be confronted with her disconcertingly sharp eyes. Sometimes they manoeuvred William into the chair opposite, where he would sit, quiet and biddable as a well trained dog. My son-in-law, since his stroke, looks older than

6

I do myself, thought Natasha a little complacently. Even though he is seventeen years younger.

The white voile bed curtains stirred and billowed in the breeze from the windows. She had caught from her English husband the habit of leaving the windows open at night, except in the most severe weather.

'Leave the windows *open*, Edmund dousha moya?' she had exclaimed, scandalised, the first time they had slept together, that joyful night in Paris, the spring after the Great War. 'The night air is poisonsome, everyone knows this.'

'Poisonous, my darling, not poisonsome,' he said, laughing, touching her lips with the tip of his finger. 'And that is foolish nonsense taught you by your Nianyushka. I have slept with the windows open all my life, and look at me!'

And she had looked at him. He still wore uniform. It was not so splendid as the Russian uniforms of her childhood, but the sober, well tailored lines defined the shape of him, filling her with longing. He started to undress, exposing the scar on his chest that he had earned at Passchendaele, still pink and vulnerable. She began to kiss it.

Now, lying in the bed at St Martins, she was filled with wonder that she could have survived this last half-century without him, after a second war, nearing its end, had taken from her the man the first war had brought to her. It seemed inconceivable – such a gulf of time. By tenuous links her thoughts slid to Anya, her troubled eldest great-granddaughter. At thirty-four, thinking her life was over. Anya was only just beginning.

She keeps too much to herself, thought Natasha. What is going on in that tight, well controlled brain of hers? Too much she thinks of things, of ideas, of theories. All beautifully categorised and indexed and filed. She never speaks of the feelings. Irina, now, my so-disappointing daughter, she speaks of feelings all the time, her own feelings. Always they are hurt or offended in some way. But Anya – no, she is like Edmund, very British. Does she even speak of feelings with this man of hers, whom she is so reluctant to bring to my party?

In the tiny bed-sit in North Oxford, which was all she could possibly afford – no, more than she could afford – Anya Kilworth lay very straight on her back under a single plain white sheet. She was not asleep. Probably she had not slept all night. She loved this room, especially when the trees were in leaf. Without lifting her head from the pillow she could look out through the uncurtained window at a rolling seascape of tree-tops, just now heaving gently in the light summer wind. The spiky candelabra of horse chestnuts, pink and white, caressed the looser, wilder, yellow cascades tumbling from the laburnums.

The back garden of this house – divided for many years amongst a shifting population of students, graduates and university hangers-on – was in a state of rampant neglect. The laburnums had seeded themselves, and were scattered about in every size from finger length to a height of twenty feet or more. If you ventured into the garden you had to fight your way through an undergrowth of cleavers and bindweed and ground elder, clawing at you to waist height. There were tunnels where the secret cats of North Oxford patrolled on their nightly business and at the far end, beneath the crumbling garden wall of brick, lay the remains of an asparagus bed, from which Anya had been able to pick a few shoots last week when Spiro came to dinner.

It had been meant as a reconciliation. They would have a pleasant, relaxed meal and talk about neutral subjects. Make a fresh start. But somehow it had gone wrong. They started to quarrel, and then they were shouting at each other. To her horror, Anya heard herself telling him to leave. It seemed to be some other person speaking – a shrewish woman with a harsh, self-righteous voice. She did not want him to go, and had been cold with shock ever since.

She had seen him once, two days ago, in the Bodleian. They had nodded at each other and walked on without speaking. He was supposed to be coming with her to St Martins today. A month ago at least, they had arranged to meet at the station, in time for the Hereford train. Should she ring him to remind him? No, it would be too humiliating. What if he did not turn up at the station? Should she wait? He had the infuriating Greek habit of indifference towards time. If you missed a train, so what? Another one would come, today, tomorrow.

I wish I could talk all this through with someone, thought Anya. Though I know I'm not the kind of person who talks about such things. I wish I were the sort of daughter who can talk to her mother, the way Lisa talks to Mum. Though Mum is hardly the best person to give advice. Granny Irina is useless. Once, I might have gone to Natasha, but she is getting so old now, and frail. I can't burden her. And although I have lots of acquaintances – colleagues, people I go to pubs with – I don't really have any close friends. Mum would at least understand the dilemma I'm confronted with.

Anya smiled a little bitterly, flung herself crossly on her side and looked at the clock. God, it was still only six.

* * *

Frances Kilworth stopped once only on her journey. Not because she needed petrol, but because she liked to get out and stretch and view the countryside away from the tunnel-like motorway with its monotonous scenery. She had turned off the M4 at Junction 15, to take a shortcut cross-country, instead of following it the long way round to the M5. Giles always wanted to keep to the motorways. It confirmed his perception of himself as busy and sought-after, dashing about the country on the blue lines radiating out from London. It was the source of one of the many irritations between them that Frances much preferred the adventure of unknown country roads. Little hidden villages, valleys concealed from the major highways by enfolding hills, were to her an enrichment of the experience of travelling. She had never been able to make him see that her cross-country routes often shortened the journey as well as making it less tiring.

'You're always getting stuck behind some damn tractor thing,' he would complain, impervious to the fact that tractors usually turned off the road within a quarter of a mile or so, while tailbacks on the motorways moved far slower and stretched out for interminable miles. He almost appeared to enjoy them, drumming on the dashboard with his fingers, exchanging exaggerated, comical faces of woe with fellow sufferers in the cars around them.

In the same way he seemed tied to the crowds and traffic of London by an umbilical cord of emotional needs. The furthest he had been prepared to move, when they had felt they could buy a house thirty years ago, was to Reading. This was not Frances's idea of the country, but she had still been in love with him then and the house would do for a few years, till they could afford something better. But that had been, as it turned out, one of their most prosperous periods. Giles had secured his first West End part, in a lightweight play that for some inexplicable reason ran and ran, so that, together with the tiny bits of money she had been carefully putting aside for five years, they were able to pay in full the £4,000 the house had cost. (No right-minded building society would have given an actor a mortgage.) Frances managed to find some work translating correspondence for a local firm exporting to Italy, which she did while Anya was at her morning play group and Nicky took a nap. The work was badly paid, but the money covered their modest daily spending needs, with a little scrimping and saving.

'A hundred and ninety thousand pounds!' she had repeated to the keen new man in the insurance office last week.

'Oh yes, Mrs Kilworth,' he assured her. 'It must be worth at least that, even with the present difficulties in the housing market. Five years ago it was probably worth well over 200 K. You really must not under-insure. If you had a fire . . . '

She found it difficult to attend to him. When they had bought it, the house had overlooked fields at the back, giving at least an illusion of the country. But in the early eighties new housing developments had begun to encroach on them, nearer and nearer. Now the view from the main bedroom and the kitchen below it – a view once moving in a cycle through the colours of the agricultural year, and framed by willows along a stream – had been replaced by the severe backs of identical houses, row upon row, whose windows were too small and whose roofs were too shallow. The stream had been culverted, and the willows cut down – one agonising afternoon – by an indifferent man with a chain-saw.

This leap in monetary value was ludicrous, almost obscene. Because the house was much nastier now than when they had bought it. And the streets were no longer safe. When Anya and Nicky were small, she had never worried about them playing with their friends up and down the road, or on the small area of grass around which the houses were grouped. Now, whenever Katya was just a little late from school she would begin to worry.

After Junction 15 she bypassed Swindon and headed for Cirencester on the A419. She thought at first that she had missed the lay-by where she wanted to stop, but spotted it at last and pulled in. It was disconcerting not to find it where she had expected it to be.

I know this road so well, I could drive it with my eyes shut, she thought. But I suppose it must be three months since I was last down at St Martins. What can I have been doing with myself all that time?

She got out, stretching slowly and luxuriously, like a cat. Then she locked the car. And not long ago I would not have done that, she thought. She pushed through the dusty, sickly-looking bushes that edged the lay-by and climbed the slight rise beyond. North and west of her the soft lines of the Cotswolds rose, looking larger than they really were in the horizontal light of early morning which dramatised their contours.

★　★　★

'I'm going to find some real mountains to climb,' Hugh said.

They were eating a clotted cream tea in one of the golden Cotswold villages, sitting outside a cottage in the unexpected sunshine of July, 1958. Their bicycles were propped against the low garden wall, the over-full saddle bags bulging into the hollyhocks and foxgloves.

She was only half listening to him. It was, although they did not know it then, their last cycling holiday together. Since their early teens they had taken cycle trips every Easter and summer, even after Frances's acquisition of the MG. Last night they had stayed at the youth hostel in Gloucester. They planned to make their way through the Cotswold lanes at a leisurely pace, then go on to Stratford and buy standing room tickets for whatever play was showing. The tickets cost only half a crown, and sometimes the usherettes would show you to an unoccupied seat at the first interval. Once, they had found themselves in the front row of the dress circle.

'There's a field trip going out to Kashmir. I'm going to try to stay on afterwards and do some real climbing after the others come back.'

'Won't it be frightfully expensive?'

'I'm going to use my prize money, and Natasha said she would help. Mother, of course, is dead against it. Dad just humphs.'

'Mmm.' Thinking about Stratford had filled her mind even more intensely with Giles, and she felt her stomach churn. It was just possible they might run into him in Stratford. He had some sort of job at the theatre for the vacation – selling programmes or something. Would they see him? Would he notice her? She was so insignificant compared with his usual glamorous girlfriends. Dark, studious, shy, she was acutely embarrassed whenever she had to mix with his set, who all seemed larger, more vivid than anyone she had ever known. They called each other 'darling', were wantonly careless about lectures and tutorials, flouted the rules about staying out of college late, left Oxford without permission.

One day in the seventh week of last term, Giles had taken her with a crowd of his friends to London to see a show. She persuaded another girl to tell lies to their tutor, saying she was ill and would have to miss her mediaeval history tutorial. The entire evening was ruined for her by her guilt and terror.

'Look at my little bluestocking,' Giles said, parading her before his friends and covertly caressing her, so that she blushed an ugly red.

They had dinner afterwards at Rules, and celebrities of the stage were pointed out to her. Giles's OUDS cronies themselves could not quite conceal their awe. Then they went on, somewhat drunk, to a Soho night-club, which was horrible. Frances thought the floor show ugly and degrading, and a swarthy, middle-aged man pawed at her in the dark corridor near the Ladies.

They began the drive back to Oxford at dawn, tired and quarrelsome. Giles seemed morose and withdrawn, so that Frances sat, biting back tears, looking out of the window, past Beaconsfield, past High Wycombe, into Oxford through Wheatley. She asked to be dropped near the Martyrs' Memorial, and wandered about disconsolately until well after the college gates were opened. The last week of term had been spent trying to avoid the Dean, in the fear that somehow she would reveal her guilt in her face.

★　★　★

At the end of that summer Hugh made his Kashmir journey, arriving back late for the start of term at Cambridge. But, as always, he was forgiven. He had managed to lose himself in the mountains. Had fallen in with a remote local tribe, and lived at their village for a month. By Christmas he had sold an account of his adventure, with photographs, to one of the major Sunday papers.

The following summer Hugh graduated, staying in England only long enough to attend Frances's wedding to Giles in the chapel at St Martins. Then he had left for a two-year expedition up the Amazon.

★　★　★

Giles Kilworth did not sleep as well these days as he used to. In the past he had stayed up till the early hours, keyed up after a performance or drinking with chums when he was resting from work. The moment he laid his head on the pillow – unless, of course, he was otherwise occupied – he had always been able to fall asleep immediately, not waking until a civilised hour of ten or eleven, in time for a leisurely shower and a half-breakfast, half-lunch with the papers.

Lately – and he could not quite trace the beginning of the change – he had found it increasingly difficult to fall asleep. And then he would wake in the dark reaches of the night, or in the early morning. Partly, it was due to the twinges of pain he sometimes felt in his hips and knees. Stupid, really. Nothing to worry about. But just enough discomfort to keep him awake. Partly, too, he was keyed up about the filming of the new series of *Vet in Hot Water*. The first series was just finishing its run on ITV, and was a smash hit. He'd never had so much fan mail in his life. Odd, when you thought about it. He'd always seen himself as a serious actor, and he'd done his Hamlet in rep in Birmingham and his Romeo (rather late, when he was nearly forty) in Huddersfield. He'd had supporting roles at Stratford and the National, but somehow had not made it to the top at either. He was looking forward to his Lear some day, but not yet, for heaven's sake!

The trouble was, there were so few good parts for Shake-spearean actors in their fifties. Though Larry Olivier had got away with it. There was Malvolio, of course. And Shylock, though Giles wasn't the right build for that – you ought to be gaunt and hungry-looking, and he *had* put on rather a lot of weight recently. As his agent kept pointing out to him, quite unnecessarily.

Caesar? Mark Antony? Not that anybody seemed to want to do the Roman plays at the moment. Derek J. was a lucky bastard getting Claudius for that great long Robert Graves thing on telly back in the seventies. A toga is quite flattering if you are, well, a bit on the heavy side.

There were other possibilities, of course. He'd like to try his hand at Ibsen's *Master Builder*, but Brian was doing a run with that. Up in the north, though. He shuddered at the thought of a Scottish tour. Those freezing digs.

Really, it was much better to stay in London. That way, people didn't forget about you. What a stupid idea that had been of Frances's, years ago when he was just getting known in the right circles – some idea that they should live in the country. He could commute to London when he had a show, she said. Perhaps have a little flat there for sleeping over. The point was, you had to be *seen* about the place, all the time. He couldn't make her understand that.

He had never supposed he'd be so good at comedy, though

he had done his share of the usual frothy things in the early days. And there had been the Noel Coward about fourteen years ago, when that stupid little cow had tried to make him leave Frances and marry her, for God's sake! He'd paid for the abortion and sent her packing. Nasty little piece of work. She'd only been trying to use him. You saw her all the time on the telly these days, in some soap, playing a brassy barmaid. That was about her level, he thought with satisfaction. She looks older than Frances now, though she must be nearly twenty years younger. Not much older than Anya. Saw her the other day at a party. That was a lucky escape, that time.

One more rehearsal tomorrow, then we'll get the last episode in the can next week. He turned restlessly on his side, grunting as a pain stabbed briefly in his back. He wasn't *absolutely* happy about the new series. There was a different screenwriter, who just didn't have Max's zest. And then Judy, that clever little kid with a face like a monkey, who'd played the part of his assistant, had already been sewed up tight in a stage contract she couldn't wriggle out of, so they'd had to drop her character from the second series. Didn't think it would matter, he thought grimly, but somehow the whole thing seemed to be falling flat without her, even though hers was only supposed to be a minor part. She has absolutely no sex appeal, not for me anyway, but she's a real pro, bright as the proverbial button.

The worrying thing was that there wasn't anything definite fixed up to follow this second series. Of course, with the reviews and the ratings, something was bound to turn up soon. Still, he hadn't been happy when Frances had said that she was thinking of giving up her part-time lectureship at the poly.

'Now that you're doing so well, Giles,' she said, 'and with only Katya left at home, I thought I might stop. It takes so much time and energy, all the preparation and marking and examining, when I'm only paid on an hourly basis for the hours I'm in college lecturing. No pension. No paid holidays. No sick pay.'

'Not for me either, darling.'

'But you knew that when you went on the stage. My full-time colleagues at the poly have everything very nicely pro-

15

vided. It's just the mugs like me – married women working part-time – who are exploited.'

'Now don't go all *feminist*,' he said, in the beguiling comic tone he used so effectively in the series.

She looked at him coolly.

'There are other things I would like to do. I think that it's just about my turn. At last.'

That was unfair of her. They'd agreed right from the start that she would take all the part-time jobs she could until he made his name. Of course she had to give up that notion of going to Italy to do a PhD – on apprentices in Renaissance art studios, or whatever it was. Boring trash. What with Anya arriving while they were still undergraduates. It wasn't *his* fault. She said she wanted to put his career first.

The trouble with women of Frances's age was that they were both too young and too old. They were too young to be like their mothers' generation, accepting their place in the scheme of things, staying at home and supporting their husbands. And they were too old to have the freedoms of younger women. But now some of them were trying to grab those freedoms in middle age. It was laughable.

Uncomfortably, he thought of Natasha, who disproved his theory. Now Irina, Frances's mother, was the old-fashioned wifely type, irritating though she was. But her grandmother! By all accounts, Natasha was quite a girl in her day, back in post-World War I Paris. Part of a real bohemian living-in-a-garret set, from the tales told by those odd characters who used to wander in and out of St Martins. All dead now, probably.

* * *

'Natasha Ivanovna, she comes from great family of Russia, you understand, my friend.' The man, a morose White Russian in threadbare clothes, has warmed to Giles over the vodka bottle, in the little back sitting room at St Martins. 'She saw terrible things in Revolution, terrible, when she was just girl. All her family slaughtered by those pigs of Bolsheviks. Not clean with gun, oh no. They make long time fun with swords taken from wall of Petrograd mansion. This she watches. Her mother,

her sisters, her little brother. Her father is already dead, you understand. They climb over his dead body to get into house.'

He pours himself another glass, staring red-eyed into the fire.

'When they finish with others of family, they turn to her, Natasha Ivanovna. All this time they hold her and she struggles. She thinks, I will throw myself on sword and it will be finished.'

'But she didn't.'

'No, my friend. Natasha Ivanovna is very beautiful. They do not use sword. They rape her. All of them. I spit on them.' He spits into the fire.

'But how did she escape?'

'One of this rabble – he was once servant of Greshlovs. He is ashamed. While pigs of Bolsheviks are stealing bottles from cellar, he manages to make escape her.'

For a long time he is silent, turning the glass of clear liquid round and round in his hand, staring into the past.

'When she is in Paris, she becomes part of bohemian set – artists and musicians, living on Left Bank. She is now painter. She comes also to quarter of émigrés, where myself I am living. She is become very wild, you understand, my friend. For some it was like this, for others – nothing but grieving. Once, there is party at Russian club, and someone begins to play balalaika, very sad songs, mourning our lost Mother Russia. No, says Natasha Ivanovna, play fast dances, play for me!

'And she dances on table amongst glasses and food, wearing nothing but her petticoat. *Nothing*, my friend! This you must believe.'

It is certainly true, what he says. His eyes gleam at the memory and his lips are wet.

* * *

Glumly, unable to sleep in the brighter light now slipping beneath the thick curtains, Giles thought of Frances. Certainly she had never shown any sign of dancing on the table in nothing but her petticoat, like Natasha. But some women did turn *odd*, didn't they, at her sort of age?

The latest red-head, stirring and moaning a little in the bed beside him, broke his train of thought. He had completely

17

forgotten about her. Disconcerted, he eyed her pink freckled shoulder with distaste. High time to end that particular liaison. He would slip quietly out of her bed now and go to his club for a shower and breakfast before tootling along to the rehearsal room in Ealing. He would send the aspiring starlet a graceful letter of farewell, with some roses and a bottle of bubbly. Something fond and fatherly, making her see that it was only a diversion, helping her to find her feet in London.

He started to ease himself out of the bed, groping for his slippers. A large, firm hand grasped him about the upper arm in a grip it would have been difficult to break without rudeness.

'Darling?' said the red-head.

With a groan, Giles sank back on to the pillows.

* * *

Irina Appleton, daughter of Natasha and mother of Frances, was not quite awake, but she was going over her lists in her mind:

Send Katya to village to collect extra cheese
Check enough glasses
Get Mrs D to wash glasses
Get Mr D to put out tables
Tell Olga to lay tables in garden
Mabel to make salads
Mabel to bake quiches
Mabel to see about tea urn
Get cakes from Sally
Nicholas to put up signs on drive about parking
Mabel to phone wine merchant about one case short
Sally to set up old dairy as crèche
Tony Nicholas & Paul to put up marquee

She stopped trying to pretend she was still asleep. In the other bed William's breathing was deep and regular. Fretfully, she felt he had fallen ill just to spite her. Not retiring from his solicitor's practice until he was over seventy, when he knew how difficult it was to deal with St Martins and Mother, despite

Mabel's splendid help. He could have been some use to her during these last ten years. Then he had a stroke and became just one more worry for her. Thank goodness he didn't seem to mind Mabel nursing him.

And I do think Frances might have come down yesterday to give me a hand.

The voice inside Irina's head was so indignant she could almost hear it in the room.

She could surely have cancelled that bit of teaching she does, they wouldn't have minded. It's not as if it is a *real* job. People are so inconsiderate. And Katya looked dreadful when she arrived last night. Why ever does Frances allow her to wear those appalling clothes? I would never have allowed *her* to dress like that.

Briefly, she recalled those disgusting short skirts of the sixties. But Frances was married by then. She *would* marry Giles, and much good it has done her. Though I will say his new show has been a real laugh. Quite made me forget my sciatica for half an hour.

That marquee. It looks awfully complicated. I hope the boys can manage it. There could easily be rain. Not that it is a marquee really. Just something the Scouts use at their summer camp, but it was kind of Mr Peters to lend it to us. Mother has no idea, really. How did she suppose we could afford a real marquee? This isn't pre-Revolutionary Russia, I ask you.

Dreading the day ahead of her, Irina climbed slowly out of bed.

* * *

Frances had left Ross-on-Wye behind her. It was fully morning now, and the Black Mountains stood out clearly on her left as she headed north through Herefordshire. The cloud cover was thinning out. It might be a sunny day after all. Oh, I hope so, thought Frances, for Natasha's sake.

Only five more miles to St Martins. She was nearly home.

Copyright © 1996 Ann Swinfen

TRAVELLING HOPEFULLY
Maggie Makepeace

'A witty and incisive book . . . quirky and sophisticated humour'
CATHOLIC HERALD

For Imogen Redcliffe leaving a man with an incurable disease was unthinkable. But it didn't stop her longing for her freedom.

Perhaps therefore it was dangerous to embark on a holiday with a group of strangers? Two weeks in Seychelles may have seemed like paradise on paper but the reality would prove rather different. In the company of, among others, a sex-starved doctor, a shrewd psychotherapist and a frightened vegetarian, Imogen is forced to face up to her own shortcomings and to take action.

It's a liberating experience but not quite in the way she intended!

Praise for Maggie Makepeace's *Breaking the Chain*

'Sparkling comedy and high-value entertainment' SUNDAY TIMES

FACING THE MUSIC
Mary Sheepshanks

'There wouldn't be any trouble if only you had a wife,' Lady Boynton had said. But Flavia Cameron was not at all what she had in mind for Gervaise Henderson. Impossibly young, with a musical talent that could have been heard in concert halls around the world, the headmaster's new wife was beautiful and sparkling and she swept the Upper Fourth off their feet.

Until Ben Forbes arrived, with a father who saw Flavia not as a prodigy, a daughter or a wife, but, for the first time, as herself. It is a discovery that will throw her life into turmoil.

Perceptive and poignant, funny and touching, *Facing the Music* is a welcome new novel from the author of *A Price for Everything*.

Praise for *A Price for Everything*:

'Touchingly wise and extremely funny' THE TIMES

'Midway between the sexual candour of Mary Wesley and Joanna Trollope's sharp observation' MAIL ON SUNDAY

THE TORTOISE SHELL
Fanny Frewen

Mulberry Cottage is the perfect country retreat, the village quintessentially English. But with a cosmopolitan London background and a lucrative career of her own, Henny Brack is not at all sure she's ready to settle down.

But the village is also home to ninety-five-year-old Cecilia Boxendale. Scratchy, dauntless and devoted to those she loves, she saves her caustic tongue for the ghastly Mrs Phillips (hell-bent on steering her safely into The Elms retirement home) and gradually becomes Henny's greatest friend. As crises loom, Cecilia remains steadfast. Ultimately, though, it is she who will face the greatest ordeal.

Quirky, original and full of life, *The Tortoise Shell* is both unashamedly touching and utterly realistic. It is a welcome first novel from an exciting new talent.

FLOWERING JUDAS
Elizabeth Palmer

Charmian Sinclair runs her own PR firm and a regular series of married lovers, one for each day of the week. Weekends are spent with Giles Hayward in Sussex. It is a rewarding way of life, but when Giles, the only bachelor in her set, falls in love with a country neighbour, Charmian realizes it can't go on for ever.

Charmian's opportunities for reflection are cut short, however, by the news that Oliver Curtis, her brother-in-law, has been brutally fired from his high-powered City job. Outraged by this, Charmian resolves to exact revenge through her own influential contacts – and discovers far more than she bargained for . . .

With wit, candour and more than a touch of brilliance, Elizabeth Palmer offers another comedy of sparkling bad manners.

Praise for previous novels by Elizabeth Palmer:

The Stainless Angel 'Beautifully executed' TODAY

Plucking the Apple 'A sharp, stylish novel of adultery' SHE

'*Old Money* seethes with possibilities . . . brisk and witty sexual episodes' THE TIMES

THE YOUNG ITALIANS
Amanda Prantera

When young, beautiful and very English Irene arrived in Florence in 1928 to stay with her aunt, she had no idea that Italy's seduction would be so powerful, nor that she would be married within six months.

Nor did she imagine that it was only the beginning of her experience of love.

Passion comes in many forms – one of them adulterous.

'I don't think I have ever read anything so good about the thin line between love and infatuation' LITERARY REVIEW

'Set in the late thirties, it traces a young woman's romantic coming of age against the background of political turmoil and gathering cloud of the Second World War . . . sharp, humorous detail and dreamy nostalgia' GUARDIAN

'A drolly original, wholly convincing portrait of life in a bourgeois Italian family . . . which is ultimately a celebration of family life, for its loyalties triumph over passion and politics' INDEPENDENT

'Reveals the black and merciless things that lie behind the façade of polite society' INDEPENDENT ON SUNDAY

PROMISES PAST

Charlotte Moore

Sarah and Adrian Stanhope are taking the plunge. They are leaving London with their three small children to live in a small market town. Adrian will commute, the children will thrive and Sarah will too. But she doesn't. Is it the seven year itch? The reality of the rural idyll not measuring up? Or the downright attractiveness of the local GP?

Standing aloof is childless Claudia Prescott, devoted to her career and shoring herself up against all manner of hurt, from an errant husband to ubiquitous references to babies, while Hilary Nightingale, singular and translucent, paints murals and attempts to conduct a fledgling affair under the eagle eye of her teenage daughter.

Promises Past is a brilliant exploration of marriages in silent crisis, unlicensed desire, motherhood and childlessness, and teenagers presiding over their parents' lives in proprietorial vigil.

'Immensely enjoyable . . . I could not put it down' Titia Sutherland

OBJECT LESSONS
Anna Quindlen

'Afterwards, all the rest of her life would seem to her a hereafter. Here and hereafter, and in between was that summer, the time of changes'

Young Maggie Scanlan begins to sense that, beneath the calm, everyday surface of her peaceful life, everything is going strangely wrong. Her all-powerful grandfather is reduced to a shadow by a stroke, and to Maggie's astonishment this causes her usually unemotional father to burst into tears. Connie, her lushly beautiful mother, whom Maggie could always be sure of finding at home, is now rarely there. And her cousin and her best friend start doing things that leave her confused and frightened about sex and sin.

In the sprawling Scanlan family in New York's Westchester County in the '60s, accommodations are made within a culturally mixed marriage and the mundanity of married life is validated by the occasional flare of passion. Maggie observes the powerplay and shifting allegiances operating behind the scenes with the sharp and dispassionate vision of a child on the verge of adulthood. A troubling, frightening time, it ultimately becomes one of liberation, an object lesson Maggie will remember for the rest of her life.

'An intelligent, highly entertaining novel laced with acute perceptions about the nature of day-to-day family life'
Anne Tyler, NEW YORK TIMES BOOK REVIEW

OTHER B FORMAT TITLES AVAILABLE IN ARROW

☐	Queen of the Witches	Jessica Berens	£4.99
☐	Letters From Prague	Sue Gee	£5.99
☐	Spring Will Be Ours	Sue Gee	£5.99
☐	Electricity	Victoria Glendinning	£5.99
☐	Damage	Josephine Hart	£5.99
☐	Sin	Josephine Hart	£5.99
☐	The Morning Gift	Eva Ibbotson	£5.99
☐	A Countess Below Stairs	Eva Ibbotson	£5.99
☐	Breaking the Chain	Maggie Makepeace	£5.99
☐	Telling Only Lies	Jessica Mann	£5.99
☐	Plucking the Apple	Elizabeth Palmer	£5.99
☐	Old Money	Elizabeth Palmer	£5.99
☐	The Young Italians	Amanda Prantera	£5.99
☐	One True Thing	Anna Quindlen	£5.99
☐	A Price For Everything	Mary Sheepshanks	£5.99
☐	My Life as a Whale	Dyan Sheldon	£4.99

ALL ARROW BOOKS ARE AVAILABLE THROUGH MAIL ORDER OR
FROM YOUR LOCAL BOOKSHOP AND NEWSAGENT.

PLEASE SEND CHEQUE/EUROCHEQUE/POSTAL ORDER
(STERLING ONLY) ACCESS, VISA OR MASTERCARD

												,						

EXPIRY DATE................ SIGNATURE..

PLEASE ALLOW 75 PENCE PER BOOK FOR POST AND PACKING
U.K.

OVERSEAS CUSTOMERS PLEASE ALLOW £1.00 PER COPY FOR
POST AND PACKING.

ALL ORDERS TO:
ARROW BOOKS, BOOK SERVICE BY POST, P.O. BOX 29, DOUGLAS,
ISLE OF MAN, IM99 1BQ. TEL: 01624 675137 FAX: 01624 670 923

NAME ....

ADDRESS ....

....

Please allow 28 days for delivery. Please tick box if you do not wish to receive
any additional information ☐

Prices and availability subject to change without notice.